Chapter 1

Long before she left the flat that evening, Alex sensed the adrenalin pumping around her veins. The job frequently got her into tricky situations, and some were downright dangerous, verging on the scary and lethal. But at least they were never the same. And they were rarely dull.

And, since she relished a change of tempo in whatever she did, her choice of career had taken considerable thought, ticking off the unlikely and the impossible, and coming down to the, um, well, maybes.

After a sketchy schooling, she was cheerfully hopeless at maths, and science was a frighteningly alien country. But geography and art had always fascinated her, and she definitely had an enquiring, not to say avidly nosy mind. So in choosing to go for the quirky instead of the predictable, she reminded herself severely that she had no one to blame but herself for whatever turned up that night, or any other night.

God, what a job description, Alex thought with a faint smile now. It made her sound more like a street-walker than a perfectly respectable private eye, however amateurish the big boys might think her methods. And at least she got results. Nearly always. Well, sometimes.

The Rainbow Cellar Club was just as she had expected it to be: dimly lit with rose-coloured lamps, and smoky with an indefinable smell that was more than just cigarettes and the overpowering scent of cheap perfume and sweaty bodies.

It was familiar territory for this kind of initial meeting. Those who turned up in her office after hesitant phone calls, were usually nervous lady clients, wanting to check up on errant

5

husbands with as little fuss as possible. For those she just needed to keep a supply of tissues at the ready, and just as great a need to keep her own emotions well under control. Beneath her air of hard-won city sophistication there beat a heart of pure unadulterated slush – or would be, if she once gave it its freedom.

She was still a sucker for a woman's sob story, which, she freely admitted, came from too many late nights watching old movies on satellite television, curled up on her sofa with the said tissues, dipping her fingers far too often into a box of chocolates, to the despair of her thighs.

But when it came to the men who found her name in Yellow Pages, they generally sought her out to investigate a crime thus avoiding the interference of the police. And if they didn't turn up unannounced at her minuscule office, then, as predictable as breathing, they invariably suggested this kind of place for a first meeting.

She guessed that what they never expected was the kind of upper-class persona she exuded, as if she'd been born to it. It could put them off, of course, but on the other hand, it also kept them firmly in their place.

As she moved across the room, her long slim legs seemed even longer in the short black silk skirt and well-fitting jacket she wore. The chocolate-enhanced thighs hadn't yet succumbed to the wearing of elastic-waisted skirts, she thought thankfully. She wasn't conventionally beautiful, but she did her best with what she had.

And how about *that* for an epitaph! She ignored the head-turning and the wolf-whistles and the blatant remarks, and let her startlingly green eyes roam lazily around the disco floor towards the bar.

'Fancy a night to remember, darlin'?' a guy in black leathers said, pressing close to her in the crush, and letting his hand slide around the silky mounds of her buttocks.

'Get lost, creep,' Alex said, giving him back the kind of language he would understand, and a stare that would freeze a polar bear at ten paces.

'Is that any way to treat somebody who's looking for a good time? How about this for starters, babe?'

He pressed closer now, and she could feel his erection pushing against her. She hid a faint smile, and swivelled round as if she was interested.

'How about *this*, babe?' she said softly, kneeing him just hard enough to make him grunt, and then twisting away from him to merge into the crowd of disco dancers.

'Bitch!' she heard him yell after her, but she was no longer interested, even though she had swiftly registered that he had a nice bum and clean white teeth, and was probably a biker. Maybe another time she might have accepted a drink or three . . . but tonight she was here on business, and the guy she was here to meet was a gent called Norman Price.

She scanned the bar area quickly, used to making instant assessments of people. It went with the job. Alexandra Best, Private Investigator . . . even now, whenever she caught sight of the title on her business cards or headed notepaper, it sent a thrill of almost sexual pleasure running through her.

She had learned the job unaided and through instinct, some of which had admittedly sent her down plenty of wrong alleys. But she finally felt she had made it – sort of – and if she was ever asked about her job, she said with as much irony as possible that turning to crime was the best thing she had ever done. . . .

There were half-a-dozen guys at the bar. She discounted the two who were surreptitiously holding hands. It was none of her business. An older man, hunched over his whisky, looked as if he was settling in for the night, and had already drunk half his weekly salary away. One guy turned away from the bar with a trayful of drinks, so he wasn't her man.

That still left two. It would be the dark-suited one, Alex decided. He was distinguished, slightly greying with a neat haircut and a furrowed frown on his face.

It certainly wouldn't be the yob with dirty fingernails, at least, she hoped not. She might often be involved in dirty jobs, but she was fastidious when it came to personal hygiene.

In the long mirror behind the bar she could see the guys watching her approach, and sensed that the barman was wondering what the hell she was doing in a place like this.

Her face, while not of the Demi Moore variety (nose too long, chin too pointed), nevertheless had a kind of autocratic quality about it – or so she always kidded herself when bemoaning that she was never going to be movie-star material. But she did have those glorious eyes, and long, pike-straight, fringed red hair that somebody once said shimmered with the richness of autumn leaves in New England.

It was a phrase that alternately charmed her and made her want to throw up. All Alex knew was that it was the kind of springy hair that leapt defiantly out of curling tongs no matter how much she coaxed it or swore at it . . . but right now, its hot colour was muted under the rose-coloured lights, and it looked pretty good, she acknowledged modestly.

What she *did* have – so she was told – was a sensual mix of innocence and hidden passion. They were assets that had got her into hot water as often as they had got her out of dangerous situations. She pushed some of the uglier memories out of her mind now, as she wove her way through the disco dancers to reach the bar of the Rainbow Club.

'Mr Price?' she queried the well-dressed gent in the suit. He looked at her, startled and wary at being approached, and she knew at once she had made a mistake.

'I'm sorry,' she said, backing off. 'I thought you were someone else.'

'I wish I was, miss,' he began with a ready smile, and she could tell he was intrigued and reassured by her well-bred voice and that Sloaney air of sophistication. It always fooled them.

'Miss Best?' she heard a thick voice say from somewhere along the length of the bar.

She smothered a groan. It was the huncher. The drunk. She hid her distaste as she moved towards him. She forced herself to remember that he was a client, no more, and personalities and lifestyles made no difference to her determination to do her damnedest for her clients.

Anyway, they were the ones who paid the bills for her tiny office and West End flat, she thought, with the inborn cynicism of somebody who had found her way to the proverbial top by her own efforts and no silver spoon.

She pushed aside the thought. Tonight, Alex Best's northern background was the last thing on her mind. She was here on business.

'I'm Alexandra Best,' she said, extending a slim hand adorned with her favourite antique silver and turquoise rings. 'And you are Mr Norman Price, I take it?'

'That's right.'

He looked at her from beneath bushy eyebrows. He was probably about sixty, but he looked older and seedier. But now that she looked at him properly, she thought he probably wasn't drunk at all. And why did something tell her the casual clothes he wore were far from his usual style?

His hair was too cropped, and too tidy around his nape; his fingernails were trimmed and ultra white. She always took account of such things; it went with the job.

But he had a worn, defeated air, like one of those dogs with sad eyes and drooping jowls whose name she could never remember. And he was desperate for somebody to find his missing daughter. Which was why she was here.

'It's far too noisy for us to talk here,' she said quietly, as the disco music reached a chest-hurting crescendo. 'Why didn't you come to my office like I suggested? We could go there now, if you like.'

God, she hoped he didn't think this was a pass. The barman, listening with eyebrows raised, obviously did.

'No,' Price said sharply, with no further explanation.

'Then we'd better find a table,' Alex said, jostled from behind once more. The biker had recovered from his kneeing, and was glowering at her now, his dark eyes gleaming with anger, but also something else.

Despite her earlier annoyance, she felt a *frisson* of excitement. After the boredom of a childhood spent in the wilds of Yorkshire, the longing for a more vibrant lifestyle was what had brought her to London and into this work in the first place. And this guy had a look of animal danger about him . . . deliciously so. And she was no nun.

She treated him to a smile and mouthed a 'Sorry, I'm here on business' at him, as Norman Price looked at her cautiously, then clearly remembered the social niceties.

'Let me get you a drink, Miss Best.'

'Just orange juice, thank you,' she said firmly. She normally went for vodka and lime, but maybe her innocent choice would encourage the guy to do the same.

He scowled as the barman asked him pointedly if he should

make that two orange juices, and then reluctantly agreed. A couple of minutes later they were heading towards a table at the far end of the room, but not before the biker had leaned towards her and whispered in her ear, nuzzling his lips far closer than was necessary. He smelled of the healthy outdoors.

'See you later, Miss Best.'

So he knew her name. Well, it didn't take a genius to know he'd overheard Norman Price mumble it. But the way the guy in the black leathers had said it was something else.

Sternly, Alex reminded herself that she fell in and out of lust too easily . . . and all too often it had nothing to do with love, just a wild sexual attraction, as inevitable as the pull of the moon on the tide. And, incongruous and unexpected though it was, it was pulling her now. . . .

'So tell me what I can do for you, Mr Price,' she prompted, when the client sat morosely looking into space. 'I can't help you unless I know every detail you can think of.'

She flipped open her notebook unobtrusively. The guy was nervous. She knew he didn't really want to be telling her anything at all. Despite his attitude tonight, Alex suspected he was behaving out of character, both in drinking heavily and coming to this kind of place. Maybe he thought he could find the kind of anonymity here that was in total contrast to his normal life, whatever that was.

Interesting. She filed away the thought for future reference. Intuition told her that he was either a very private person, or somebody with secrets. She plumped for the second, knowing what little she already did. Somebody had invaded the privacy of his life and snatched his daughter. Or so he suspected. And for some reason he didn't want the police involved. QED.

'It's my daughter.'

'Yes?' she prompted again, knowing he couldn't be rushed.

Sometimes you had to winkle information out of them with the proverbial pin. She gave a mental shrug. It was her time, but it was their money that was paying for it, and she had her eye on a winter cruise that was going to be her reward for finding the Price girl.

'To my knowledge she's been missing for two weeks now, and it's vital that I find her by the end of next month.'

'And why is that?'

Encouraging him, Alex calculated that six weeks' work would produce a healthy sum towards her cruise.

'What?'

'Why is it vital to find her before the end of next month?' she repeated, as patiently as if she was questioning a child.

There was something odd here, thought Alex. The guy had a clipped Yorkshire accent, like hers had once been before she had spent months in smoothing and rounding it after moving south. He spoke with a sense of desperation when he mentioned his daughter, but also with some irritation that didn't sound like genuine parental concern.

She had noted it on his initial phone call, well attuned to an accent and the nuance of a disembodied voice. But why such precise attention to detail – and why not get the police on to it, or Interpol, for God's sake?

'She comes into a large inheritance then, and she must be in good health to claim it. If not, it all goes to a cousin.'

Alex could hear the anger in his voice now, and felt a ridiculous sense of disappointment and betrayal. So it all came down to money. And where was the love he should be showing for his daughter? She was indignant at what she imagined was the girl's loveless childhood, knowing the signs all too well, and she felt a brief pity for the kid.

'How old is your daughter, Mr Price?' she said carefully.

Good God, he even had to think about that, she thought, as he hesitated. But apparently it was simply reluctance to reveal his daughter's age.

'She was twenty-nine on her last birthday, but of course she'll be thirty at the end of next month—'

'For Christ's sake, I'm sorry – but I had assumed from your phone call that she was a child,' she said, momentarily floundering. 'It's hardly unusual for a woman of twenty-nine to take off on her own for two weeks, is it?'

'It is for Caroline,' he said, clearly annoyed at her involuntary reaction, just as Alex herself was at making it so clumsily. 'She doesn't go walkabout. And she's deaf.'

So she was looking for a deaf adult woman, three years older than herself, who could be anywhere in the world, especially if she had something to hide, or something she wanted to escape from. Great!

11

'Have you tried the usual places – friends, acquaintances, workmates, local hospitals?'

The morgue? she added silently.

'She doesn't have any friends, and she works at home. She's a crossword compiler.'

'Her publisher then, her agent?' Alex went on relentlessly. 'They must be in contact with her.'

'No. She's totally freelance, and I have to tell you, lass, we don't get on. She's been a recluse since meningitis left her deaf about ten years ago. She had a hard time dealing with it. She works alone and lives on her own in her cottage, and she's as touchy and defensive as a cat. I check on her every few weeks, and she even hates that. Last time I saw her she said vaguely she was between commissions. Or, as actors would say, she was resting temporarily.'

Alex jotted down the details as he spoke. She knew a bit about acting in an amateur way. Right now she was playing her best part – Alexandra Best, confident super sleuth, and with as much idea of how to go about each new case, as flying to the moon on a broomstick.

She also played to perfection – and sometimes far too well – the kind of upper-class girl who turned men horny the minute they discovered her outgoing nature, and thought that even if there was nothing much between the ears, there was considerably more between those great legs.

Nobody would ever connect her with little Audrey Barnes from a farming family in the remote Yorkshire Dales, who'd missed out on schooling through caring for elderly parents. And who, with true Little Dorrit melodrama, had vowed to make A BETTER LIFE for herself if she had to kill for it. . . . She never had, thank God, but by now she had met others who had.

Through learning by trial and error to be streetwise, she had seen how the minds of those people worked, and the idea had begun to form of solving some of those crimes. During all the tedious hours at home caring for her parents, she had read voraciously, learning about the way the police and other investigators operated. She could solve most TV crimes as soon as the suspects were presented on screen.

When the farm eventually became hers, she had sold it for a surprisingly decent amount, and had come to London. And she knew at once that she was in a different league. So the invention of Alexandra Best, née Audrey Barnes, had been an essential part of the transition.

'Look, miss, perhaps I'll leave it after all,' Norman Price was saying now, as if her intense green stare had begun to unnerve him. 'I'm sure Caroline will turn up soon—'

'And if she doesn't?'

Alex leaned forward and placed one hand on his arm, feeling the tension in it. 'Mr Price, I don't know if I can help you, but I promise I'll give it a damn good try, so why don't you go home and sleep on it and give me another call tomorrow? And if you'd rather not come to my office, why don't we meet at Caroline's cottage in a day or two? It can often provide clues that even close relatives miss.'

She wondered if Norman Price had even bothered to look for such clues. He was an oddball if she ever saw one. And he wasn't half as drunk as she had at first imagined. Just keen to get his hands on his daughter's inheritance. Maybe. As yet, she couldn't really fathom him at all. She saw him nod slowly.

'All right. I'll call you tomorrow morning with my decision. And thank you for your time.'

He shook her hand, and Alex noted that his was clammy. There was nothing unusual in that. Her clients were frequently either distressed or hyperactive. It was to be expected. Nobody liked airing their private thoughts in public, and it took some people a lot of courage to do so.

After he left, she scribbled a few details in her notebook while they were fresh in her mind. Yes, definitely an oddball. And he hadn't told her everything yet. In fact, he'd hardly told her anything at all. . . .

'Are you sticking with orange juice all night, or do you fancy something a bit more exciting to tickle your taste-buds?'

Alex didn't need to look up from her scribblings to recognize the voice, and nor did she miss the *double entendre* in the words. The biker lounged in front of her, arms folded, powerful and dark against the smoky background of the club. He was every inch the Clint Eastwood of his day – or maybe James Dean reincarnated, she thought faintly.

. . . But why not? The night was still early. . . .

'I'll have a vodka and lime if you're buying,' she said, a damn sight cooler than she felt inside.

'If you're selling, I'm buying,' he said with a lazy, seductive smile.

She watched him as he moved smoothly back to the bar, and adjusted her earlier opinion of him. He didn't just have a nice bum. He was a wow, even if he was a pick-up, and she felt the familiar tug on her nerve-ends at the thought.

And there was no way she could misinterpret his words: he was as blatant as they come. She smiled faintly as the words entered her head and tried to concentrate on Norman Price.

Usually, after her first meeting with a client, she went home and tried to assess everything she had learned so far which wasn't much, she admitted again, but as always, it was far more than the client thought.

For a start. from his generous agreement to her fees, she guessed that Father Price was well-heeled, despite tonight's cha-rade of dressing down for the company. Maybe he was in disguise too, acting a part in life, the way she did.

It was an intriguing thought. She'd already looked him up in the phone book and he wasn't listed, even though he'd given her a number where she could reach him. So he was ex-directory, and he was using a contact number ... or a private one that could mean anything, from a mistress's address to a hideaway holiday place.

But now that she knew a little more about the missing daughter, she would start on the trail of both of them tomorrow. If the woman was a crossword compiler, she shouldn't be hard to trace. She noted that Price hadn't volunteered the name of any newspaper group, but that wouldn't be hard to find either. Caroline sounded like a loner, so there may not even be an agent involved. Pity. That would have been a start.

The biker was coming back to the table with two drinks in his hand, and Alex abandoned all thoughts of work for tonight. Sometimes it was best to do just that. Make her mind a blank and let her subconscious ask the questions and sort out some of the answers. It could work spectacularly well.

And sometimes there were more important things to think about, anyway. She crossed one silk-clad leg over the other, and her short skirt revealed the lacy top of her sheer black stockings.

The guy noted it and grinned.

'If we're going to spend the night together, we'd better get properly acquainted,' he said, as brash as you like.

'You're taking a bloody lot for granted, aren't you!'

He laughed, showing those amazing white teeth. Alex could almost taste his minty toothpaste already.

'Am I?' he said, oozing sexiness as he reached forward and caressed her velvety cheek. 'You tell me.'

'I don't have to tell you anything—'

He shrugged. 'OK. So I'll tell you what I see. I see somebody way out of her environment in the Rainbow Club. Slumming it, I guess. The question is – why?'

'And what's the answer?' Alex said, despite herself. Who was the detective here, for God's sake!

'Well, you're not a hooker, that's for sure.'

'Thanks!'

'So you're either a snoopy journalist taking notes for a magazine article, or you're doing research for a book – or you're looking for somebody.'

'How clever you are!' Alex murmured, giving nothing away, but thinking at the same time that at least the guy had a brain. And she liked that. She liked it a lot.

'So which is it?' he asked, taking a long drink and not taking his eyes off her face.

'Guess.'

'The journalist.'

'You're wrong, but thanks for the compliment. I've always fancied working in that line,' she lied. 'Now forget it.'

'OK, but I know you're into something from the way you kept jotting down notes in that little book of yours.'

Alex was glad it was safely tucked inside her bag now. Among tonight's doodles was a rough drawing of Norman Price, and another of the guy sitting opposite her now. It was gratifying to know that her aptitude for art had come in handy for something. She wasn't wonderful, but she wasn't bad, either, and she could create a passable likeness. Even a passable mug-shot on occasion.

'I'm Gary, by the way. Gary Hollis,' he said, when the silence between them lengthened.

'Alexandra,' she said non-committally.

'Classy. So, Alexandra, where are you taking me tonight?'

15

'What's the matter? Don't you have a place to sleep?' she said, suddenly suspicious.

She'd met pick-ups before. Drifters who came into town and played up to anybody who would give them a free bed for the night. She was mildly disappointed. Somehow she hadn't expected this guy to be one of the transient kind.

'Sure I do. But I'd far rather sleep at your place,' he said. 'And don't tell me you're not interested.'

She could see the sexual challenge in his eyes, and she was aware of her own weakness.

Virile guys with sexy eyes could always turn her on, and she could already imagine her fingers running through that collar-length dark hair . . . she gave a small shiver.

'Alternatively, how about a blast on the bike while you think about it?' he went on.

A different kind of excitement ran through Alex's veins at the words. 'You do have a bike then?'

'Only the very best. A Harley is at your disposal, ma'am, ready, willing and eager, just like its owner.'

She ignored that, but she knew enough about motor bikes to know that if he owned a Harley Davidson he was no drop-out. And his leathers were of good quality that hadn't been bought at some cheapskate everything-must-go warehouse sale.

And, thinking ahead, she also registered that he might be useful if ever she needed to get somewhere in a hurry while trying to track down the missing Caroline Price. A motor bike could often reach the parts that a car couldn't.

As always, her client's needs were never far from her mind, even when she tried to abandon them for the time being.

But that was what being professional was all about. Let the ideas simmer on the back-burner of the mind, and eventually, with any luck, they would burst into flame.

'All right, I'll take a ride with you,' she said, seeming to capitulate. 'Providing you've got a spare crash helmet.'

'Lady, I've got all the protection you'll ever need,' Gary said with a grin that told her he definitely wasn't just talking about biking gear.

They surfaced a joyful couple of hours after getting back to Alex's flat. By then, the duvet and pillows had found their way to the floor, to join the frantic scattering of clothes that had been shed between the sitting-room and the bedroom. The leathers and silk skirt mingled with the trail of stockings and lacy under-wear. . . .

'Nice,' Gary murmured against her breasts as he carefully shifted his weight to circle each stiffened nipple with his tongue. 'I think I might move in.'

Alex hoisted him off the bed so fast that he hit the floor with a howl of rage.

'What the hell did you do that for?'

She rose naked from the bed. pulling on her red kimono dressing-gown to hide the burgeoning thighs, while briefly won-dering why she was getting so paranoid about the damn things. He'd seen it all, and he certainly hadn't minded . . . he reached for her and they both fell onto the bed again.

At once, she knelt over him, holding his arms back over his head. She was surprisingly strong, and she could see by his expression that he hadn't expected her to be. It was a legacy from tramping the Dales in all weathers, and her fair-weather keep-fit sessions at the gym.

In her job, you never knew how much sprinting you might need to do, nor how much physical strength would be needed to overpower an assailant. It wasn't all chicken-feed stuff.

'You can forget any ideas about moving in,' she snapped. 'We had a great time. Gary, but that was it.'

'So now it's goodbye? You disappoint me, Alexandra. Anyway, I thought that was supposed to be my line.'

'Not unless you've been living in a time-warp for the last couple of decades,' she whipped back.

But she was all too aware that his passion was on the rise again. And she fancied him like mad, damn it, as she freely admitted now that she had done from the moment she saw him. His sensual mouth curved into a smile as he saw the matching desire in her eyes, and his hands slid down to push the dressing-gown aside and stroke between her thighs.

Oh well, what the hell, she thought weakly? She'd probably never see him again anyway. . . .

She was still waking up properly as she heard the roar of the Harley departing around 7 a.m. Gary had kissed her thoroughly before he left, and her own musky smell had wafted around his lips.

'I'll see you around,' was all he had said.

And then he had gone. But that was OK. She had work to do, and too much involvement usually got in the way.

She got up half an hour later, had a shower and grimaced at the love-bites on her neck. He was an enthusiastic and inventive lover all right, she'd say that for him. She felt her heartbeats quicken, remembering just how good it had been, then resolutely washed every vestige of him out of her mind and body.

As she rinsed away the sweet-scented shower gel with the spray, she found herself wondering about Caroline Price's love-life, or if she'd even had one. She realized she was unintentionally thinking about her in the past tense. and she revised the thought at once.

Missing nearly-thirty-year-olds were more likely to disappear for some personal and private reason rather than from anything sinister. And if they did so, they would certainly have the nous to cover all their tracks, so that no inquisitive father could find them.

But in this case, there was a large inheritance waiting to be claimed in about six weeks' time. And if it wasn't claimed satisfactorily, then, according to Norman Price, a cousin would be waiting in the wings to claim it.

Alex's first instinct was to ask herself what was in it for the father? She sensed that it wasn't just for his daughter's well-being that he wanted her to claim what was rightfully hers. Her second instinct was to remember that in all traditional detective stories, the villainous cousin would be the most likely suspect to have abducted Caroline until it was too late for her to claim her inheritance, and everything would be rightfully his.

So usually, he was the *least* likely suspect. Except that you could never *quite* ignore the possibility, damn it. It was all too easy to dismiss what was right under your nose. And besides, what would he do with the girl after abducting her? He couldn't just return her home again.

The gnawing likelihood of what frequently happened in such circumstances was something Alex didn't care to think about too deeply.

She'd grown up in a harsh environment, and she'd had to

hold on to that toughness to survive. But she could never get used to seeing some poor sod zipped up in a plastic body bag after a violent death had occurred.

Or having to stand by while some grieving relative identified a loved one. Somebody had to do it, and she knew she had the reputation among the local plods for being as cold as ice on such occasions. But she wasn't. Inside, she was always falling apart.

The phone was ringing as she was drying her hair and waiting for the toaster to pop up with her wholemeal slice. She wasn't the world's tidiest person, and her kitchen was in its usual state of chaos, but the area where she lived now reflected her pride in building A BETTER LIFE for herself by her own efforts. Her life was definitely upwardly mobile since Audrey had become Alexandra. Despite the chaos.

'Alexandra Best,' she said into the phone.

'Good morning, Miss Best. I hope I'm not too early. This is Norman Price. If you're prepared to continue with the investigation, I'm happy to retain you. So would you meet me at my daughter's cottage at twelve o'clock? And I apologize for any lack of finesse on my part last night. I'd like to make up for it by buying you lunch.'

'Thank you. I accept,' Alex said at once, registering the polished smoothness in the voice now.

Oh yes, this was the real McCoy all right, and last night's show had been just to capture her sympathy. But she was wise to that game. As a pathetic old man, lost without his daughter, it hadn't rung true.

She didn't accept his lunch invitation for the joy of eating with the slob, but because informal meetings often gave out the unwitting clues the clients were too inhibited to reveal otherwise. She quickly noted down the address of Greenwell Cottage. It sounded rural and picturesque, and was situated in a small village north of Bishop's Stortford.

And she was on a very healthy retainer. Alex's normally good spirits lifted still more, visualizing a trip to the country on expenses, and her cruise becoming even more of a reality. But first, she had some detective work to do.

Dressed in a casual trouser suit in her trademark black, she left her flat and drove to the building where she had her office.

She felt the familiar glow at seeing the gleaming gilt lettering on the nameplate, Alexandra Best, Private Investigator. She unlocked her glass-panelled door and went inside, picking up the mail as she did so and tossing it into a wire tray after a cursory glance at the envelopes. There was nothing that couldn't wait until later.

First, she switched on her computer and opened the file for Caroline Price. She ran down the usual leads to follow, checked the necessary volumes of *Who's Who* and other directories on her shelf, and spent some time making phone calls. Her frown had deepened by the time she had finished.

None of the big newspaper groups or magazines had ever heard of a crossword compiler called Caroline Price. Nor had any of the literary agencies she tried as a last resort, though she hardly expected them to be interested in such small commission stuff.

Even if the woman used a pseudonym, those people would have known her real name. And not even the additional tag of being a deaf woman could identify her. Alex checked the local hospitals, but no woman of that name had been admitted during the past two weeks. She checked the airports and ferry terminals and again she got nowhere.

It seemed that Caroline Price had simply vanished off the face of the earth. Transported by aliens, maybe . . . which was crazy, and just the kind of thing that Alexandra in her dumbest mode might imagine, Alex thought in sudden annoyance. But she was shrewder than that.

Caroline had to be somewhere. People didn't just vanish. People must know her. People must be missing her. Unless it was Norman Price himself who was crazy, and there was no daughter, and no inheritance at all.

And Alex had just arranged to meet him alone in a cottage in a remote Hertfordshire village at noon.

Chapter 2

The likelihood of it all being some bizarre hoax was ridiculous. Alex had heard some stories in her time, but never a man who had invented a missing daughter. There were women who wanted a child so much they imagined they'd given birth, and even resorted to snatching another woman's baby. Even though the new thinking was that women who had had miscarriages or had lost a child through cot-death were the least likely to want any other woman's child, she'd had one traumatic case like that, and she didn't particularly want another, thank you very much. But nobody invented a missing daughter of thirty years old!

'So where the hell are you, Caroline?' she muttered.

She saw a shadow outside the glass door of her office and visibly jumped, feeling as if she had somehow conjured up the missing woman out of her imagination. Quickly, she told herself not to get twitchy. Nobody could get into the building without pressing the security button and getting official admittance. She wasn't expecting anybody, but there were one or two who were admitted on the strength of their ID cards. She must speak to the guy on the desk about that. . . .

Her door opened after a brief knock, and a face she knew all too well came around the door. DI Nick Frobisher from the local constabulary had been chasing her for months now, even though she had only given him minimal encouragement, having decided early on that it would be fatal to mix a useful business contact with pleasure.

Though she had to admit that Nick was a super guy if you liked the tall, lean, black-moustachioed type, and she supposed his Latino appearance helped to disarm the crims he came into contact with. He often said proudly that his rough looks were identifiable with theirs. Alex liked him a lot, but that was all. He was a useful inside contact because he often gave her tips she'd never get from the police otherwise.

She wouldn't want it put into words that she used him, but in this business people used one another in all kinds of ways, didn't they? And she had learned very early on that you got your information where you could and by whatever means. There was no university course for private eyes, and the sources weren't always as savoury as Nick. All the same, he shouldn't take it for granted that she was always so damn accessible to him. Or pleased to see him.

'You scared me half to death, creeping up on me like that,' she yelled. 'And if you want coffee, you'll have to make it yourself. I'm going out of town in exactly twenty minutes from now.'

He grinned at her scratchiness, helping himself to the coffee she always kept percolating, and took no offence. In Alex's opinion, that was part of his trouble, charisma-wise. Despite his great looks, he still had the ability to merge into the background, as effortlesly as a chameleon.

In his job, it was a rare strength too, of course. Everybody, crims and contacts alike, thought his personality value was zilch, while Alex knew that it wasn't. Underneath, he smouldered. As the word came into her mind, she felt more than a stirring of interest at the thought, and quickly smothered it. Now wasn't the time. She had too much to do.

'Do you know how you turn me on when you're angry?' Frobisher said, mentally backing off as the emerald eyes resembled chips of ice. 'Actually, I was in the area on business, and thought you might be interested in hearing about a body we recovered from a lake yesterday. The circumstances sound just about up your street,' he added, with the usual callous patronage he could never quite resist.

'Sorry, Nick. I'm already on a case,' she said coolly, her accent as cut-glass now as the proverbial Austrian crystal, and betraying no interest at all.

'OK. I just thought this one might have stirred even your hard heart. It was probably a crime of passion, though as far as the clothes went, she looked like one of those Stepford Wives before the drugs got to her. She was no oil-painting, mind, though she might have been once. Still, they never look good in the state I get to see them. Once the water's got to them for a few days, and blown them up—'

Alex was no longer listening to detail, knowing he'd go to town on the gory bits if she gave him the slightest encouragement. She didn't want to know about bloated bodies and green-tinged skin right now, thanks. But her interest had definitely been caught.

'She? Did you say *she*? Where? And how old?'

She musn't sound too eager. Bodies weren't found every day of the week, even in Nick's job. And there was no possible reason to suppose that this one had been Caroline Price. Only a fool would think such a coincidence could happen. And so quickly. But just sometimes Alex knew you had to let the long arm of coincidence in for a few minutes.

'She was a well-preserved forty, the doc thought, though the autopsy reports haven't come through yet as to actual cause of death. She could have been killed and then dumped in the lake. Why? Is it any interest to you?'

Frobisher's eyes became keener. His laid-back manner hid a canny ability to sense when somebody else was on to something. Especially something he should know, and which the other party wasn't telling. Alex recognized the trait in him, since it was part of her own make-up. Trading information or keeping it to yourself was very much a two-way affair. She gave an unconcerned shrug, not yet prepared to confide in him.

'Oh, it just triggered my memory about something I read in the paper, that's all. Wasn't there some group being suspected of starting up that kind of caper in deepest Wales recently? Stepford Wives and all that stuff, I mean,' she added vaguely, thankful that he'd given her a lead by mentioning them.

'Yeah? I don't remember seeing it. But I wouldn't mind seeing you play up to my every whim like one of those Barbie dolls, kiddo,' Nick said with a grin, his eyes roaming over Alex's curvacious figure.

'And I'd like to see you out of here before I have you thrown out,' she said crisply, her smile firm.

He laughed, draining his coffee and getting to his feet. He was never riled by anything she said. He often told her he fancied her rotten. They both knew the routine, just as they both knew it was probably never going to get him anywhere. It didn't stop him

rising to the challenge though, in more ways than one, as he frequently hinted.

'All right, I'm going. But one day, Alex, one day. . . .'

'In your dreams. And it's Alexandra.'

She didn't know why she bothered to say it, except that the
grandiose name she'd bequeathed herself gave her a feeling of
superiority. It distanced her from the punters, and anyone else
who came too close for comfort.

But she was still smiling when he'd gone, wondering, just for
a minute, how he'd be . . . there was a damn sight more to him
that he showed on the surface, and she wasn't being facetious in
her thinking, either. He had a calculating brain, and a relentless
way of never letting go of a case . . . and she liked a man with
brains.

But she had her own case to think about. She reverted at once
to business mode and dismissed the thought of considering Nick
Frobisher as anything more than a good mate. She gathered up
everything she needed in her leather holdall, switched off the
coffee percolator and watched from her window until she saw
Nick drive away.

Then she gave him ten minutes more before she switched on
her answering machine and fax, and went down to her car.

She wasn't born yesterday and she wouldn't put it past him to
follow her out of sheer bloody-minded curiosity, and even
though the thought of police back-up had its merit at times, it
wouldn't do her any good at all with this particular client. He
had made that abundantly clear, and she didn't want to lose her
retainer before she'd even begun.

Part of her morning's work had been to track down just what
Norman Price did. It had been pathetically easy to discover the
name and address of Price Chemicals. Alex found the rambling
buildings just outside London in an unsalubrious area. The company may have prospered once, but there were several
incongruities that hit her at once. From the look of the peeling
paintwork and general shabby appearance – compared with the
sleek forest-green Mercedes parked in the company director's
parking space – Alex made a shrewd guess that if the CD needed
his daughter's money, there had probably been too many dips
into the profits to make the company viable any longer.

Before she made her way to his daughter's cottage. Alex sat in her car at a discreet distance for some while, watching the comings and goings of the various folk who inhabited Price's world. She was definitely curious about him, wishing she could be a mind-reader when it came to the deviousness of some of her clients. And she was damn sure that applied to this particular charmer.

From the look of the run-down buildings here, and the fact that he was so interested in his daughter's future inheritance, she'd put even money on his Achilles heel. She'd seen too many just like him. Throwing their money about like water, gambling the profits away. Men like Norman Price often had a habit that was hard to break. It was how so many of them came to grief. They got in deep before they knew it, and the consequences often led to crime or suicide.

It was all speculation so far, of course. But she prided herself on her woman's intuition when it came to such things. And if it happened that a man who had got so badly out of his depth was lucky enough to have a daughter with a promised inheritance waiting in the wings, what then?

Norman Price was thinking about Alexandra Best at that precise moment. She was nearer the truth in her assessment of him than she realized. His gambling debts hadn't seemed any problem until six months ago when he realized he was taking far more out of the business than was coming in.

Now he was in Queer Street. And if he couldn't persuade Caroline to invest heavily in the family business once she came into her money . . . well, Price didn't want to contemplate what would happen in that case, with the blood-sucking creditors already breathing down his neck like vampires. He hadn't anticipated any problem in persuading Caroline that being a sleeping-partner in the firm would be a good move. She didn't have a head for business, and the second set of books he would show her would convince her of the annual dividends she could expect.

But why the silly bitch had disappeared just when he was going to make his move, was a complication he could do without. She had no men friends that he knew about – although, as they had never communicated on such delicate matters,

Caroline's little country cottage could be the scene of raving sex orgies for all he knew.

He scowled. Knowing her as he thought he did, he doubted anything of the kind, and anyway, he didn't want to think about it. Sex was the last thing that mattered to him these days, and if ever there was a case of anxiety – not to say panic – squashing what little libido he'd ever had, he knew it in full measure now.

Anyway, if this bloody drop-dead gorgeous detective woman with the child-bearing thighs couldn't even stir him to erotic thoughts, then he might as well forget them for ever. He was cute enough to have seen the glances between her and that leather-clad sleaze at the Rainbow Club last night though, and even his limited imagination had put two and two together. Or even one and one.

And for a man with no sense of irony, let alone humour, that little notion wasn't half bad.

He switched his thoughts away from the two of them, and con-centrated on getting ready to drive to his daughter's cottage to meet the woman. There had never been any love lost between him and his daughter, and the distance between them had widened considerably since Caroline had become so hostile and defensive because of her deafness.

Norman Price was a cold customer, but since father–daughter affection had never rated highly for either of them, they were better apart, and they both knew it.

But he had to find her now, he thought savagely. It all came back to that. He had to find her, and make up to her, because without her bloody money he'd probably end up in a debtors' prison, if there was still such a thing.

His face was dark and furrowed as he slid behind the wheel of his Mercedes. He breathed in the clean, expensive smell of the interior and caressed the wheel more lovingly than he'd ever caressed a woman. He was in danger of losing everything and if that included the motor, it would be comparable to almost reaching orgasm and never quite making it. The worst kind of hell.

Alex reached the small village of Wilsingham just before noon, having been held up on the motorway by an accident. Not that she had wanted to arrive before Price himself, but the delay had given her no time to call in at the village post office to make a few casual enquiries about Caroline Price, nor to stroll around the village green where the old men were gathered on the wooden seats circling an ancient oak, as predictably as summer follows spring. But there would be more opportunity for strolling later, if not today, and for buying a pint or two for the more garrulous locals in the village pub.

Right now she followed Norman Price's directions to the far end of the village, where the isolated cottage stood in tranquilly rustic surroundings. It really was picture-book stuff, Alex thought, if you liked that kind of thing.

But she had left such isolation behind long ago, and vastly preferred the hectic, noisy vibrancy of the city. The country was nice for a day of nostalgia, but to her, civilization meant London.

She saw the now-familiar Mercedes parked outside Greenwell Cottage. She had deliberately taken her time so that she wouldn't arrive there before him. She mentally noted that a guy who could afford such a car was unlikely to need the daughter's money on his own account and was still unconvinced that Price was all he appeared. A bit more investigation on the man himself was definitely on the cards.

The cottage was partially hidden by a dense thicket of evergreens, and it was the ideal place for somebody who didn't want to be disturbed by neighbours. Caroline was obviously a very private person, and she could be as isolated as she chose here without performing some disappearing act.

Norman Price must have seen her coming, because the cottage door opened even before she was halfway up the path. The scent of roses in the white-picket-fenced garden was almost nauseatingly sweet, but it was also clear that no one had dead-headed them, nor weeded the borders, for some time. The paintwork on the cottage was spruce enough, the floral curtains were neatly drawn back with schmaltzy ties, but the garden looked sadly neglected and forlorn.

'I thought you weren't coming,' Price complained.

'Sorry if I'm a little late. A traffic accident on the motorway,' she said, perfectly aware that his accusing voice hid unease as well as annoyance.

He didn't really want her here at all, thought Alex immedi-

27

ately. She had probably been his last resort in looking for his daughter. And maybe he'd thought a woman would be less inquisitive into his private affairs than a man. She bridled at the thought, because he couldn't be more wrong. She had a tenacious habit of never letting go, if she thought there was something more to discover. Like the Mountie, she always aimed to get her man . . . or woman, as the case may be.

Price was also clearly the sort of man who didn't take kindly to inefficiency in others – even if they were sloppy enough in their own dealings. She didn't yet know if that applied to him, but it was hard not to make prior judgements when it was someone you instinctively disliked. And she disliked him intensely.

She entered the cottage and stood perfectly still in the small living-room, the way she always did when entering someone else's place for the first time. It was the perfect way to absorb the essence of someone else's aura. The room had a slightly musty and unused smell. She breathed in deeply, noting the heather mixture carpet and the no-nonsense armchair and sofa, grouped around the TV set. There was no smell of furniture polish, and all the wooden surfaces had a faint film of dust on them.

All the same, Alex felt that this was the home of someone efficient, yet homely. Someone who might not be a mad keen housekeeper – any more than she was herself – but someone who liked a reasonable sense of order (viz the compiling of crosswords), and most days would be satisfied with giving everything a casual flip with a duster to keep the dust down.

Masses of books spilled out of bookcases and shelves, but magazines of the geographic and information variety were stacked neatly. There were no women's mags in sight, and no *Homes-and Gardens* either. There were a few novels, but most of the books were reference books of all descriptions.

The main focus of the room was obviously the area taking up the whole of one side of the room. There was a large desk on which there was a computer and printer, with piles of crossword grids alongside, and a photocopier.

At a cursory glance, Alex saw that some of the grids were still in their virgin state, and others had already been partly compiled. She also noted that the drawers of the desk had keyholes, and she'd be willing to bet good money that the drawers were locked. There was no telephone. Presumably there would be no reason for a deaf person to have one. (Wasn't there some way that BT could get around that? She wasn't terribly *au fait* with the details, and anyway, it didn't matter right now.)

'Are you going to make a start then? I don't have all day to waste,' she heard Father Price say as she roamed around, his voice oozing impatience. He seemed oddly uncomfortable in this environment, and Alex could see that he didn't want to stay any longer than was necessary.

'Actually, I've already started,' she said crisply. 'And you must let me do things in my own way, Mr Price. I need to feel and absorb the place where Caroline lived – lives,' she corrected quickly. No sense in worrying him unduly yet.

'I'd like to take some photographs if you have no objection,' she went on. 'And I'd also like to phototcopy a few of these crossword grids. There's always an individual pattern to every compiler's work, and it could be a help in tracking her down through her own particular style.'

He looked at her as if she was stupid, and she guessed that he had never had the wit or the inclination to unclue a crossword puzzle in his life. She widened her green eyes to disarm any suspicions he might have of her motives. Though why should he, for God's sake? He was the one retaining her. Yet the feeling that he too had something to hide was very strong in her gut at that moment.

'I suppose it's all right,' he said guardedly. 'Though Caroline's photo album is probably around here somewhere, and surely you can take what you want from that.'

'That will be useful. but it's not just photographs of Caroline and any acquaintances that I need: I also want to photograph the cottage as it is today.'

Blow-ups could often reveal what the naked eye missed. They had been her godsend on other cases. But as she got her Leica out of her bag and adjusted the lens she saw Price give a shrug and stand well back out of camera-range. Interesting.

'Do you have any objections if I go upstairs and look around?' she asked next. 'And perhaps you could hunt out that photo album for me to look through while I take a few pics. I'm sure it will be useful.'

'If you like.'

For somebody supposedly keen to find his daughter, he wasn't the world's most communicative man. He was cold and distant, and if Alex had been his daughter the less she had to do with him, the better she would have liked it. But, as she knew now, his need to find her all came down to money.

Poor Caroline. Poor little rich girl. Poor little *dead* rich girl, maybe. Alex shivered as the hated thought tripped into her mind. But you had to examine all the possibilities without shirking, and that was one of them.

She went up the narrow spiral staircase to the two bedrooms and tiny bathroom. The cottage was what was popularly known in estate agents' jargon as quaint, providing you liked a place where there was no room to swing a cat. (Why a cat, particularly?) She realized she was letting her mind wander, and told herself to get on with the task in hand.

Caroline Price's bathroom was quite a revelation. From the rather dour, reclusive conception Alex had been given of her, and which she had totally accepted, here were expensive bottles of bath oils and perfumes and, even more surprisingly, a bottle of sensuous massage oil. And whose fingers would be busily using *that*, she wondered? And on whom?

She took several pics of the bathroom from different angles, and noted the names and makes of the various oils. They gave her no real clues, for there was no consistency in any of them. Still, you never knew. Then she went into the larger of the two bedrooms. Here again, it was the bedroom of a far more sensual woman than she had been led to believe. The pristine coverlet was of white lace, and the twin white satin fun pillows were frivolous rather than functional.

Silently, Alex opened several of the dressing-table drawers, and noted the silky underwear. The scent of an expensive perfume that hadn't come from Woolworths, rose seductively from every drawer. Alex fingered the softness of a black satin nightgown, lifting the sensual fabric to her nostrils with a sense of vicarious pleasure. She wouldn't mind a few of these items herself.

As she replaced the nightgown, her fingers encountered something hard at the back of the drawer. She pulled it out, saw that it was a diary, and slipped it into her bag as she heard Norman Price laboriously coming up the stairs. There was also a large key in the drawer that she guessed was a spare key to the cottage, and she took that too.

'Well? Any clues?' he said, as if the solution to Caroline's disappearance was going to jump out and hit her.

'Not immediately,' Alex said. 'But once I get my film processed I'll be able to study things minutely, and I'll get back to you as soon as there's anything to report.'

'Fair enough. And here's the album you wanted to see. There's some good likenesses of Caroline in it.'

He opened the album and pointed out several photos. Alex didn't betray her thoughts, but in no way could she associate the woman who bought erotic underwear designed for a man's pleasure, or the sensuous bath and massage oils, with the plainly dull woman she saw pictured here.

The term Stepford Wives leapt to mind, partly because of her recent conversation with Nick Frobisher, but also because of the ankle-length Laura Ashley dresses that Caroline seemed to favour. The face wouldn't have launched a thousand ships though, she thought, a mite uncharitably. The nose was too big, the jaw too square, but there was a determination in the face that stamped her as a fairly dominant person. She had probably had to be, with Norman as a role model.

But all credit to Caroline for enjoying a more sensuous life than her father gave her credit for, Alex thought, mentally cheering womanhood *en masse*. And she wouldn't mind betting that Norman had no idea of whatever alternative kind of life his daughter was leading. He would merely see the pristine white bedroom as virginal, ignoring the sensuous fabrics. But the woman was clearly more of an enigma than Alex had been led to believe.

'Can I take a couple of these photos?' she asked now.

'Take the whole damn' album if you think it'll help. Though there's nobody in there but childhood friends and family. The names are marked underneath in most places. She was hardly God's gift to womanhood, as you can see, and I doubt that any man ever looked twice at her.'

'That's hardly a kind way to describe her, Mr Price—' Alex said reproachfully, annoyed that she had been thinking the same thing herself, just seconds ago.

'Maybe. But I think I know my daughter better than you do, lass.'

And maybe you don't, thought Alex.

She was still thinking about the key she'd found tucked away at the back of the dressing-table drawer. If it wasn't a spare key to the cottage, she'd be very surprised ... and if she wasn't going to make good use of it at some future time, her name wasn't Alexandra Best, super-sleuth.

She grimaced, knowing she was more likely somebody just floundering in the dark as always, until inspiration struck. She was sure there were PIs with magical methods of detection, but hers were just instinct. And luck. Sometimes.

'We'd better have that lunch,' she heard Norman Price say, somewhat grudgingly now. 'I'm told the local pub here does quite good food, if you can bear to go native.'

He was trying to cover his disgruntled manner and be more sociable, but it didn't work. He didn't have a gracious bone in his body. For all his business suit and his swish car, he was a brusque Yorkshireman at heart, and Alex guessed that he didn't really want to sit and eat lunch with her, any more than she wanted to eat with him. All she wanted now was to get back to her office and take a good look through Caroline's photos, and especially her diary, which would give her a good insight into her character. And maybe a lot more besides.

'Would you mind awfully if we skipped lunch?' Alex said, in her best Sloaney voice. 'I've got another meeting this afternoon, and I'd also like to get started on a line of enquiry into Caroline's disappearance right away. So if you haven't actually booked a table anywhere. . . .'

She left it vague, knowing damn well that he hadn't. The village pub wasn't that kind of place. And from the relieved look in his eyes she knew she'd said the right thing.

They remained at the cottage just long enough for her to photocopy several crossword grids, and then she waited until he had locked the cottage door and shook hands with him. His were clammy again, and she was doubly sure that this investigation was not what he wanted at all.

He wanted his daughter back, but he was resentful, maybe more than resentful, of the necessity to have someone probing into their private lives. Odd – and intriguing. Or, as Alice would have said – curiouser and curiouser.

*

Alex drove back to London at speed, except during the inevitable hold-ups that seemed to occur on motorways, especially in the summer months. She reached her office by mid-afternoon. The anticipation of reading the diary had almost made her pull into a lay-by outside Wilsingham and take a look there and then, but that would have been careless, since Price might well have seen her on his own way back to town and stopped to see if anything was wrong.

But once in the office, she tossed her bag onto a chair and took out the diary eagerly. She flipped through the pages, feeling a growing sense of frustration as she did so, because every page was written in some sort of code. It could be a relatively easy one to crack, but it certainly wasn't one she could do instantly.

She stared at it in disbelief, wondering what would make a reclusive woman like Caroline Price write her diary in code. Who would ever see it? And what could possibly be in it that had to be kept so secret?

Unless she was running a call-girl service, Alex thought with a grin, remembering the underwear ... but she dismissed the wild idea at once. For that kind of caper, the minimum you'd need would be a phone, and Caroline didn't use one.

She flipped through the diary pages and then paused with a sudden lurch of excitement. Every page had been written in a kind of gobbledy-gook, except one.

The date of Caroline's birthday was 30 August, which was when she was due to inherit a small fortune, apparently. The date was ringed in black, but not only that: in the space provided was one word – FREEDOM.

It was too hot to spend hours in an office, even an airconditioned one, and Alex's clothes were beginning to stick to her. The lure of a cool shower was irresistible, and by 5 p.m. she was heading home through the traffic. It would be more comfortable to try to decipher the diary and the crossword grids with the whole evening ahead of her, wearing something long and loose and with a glass of something cool by her side. And there was still the photo album to study. The leisurely anticipation of an evening browsing, even if it was work, gave her a squidge of pleasure.

She shed her clothes in her bedroom, hanging them up carefully. She'd gone too long without being able to buy her things from expensive boutiques to treat them carelessly. She went into her bathroom, covered her hair, and turned on the shower, letting the hot water run down her back before turning to let it caress her voluptuous curves.

She gave a blissful sigh as she began to smooth the aromatic shower gel into her body. Her hands ran over her skin quickly, ignoring the small tingles of erotic pleasure that coursed through her. She didn't intend to linger in the shower. As always, once bitten by the intrigue of a case, she was eager to do some detective work, and the missing Caroline Price was interesting her more by the hour.

She wanted to know her, but so far she was a complete mystery from the various bits of information she had gleaned or been given so far.

Half an hour later, wearing her red silk kimono over an oversized T-shirt and with her hair tied up in a topknot away from her neck, Alex stretched out on her sofa sipping a vodka and lime. On the long table beside her she had spread out the several crossword grids, taking special note of the way Caroline worked.

The pages were roughs only, and each of them had two grids at one side, with the majority of the paper left blank for working and writing out the clues. At a guess, Alex assumed that the crosswords were sent in with one grid filled in for the editor's benefit, leaving the other blank for transcribing into the newspaper with the clues. It was probably not a unique method of working, but Alex hadn't seen it before, and it certainly made for clarity.

She couldn't forget that diary entry though, still puzzling over what that word FREEDOM – in capitals – actually meant. Caroline didn't seem like the kind of woman who would be over-interested in money, or acquiring possessions, so it didn't seem reasonable to think that coming into considerable wealth on her birthday would warrant such a special note. And if she had intended to disappear, why hadn't she waited for the loot to do it in style?

Her intercom buzzed, making her jump, and she got up to answer it irritably. She didn't want company tonight, but she couldn't ignore it either. It could be something important.

'Alexandra Best,' she mouthed briskly.

'Can I come up?' said a voice she knew only too well, a rich, sexy voice.

She hesitated, and then: 'Gary, I'm busy. It's not a good time—'

'OK. Some other time then. I'll call you.'

'Oh no, wait—'

But it was too late; he'd gone.

She chewed her lip in annoyance. He could have said *something*. . . . A few minutes later the intercom buzzed again. Before she could say her name, the voice spoke.

'Have you changed your mind yet?'

'It's open,' she said abruptly, pressing the button.

She was mad and she knew it. Here she was, practically naked, if you could call an oversized T–shirt and a red silk kimono practically naked, and she'd just invited the sexiest man she had met in a long time up to her flat. And this evening had definitely been intended for work. . . .

He came into the room and stood in front of her, arms folded like a dark Colossus, a frown on his handsome features. There was a smear of oil around his chin and she guessed he'd been tinkering with his bike. Combined with his leathers, the whiff of it was not unpleasing. It was virile and manly – and she was weakening by the minute, dammit.

'You're a private dick,' he accused her.

Alex started. This was *not* what she had expected to hear, nor the way she had expected to be greeted.

'A *what*?' she said, starting to laugh at the unlikely description.

'All right then, a dickette,' Gary snapped.

'And you're a dick-*head*, if it bothers you,' she said mildly. 'How did you find out, anyway?'

'Yellow Pages. Had to find a business address in the city to make a delivery, and came across you.'

And not for the first time . . . but he was clearly not finding this in the least funny, or in the mood for seeing *double entendres*. Alex was shocked by the annoyance in his eyes. So what, she thought defensively? If he'd discovered she was the Queen of England it might have been different, but she was only doing an honest day's work, for God's sake. Even if some people might call snooping around other people's private affairs a dubious kind of honesty.

'It *does* bother you,' she stated, sure that this was goodbye, and knowing it with a feeling of regret. They had been good together, and it didn't have to end like this.

'Sure it does. I've never fu— I've never slept with a private dick before.'

She didn't say a word. She just looked at him, unblinking, her green eyes wide and innocent, willing her laughter down, and willing him to see the funny side of it.

And certainly not daring to say airily, 'Oh, were all the others in public then—?'

And wishing her quirky sense of humour wasn't making a pig's ear out of what was obviously a very serious moment to Gary . . . and then she saw his mouth twitch.

'Mind you, I wouldn't mind doing it again.'

'So now can I get on with my work?' Alex said, a considerable while later.

'Sure, if I can help,' Gary said lazily, his arm sliding round her silk-kimono'd shoulders on the sofa.

'You?'

'Why not? Two heads are sometimes better than one, and I've got plenty of contacts in my job. Besides, I always fancied myself as a—'

Alex grinned. 'Yes, I know. A private dick. I'd say you've rather proved that already.'

It was corny and Raymond Chandlerish, but she felt as if she could say anything to him. He was the most refreshingly open guy she had met in a long time. She knew next to nothing about him, but she was strongly attracted to him, and not just for his body.

Though that helped, of course. That *definitely* helped. But she wasn't falling into the trap of thinking about forevers, any more than she suspected he was, and even if it only lasted a few days or a few weeks. . . .

'So let's get down to business,' Gary said. 'I presume it's all to do with the old boy you were talking to at the Rainbow Club last night?'

Alex blinked, trying to co-ordinate her thoughts away from the dreaming mode they had temporarily moved into, when Norman Price and his elusive daughter were the last things on her mind.

But meandering *would not do*. She had to earn her money, and to start while the trail she intended to follow was simmering, if not yet hot. And if Gary wanted to help. . . .

For a moment she felt a strange sense of selfish resentment at the very thought. She had always worked alone apart from the nuggets of help that Nick Frobisher had occasionally thrown her way. She didn't get much assistance from any other police source. They still viewed her efforts as those of the little female trying to do a man's job. And she had always jealously and triumphantly thought of her successes as her personal achievements. Down to her alone.

She eyed Gary's strong young body, sprawled out on her sofa now, his shirt half open, his broadly tanned chest sparsely covered with dark body hair, and sighed.

'OK,' she said.

Chapter 3

It probably wasn't ethical to show a stranger her client's diary, but there were two things that made Alex easily overlook such a minor matter. One was that Gary was certainly no stranger to her now, at least, not in the Biblical sense; and two, because nowhere in the diary was there any mention of Caroline's name.

The first thing most people did was to fill in the details at the front of each annual record; name and address first; then their National Health number, blood group, doctor's and dentist's numbers, car registration and passport number. There was none of that in Caroline's diary, despite the provision for it. It was as anonymous as the woman herself, and Alex decided to keep it that way, at least for the time being. In her business, it paid to be cautious.

More disturbing thoughts cascaded into her mind without warning. How did she know how far she could trust Gary Hollis, anyway? Who was he? It was probably sheer coincidence that he'd turned up in her life on the same night that she had met Norman Price.

But what if it wasn't coincidence? What if there was some connection? What if he was Caroline's cousin, destined to inherit the loot if she failed to turn up in good health within the next six weeks, and he was monitoring her every move, and reporting back to Norman – or *not*, as the case may be? What if he was as anxious to find Caroline as her father, and for a much darker reason?

God, she was really letting her imagination run away with her now, she thought in disgust, staring into space as Gary flipped through the pages of Caroline's diary. Hadn't they just made glorious love together? (But so what? a small inner voice mocked her. What did that have to do with anything?)

She just about managed to resist the urge to snatch the diary away from Gary at that moment, wondering if she was going completely mad.

'My dad used to take me to see spy movies when I was a kid,' he observed, startling her. 'They were his favourites. Our local cinema used to show them on Saturday afternoons.'

'Oh? And is there a point to all this?' Alex said, hoping her sudden attack of nerves didn't show in her voice. But there was nothing to say that a private eye couldn't have nerves, or be scared witless like any other person.

He looked up from the diary. 'Are you OK? You look kind of funny.'

'Funny peculiar. or funny ha-ha?' she asked, using one of Nick Frobisher's boring expressions. 'Anyway, if I do, it's because of what you just said.'

'What did I just say?'

'Are we going round in circles for any particular reason, or are you going to tell me the point of mentioning the fact that your dad used to take you to see spy movies?' she said patiently.

But she felt her face break into a half-grin, because it sounded so nice and ordinary. A dad taking his son to the pictures on Saturday afternoons . . . *her* dad had never done any such thing – or been able to, she admitted. There were no cinemas within miles of the farm. But her dad hadn't been interested in such things, anyway, and therefore it hadn't come within her small range of activities.

She felt a brief sense of grief not to have known the kind of childhood other kids did, and immediately told herself not to be so bloody feeble.

'It's this,' Gary said, stabbing a finger at some of the gobbledy-gook. 'Michael Caine or Alec Guinness could have deciphered this in a trice.'

'Oh yes? I thought they were movie-stars, not human decoders.'

'And I thought you were the bright private dic— private eye, sweetness,' he said mockingly. 'Can't you see what I'm getting at?'

She began to find him irritating. He might be great in bed – he was great in bed – but there was no way he was going to show his male superiority over her job. It had been a mistake to let him stay, and to let him see the diary at all. She grabbed it out of his hands and snapped it shut.

'I think you'd better leave the detecting to me,' she said pointedly. 'And it's getting late. Don't you have somewhere to go? Where do you live, by the way?'

'Kingston on Thames. And what have I said now?'

Alex had visibly jumped on hearing the name, her skin crawling uncomfortably. Kingston on Thames was where a body had been found in a lake, according to Nick Frobisher – and there was no reason on earth to think there was any connection between it and her case, or with Gary Hollis. She swallowed.

'Just nerves. Wasn't there a murder there yesterday?'

He shook his head and spoke quite gently. 'Are you sure you're in the right business, Alex? Anyway, it wasn't a murder; it was suicide. The woman left a note. Haven't you seen this evening's paper? It's all in there.'

'I'll catch it on the TV news later,' she mumbled.

He folded her in his arms, and she wondered if he could tell how sickly her heart was beating. There wasn't much clothing between them to disguise it. She was a fool, and he may be right about one thing: was she *quite* sure she was in the right business? She could be serving behind the counter in a nice little corner shop, where nothing exciting ever happened and life meandered on blandly from day to day. . . .

'So do you want me to tell you how to decode this diary or not?' she heard his voice vibrate against her cheek as she leaned weakly against him.

She jerked back, instantly alert, and saw the laughter in his eyes.

'You *know*?'

'What the hell do you think I've been telling you all this time? When you were addicted to spy movies the way my dad and I were, we used to spend a high old time making up our own codes and seeing who was the first to crack them.'

It sounded even more like an idyllic childhood to Alex. A father who took time to be with his kid and share his interests. . . . She shut her mind to such sweet images, knowing there were more important concerns to deal with now than wishing

41

for something she had never had, and could never have.

'So *tell* me,' she said aggressively.

'I'm surprised you haven't worked it out for yourself. It's pretty basic stuff. It'll just take a little time, that's all,' Gary said, his voice hopeful.

'All right, so I'll make us supper when we've cracked it, OK? And then you go.'

'Really?'

'Really.'

He gave a heavy sigh. 'Get a pad and some pens then, because you can't work it all out in your head.'

She did as she was told. Part of her was glad of his help, and part of her was wishing she'd had the sense to discover just what it was he had seen in the coded rubbish. But since she'd never had to deal with this before, she might as well look on Gary's knowledge as a useful learning process. And in the end it was unbelievably simple, if time-consuming.

It was the kind of thing any intelligent child could do. Alternate letters in the mangled words were either three or five letters away from the correct one in the alphabet. Except that every fourth and sixth time they occurred, they went backwards through the alphabet instead of forwards.

Only somebody with a mathematical mind and the kind of brain that could compile cryptic crosswords could think of such a tortuous way of rendering her diary useless to anybody else, thought Alex. And it took a hell of a long time to make any sense of the sentences. But when they did. . . .

'It looks as though your client was a goer all right,' Gary said, whistling through his teeth in admiration. 'Torrid nights with M figure more prominently that anything else, and in plenty of graphic detail, too. Who's M, do you think? Must be a secret lover, and married, I bet. And who's the lady in question? Am I going to be told?'

'Fancy her, do you?' Alex parried. 'How do you see her, anyway? Small and fluffy and blonde, or a bit on the horsy side, with a large nose and no-nonsense stare?'

He laughed. 'She's certainly no horse-face, if all this is anything to go by. Just reading it is turning me on. She's living every moment on these pages. Either that, or she's got a bloody erotic imagination.'

If she had tried to trap him by mentioning Caroline's lack of beauty, it hadn't worked. She didn't really know why she had said it. It was just her suspicious nature. Sometimes it was one of the less delightful aspects of the job. But just in case he *was* the cousin, she'd had to test him.

She felt suddenly weary of the whole thing. She hadn't even started the investigation properly yet, and already there was far more to Caroline that met the eye.

Missing adult daughters either turned up in due course after going on a high old binge, or were tracked down fairly easily, and sometimes the search ended up in the gruesome body-bags. More often, missing daughters were defiant teenagers who weren't about to inherit vast amounts of money. There had to be an angle to this, but, as yet, Alex simply couldn't fathom it.

'Have you ever heard of Price Chemicals?' she asked Gary abruptly, her gaze unwaveringly on his face, watching for the slightest flicker in his eyes.

Lying or not, he would deny it, of course. Why was there any reason for him to know of the place? Why, unless he was connected with Norman Price in some way? She still couldn't quite overlook the coincidence that he had been around at the Rainbow Club last night, coming into her life at the same time as her client. And conveniently overhearing her name.

Or had he known it already? Had Norman Price told him to be sure and worm his way into the girl's life, to keep an insider's check on her investigations? She chewed her lip savagely. Imagination was all well and good when trying to puzzle out a case, but when it went way over the top, it did no damn good at all, except to send your nerve-ends soaring.

'Sure, I've heard of it,' Gary told her now. 'Run-down place, seen better times, I reckon. Why?'

'How do you know it?' she countered.

His eyes narrowed. 'What is this, twenty questions? Is this something to do with the case?'

'Maybe.'

His arms went round her, vice-like, and her heart leapt as she heard the aggro in his voice.

'Come on, Alex, we've come too far for you to go all coy on me. You've trusted me this far, so what's changed all of a sudden? And what does Price Chemicals have to do with it?'

'You don't know him then? The owner, I mean.'

Gary shook his head, his grip loosening a little, but not enough to make her feel comfortable.

'Never seen him. I've only ever dealt with his minions.'

'You've *been* there?'

'I *am* a courier, darling. It's my job. I've been there a few times to deliver packages. So? Are you going to tell me why I'm getting the third degree?'

She gave in. 'You have seen him. He's my client, and he's the man I met at the Rainbow Club last night—'

'That old fruit? You want to steer clear of his type, sweetheart—' and then he paused. 'So where does the girl come in? The girl with the hots for this guy she calls M. Hell's teeth, it's not him, is it?'

'She's his daughter.'

'And?'

'And she's missing. She's been missing for two weeks, and he wants to find her.'

She wasn't telling him why. Not yet. Maybe not ever.

Gary shrugged. 'I'd say it's a normal reaction when a kid goes missing, for a father to want her found.'

'So you think she's a kid, do you?'

'Well, now that you come to mention it, no. Not with all the expertise she's showing in that diary. And I don't just mean her ability with coded information. I don't blame her, though. Some of that stuff's hot enough to burn the pages to a crisp. She could make a fortune selling it to some sleazy tabloid,' he added with a grin.

Alex sighed. She wasn't in the mood for discussing Caroline's pleasure in M's sexual prowess, and her natural suspicion of Gary was becoming a nuisance. It was hindering things, and she wanted to trust him. She reached into her bag for Caroline's photo album and opened it.

'This is the missing daughter,' she said.

Before he spoke, he whistled again in the way she was beginning to find more than irritating.

'Christ, she must have something pretty potent between her legs to keep M so interested, because she sure as hell ain't got much up top!'

44

Alex slammed the album shut. 'That's just about the most sexist remark I've heard tonight,' she raged, feeling ridiculously protective of Caroline. 'If that's all you've got to say, then you'd better get out before I throw you out.'

'What in hell's the matter with you? You can't tell me you think any guy in his right mind would fall for *that* mug without some other incentive!'

When Alex didn't answer, he ranted on.

'What's she got then? Is she an heiress or something? If she's expecting to come into Daddy's money, I'd say she's in for a big shock because from the look of his business premises, he's probably frittered it all away by now.'

He was suddenly shrewder and calmer.

'Or is the reason he's looking for her because she's coming into money from some other source, and he's expecting her to bale him out?'

'Are you sure *you're* in the right business?' Alex said sarcastically. 'You're obviously wasted doing courier work.'

'Not necessarily, though the two combined might come in very useful at times. So am I right?'

'Maybe.'

He moved away from her and stood up so fast she almost fell off the sofa. He shrugged into his leathers.

'When are you going to start trusting me, Alex?'

'Why should I trust you? Haven't you ever heard of client confidentiality? Besides I don't *know* you.'

'I'd say you know me as intimately as anybody in this world,' he said, full of innuendo. 'So what are you afraid of? Do you think I'm some kind of spy for the old boy, checking up on you to see you do the job right?'

Alex hadn't blushed in years. But seeing the tell-tale reddening in her cheeks now, Gary pulled her to her feet and shook her, his fingers digging into the tender flesh of her forearms.

'Christ, that's it, isn't it? You think that because I happened to be at the Rainbow Club last night when you made your contact, me and the old fruit were in cahoots. You think that was why I made a pass at you.'

'I don't think that—' Alex said, wishing he would let her go before the bruising on her arms matched the colour of the love-bites on her neck.

45

'Good. Because I don't screw a woman just to give some old fruit a turn-on,' he said crudely.

'Why then?' she said faintly.

'Why what?'

'Why did you pursue me?' She was frosty again, with no intention of using the words he did.

Gary grinned, and the harsh pressure on her arms faded into a sensual caress.

'Don't you know? Do I have to spell it out that you're the sexiest, classiest woman I've ever met in my life? And any minute now, you're going to get the proof of it again.'

She couldn't doubt what he meant. Her frostiness vanished as she felt him hard against her through the thin silk kimono. She wound her arms about his neck, feeling the leathers cold against her warmth.

'Much as I'd like to take you up on it, Gary,' she said, her voice husky, knowing just how much she *would like it*, 'I've got work to do, and if you really do want to help—'

'OK, so we'll leave it for later,' he said. 'I never forced a woman yet.'

He wouldn't have to do much forcing now, thought Alex weakly, but she had already discovered that his brain wasn't totally housed in his jeans. And if there was no devious reason for their meeting, then it must surely have been fate that sent him to her. He had decoded Caroline's nonsense, and he knew about Price Chemicals.

So, unless anybody could prove otherwise, she was smothering her doubts, at least for the moment.

'It's not that I don't want to, Gary,' she said, her hand on his arm, and not at all sure why she was adopting this little-girl attitude. It wasn't like her. It damn well *wasn't* like her at all! 'But this is work. You understand?'

'Sure, I told you; it's no problem. So you're on the trail of this missing woman who, despite her looks, is a raving nympho. Tell me what you know so far.'

He sprawled out in one of her easy-chairs now, legs wide, and looking as though he owned the place.

She sat down again, her kimono tucked around her as prim as a nun – if a nun ever wore such a hot, frivolous colour. After studying him for a moment, she spoke abruptly.

'Do you want a drink? I've got whisky and vodka, and there may be a few cans of beer somewhere—'

'Whisky will be fine. Stop being so nervous, Alex. I'm just a guy who works for a living, same as you, and ready to help any way I can.'

She poured him his whisky, and then poured herself a generous glass of vodka laced with lime. And then she gave him a brief outline of what Norman Price had told her, and of her visit to the cottage at Wilsingham that morning. She didn't mention the cousin, just that Price needed Caroline's money to bale him out, as Gary had suggested.

Thankfully, Gary merely listened attentively. His whistling had reminded her all too vividly of her father whistling for the dog to recover their renegade sheep in the Dales, and she hadn't connected it until that very moment.

'Is this case bothering you?' he asked.

'No more than usual. They always do at first.'

'So why are your hands shaking? I really think you're in the wrong job, Alex. She's nothing to you, is she, this Caroline woman?'

'No. except that I take every case seriously, and her father seemed so callous about her, so uncaring—'

And oh God, if she wasn't careful, she was going to start blubbering about how she knew all about a father who didn't care . . . except that hers had, deep down. He just hadn't had the vocabulary to tell her so, and she didn't discover it until he was gone and it was too late.

Leaving her the farm and everything he owned had been his heartbreaking legacy of love, and she had upped and sold it the minute she could. The thought of it didn't sit comfortably on her conscience, even now, and she didn't need reminding.

She took a deep breath, knowing she was being ridiculous, and that she had no intention of telling Gary Hollis. or anyone else, about her past. Everyone had secrets, and this was hers.

'You saw Price last night,' she went on more harshly. 'I didn't like him from the moment I saw him, and from the way he carried on at Caroline's cottage, I guessed he didn't really want her disappearance investigated at all. If it wasn't for what was in it for him—'

'And what's that – exactly?' Gary asked casually.

Warning bells sounded in her head. In the early days, she'd bought a self-help manual on being a private detective, and one of the basic things it had told her was never to give too much away to would-be assistants. Not even assistants who were great in bed . . . *especially* not assistants who were great in bed. It hadn't put it in so many words, but the implications had been there for all to see: careless pillow-talk, to put it at its most blatant.

'Not losing face, for one thing,' she invented quickly. 'Friends and relatives must know he has a daughter, so he could hardly seem to be so unconcerned about her, could he?'

'So your first job should be to look for these friends and relatives, shouldn't it?' Gary said. 'Maybe she's staying with one of them, or at least they could tell you where she's gone, or give you some clues. I presume Price's given you a list of names.'

She glared at him. After Norman Price's dismissal of the idea of Caroline having friends or acquaintances, she hadn't got around to asking the father for such a list. She'd been too concerned with checking out the clinical, crossword-compiling side of Caroline's life that seemed to have got her nowhere; and now there was the intimate, personal side of it, thanks to the contents of the cottage bedroom and the diary that seemed to bear no relation to her business persona. But she knew damn well she should have asked for the name of the cousin at least. He was obviously worth a visit.

'I'm dealing with that,' she told Gary coldly.

Without warning, she gave a huge yawn that was perfectly genuine. She wanted to think, and she couldn't concentrate any longer while he was around.

'I'm sorry, but we'll have to call it a day, Gary. Sorry, but I'm out on my feet. Sorry.'

God, she sounded like a parrot now. Why the hell should she apologize anyway? She hadn't invited him in. Not exactly.

'It's all right, I'm going. Oh – and the reason I said I knew Price Chemicals is because I have to deliver a package there tomorrow.'

'*What*? Why didn't you tell me before?'

'You never asked. You were too busy thinking I had some ulterior motive for being interested. You can come along for the ride if you like. I'll pick you up at your office around ten o'clock, OK?

And you can forget about supper. I'll get a Chinese on the way home.'

She had forgotten she had even mentioned supper, but seconds later he was gone, while her mouth was still watering at the thought of spare ribs smothered in sweet and sour sauce, and succulent stir-fried vegetables. Her thighs positively swelled in anticipation. . . .

If there was anything to compare with sex, it was food, she thought longingly. And then reversed the thought. There was no comparison at all.

She didn't like being organized, and if it hadn't been for the tempting thought of taking another look at Price Chemicals she would have told him to get lost. In any case, she had already decided that her next move was to return to Wilsingham village and check out the locals, to get a better picture of Caroline. But she realized she couldn't contact Gary to tell him she had changed her mind about tomorrow. She had no address for him, other than Kingston on Thames. Nor did she have a telephone number, nor any knowledge of the courier firm he worked for. In a way, he was as anonymous as Caroline Price. She had decided to trust him, and she did, more or less, but she knew as little about him – less in fact – than she did about Caroline or her father.

It still bothered her. not least because she was sure he'd seen her as an easy pick-up. Which she had been, of course. Anyway, there was no changing things now, but the courier delivery shouldn't take more than an hour there and back, allowing for traffic.

And then she would do as she intended and go to Wilsingham. Alone. It might be a good idea to check into the local pub for the night, she decided. People always opened up more if strangers were seen to be spending money. Her thoughts rambled on as she tried to sleep on a night that was hot and sticky and airless, and far better spent without company.

Next morning, sitting in the shade on the pillion seat of the bike while Gary did his delivery, she wondered why she had agreed to go with him at all. There was no point. She could hardly march into Price's office and ask him for the cousin's name and address, since she wasn't supposed to know the details of his business, anyway. She knew Price was there because his car was in its prominent parking space, and while Gary was delivering his package and taking stock of the interior she removed the heavy crash helmet for a few moments to wipe away the dampness in her neck.

'Nothing to report,' he said regretfully when he came back to the Harley. 'I couldn't get further than the warehouse, and was sent on my way sharpish. Whatever's going on in there, the mood's pretty scratchy. So where next?'

'Back to my office and a parting of the ways. I need to think, but thanks for the ride, Gary,' she said firmly.

'And that's it?'

'That's it. Don't you have other work to do?'

Or are you just playing with me, keeping tabs on me?

He shrugged. 'Yeah, you're right. Back to London then, and I'll see you around.'

The bike roared back to town, and Alex knew the exact meaning of her heart being in her mouth. She waved him off with a feeling of relief, thankful to have survived a hair-raising journey, and with no mention of another meeting.

And then it was down to business. She found the number of the Little Harp Inn at Wilsingham, and called to book a room for the night. She had already brought her overnight bag from home. Better to do it in advance as a regular tourist than just turn up and create undue curiosity.

The phone rang just as she was leaving, and she had switched on the office answering machine, so she didn't bother to pick up the receiver. Then she froze as she heard Norman Price's furious voice.

'I don't like snoopers, Miss Best, and I understood you worked alone. I told you I wanted no police or outside interference, which includes boy-friends on motor cycles. Our contract is now terminated.'

The line went dead, and Alex felt her blood boil with fury. Snooping was *exactly* what she was expected to do in order to find his daughter. But how did he know she had been to his factory?

Unless Gary had informed him. The idea hit her with the force of a bullet, and she didn't like what she was thinking. If Gary was the cousin, with some devious double-dealing game of his own, he could have done this to stop Norman continuing to hire her.

But why the hell would Gary have deciphered the diary so cleverly if he was involved? And he wasn't M. Even in her state of heightened nerves, she knew that the way Caroline had described some of M's salacious love-making that bordered on perversion, wasn't Gary's way. She felt the slow trickle of sweat down her back, and then her heart slowed down as she realized how Price knew she'd been at his factory.

The memories clicked into place. She had taken off her crash helmet, and for those few minutes her distinctive red hair had been clearly visible. Price must have seen her from his office window. It had to be that. And since he now knew that she was aware of his business concerns, she switched off the answering machine, picked up the phone and dialled his business number.

Once she had contacted him, she snapped into the mouthpiece, 'Mr Price, I assure you I am working entirely alone, and it was total coincidence that my friend gave me a ride to your premises this morning. But I wouldn't be worth much in my line if I hadn't already checked out your business. You wanted a professional and you got one.'

She held her breath. If Price was acquainted with Gary, if he was the cousin – he would surely give the game away. She was well attuned to nuances in a voice, and in Price's now there was nothing but continued rage.

'I told you our contract is teminated—'

And Alex could see her winter cruise disappearing like a mirage.

'That's up to you, of course. But as I've already begun my investigations and am fully aware that a missing person is a serious matter, I might feel it ethical to hand over the details to the police,' she said silkily.

Alex held her breath, wondering if she had gone too far, and if he would believe her. Missing adults never produced such poignant or frantic enquiries as a missing child, though they had to be investigated too, of course. Her legs shook and she had to lean against the desk for support, as the silence at the other end lengthened.

And then he snarled, 'This is blackmail, you bitch—'

'Not at all. It's normal procedure,' she invented wildly. 'But if you decide to continue to retain me, I suggest you give me some details about your daughter's cousin, Mr Price. He may be able to help me in tracking down her disappearance.'

And if he's young and dark and horny and rides a Harley Davidson motor bike, I don't want to know.

The silence lengthened again, and then the voice was more clipped, but still full of anger. 'Very well. His name is Jeremy Laver and he calls himself a classical musician. I haven't seen him in years and have no idea where he's living now, but if you're any good I daresay that's enough for you to go on. But I'm not paying you to find him: it's my daughter who's missing—'

'I'm aware of that, Mr Price. And I'll be in touch as soon as I have any news.'

She put down the phone before he could reply, and switched on the answering machine again before scribbling down the name of Jeremy Laver. Her hands were still shaking, but partly with relief because the cousin didn't sound remotely like Gary Hollis. The memory that flashed into her mind at that moment, was the sight of him briefly dancing with some girl at the Rainbow Club, and his sense of rhythm was zilch.

But contacting Jeremy Laver was going to be put on the back burner for the present. She was going to continue with her plan to go to Wilsingham to talk to the locals and find out what she could about the occupant of Greenwell Cottage.

If Gary deigned to call her again, here or at the flat, too bad.

She reached Wilsingham late in the afternoon and checked into the Little Harp Inn. Her room was low-beamed, creaky and chintzy, with an *en-suite* corner that had once been a cupboard but did the job adequately enough. Once she had unpacked, Alex returned to the bar and spent a few minutes chatting to the open-faced landlady as if she was an enthusiastic city girl who had just discovered the delights of the countryside.

Even though the words 'darling little thatched cottages' and 'quaint old country ways' stuck in her throat, she uttered them sincerely and loudly, aware that several old salts in the corner of the bar were listening to every word.

'They'll be able to tell you more about our old country ways, if you've a mind to learn more, miss,' the landlady said, nodding towards them. ' 'Specially if there's a jar or two alongside 'em for wetting their whistles, if you get my meanin',' she added with a wink.

'I certainly do,' Alex said. 'I want to wander around to get a feel of the village right now, but do you think those people will be in here tonight?'

She felt slightly light-headed, talking about the two old men as if they were waxworks, but the woman merely laughed.

'Bless you, my dear, they're as good as fixtures. You go about your business now, and I'll tell 'em to keep a seat warm for you tonight.'

Alex smiled at them as she passed through the bar, guessing that the landlady would soon be telling them they were in for a night of free beer if they dug into their store of village lore. She wore a T-shirt, jeans and trainers now, her camera slung around her neck, the typical tourist. And her heart lifted as she began the stroll around the village.

This was the best part of her job, she admitted, and on a day like this, blue and golden with summer, it was easy to forget she was here to do a job at all. But she was . . . and in the post-office-cum-shop she bought some postcards.

'This is such a pretty village,' she said to the woman in the flower-patterned overall behind the counter. 'It's like stepping back in time – in the nicest possible way, of course,' she added. 'The thatched cottages are really adorable.'

'You might not think so if you lived in one, miss. They can harbour insects and even mice when the thatch gets a bit tatty. And the birds like to nest in 'em too. We've had ours done up recently,' she added proudly.

'Oh, but they're part of our heritage, aren't they? I want to photograph some of them for my parents. Would people object, do you think?'

'Shouldn't think so.' Alex could almost hear the regret in the woman's voice that her done-up cottage wasn't going to be one of the ones photographed for posterity now.

'Are any of them unoccupied, though? I wouldn't want to offend people.'

The postmistress shrugged. 'There's not many that stay unoccupied for long. Soon as they're for sale, city folk come and snap 'em up. No offence, mind.'

'None taken,' Alex murmured, falling into the same mode of talking. 'There was one I noticed at the end of a lane, very secluded. Does anyone live there?'

'That'll be Greenwell Cottage. Belongs to a woman, but she keeps herself to herself. They say she's mute, but I don't know about that. She has a visitor in a big car now and then, but she don't bother us, and we don't bother her. That's the way folks are here, miss,' she added meaningfully. 'Now, do you want stamps for them cards or not?'

'Oh – yes please,' Alex said hastily, knowing she should keep up the illusion of tourist.

It was odd. She always thought village folk had their noses in everyone else's business – but if Caroline was as cold and stand-offish as she appeared to them, it might well have resulted in the villagers shunning her and leaving her strictly alone.

Which wasn't going to help Alex Best's case at all.

She stepped out into the sunshine with her purchases and strode more purposefully towards the end of the village and the lane leading to Greenwell Cottage. In her bag she had the key of the cottage, and she knew perfectly well there was nobody in it. There was only the aura that Caroline had left behind, and what-ever clues to her disappearance that Norman Price had been too impatient to let her find on her first visit. But this time she was alone, and her sense of anticipation was high as she pushed open the gate, ignoring the encroaching weeds that brushed against her legs as she walked up the path to the front door.

Chapter 4

The familiar scent of the cottage enveloped her. Every house had its own distinctive smell, whether of history or ownership. and this one was no exception. Alex stood perfectly still as she had done before, but this time it was not merely to absorb the atmosphere; this time she was listening for the slightest sound that would tell her she was not alone. There was always the chance that Caroline might have returned, and the case would be over before it had properly begun.

It was pointless to call Caroline's name, of course, since she wouldn't hear it. Alex wondered why she hadn't kept a dog to alert her to visitors, since the cottage was so isolated from the rest of the village. Though from what Price had told her of his daughter's resentment and strong will, she probably wouldn't admit to any kind of nervousness.

But the character sketch Alex was building of the missing woman in her mind was far from complete. Caroline was still an enigma. The staid, reclusive workaholic and the raving nympho, to use Gary's term for her, didn't altogether add up.

Or maybe it did. Everyone showed a different face to different people. It was one of the first rules you learned as a private eye. Never take people at face value. Always look deeper. Scratch the smoothest surface and see what rough edges are there. She could almost recite the clichéd words of the self-help manual.

And wasn't she just the same? She wasn't at all what she appeared to be. She was just a small-time girl from the Yorkshire Dales who'd polished up her accent and citified her appearance, and set herself up doing a sometimes dangerous job, but one that was more often mundane and plodding. And only occasionally exciting.

A sudden noise set her nerves jumping. A stealthily moving cat in the unkempt garden had leapt at a bird, and sent it squawking for the safety of the higher branches of a tree. Alex pressed her hand over her thudding heart.

'Slow down, you fool,' she informed it. 'A missing client is one thing. The corpse of the PI in a deserted cottage is quite another.'

She shivered. There was no real reason to suspect FOUL PLAY, which she always thought of in capitals to reduce it to farce, and to dismiss the idea of discovering anything nasty. But all the same, the possibility was always there.

'Where are you, Caroline?' she muttered. 'Give me a clue, there's a sweetie.'

Her gaze was caught by the crossword grids, still neatly stacked, and the carefully covered computer and copier. Caroline was methodical in all things, she observed, and she'd be willing to bet the desk drawers were just as tidily arranged. The door key didn't fit them and she was reluctant to force them. It wasn't in the rules. . . . But try as she might, she couldn't find another key anywhere.

Anyway, there was nothing here to help. There was nothing. If Caroline received letters, she kept them well hidden, and how she received payment for her work Alex had no idea. However it was, Caroline seemed to have successfully turned herself into a one-woman self-sufficiency.

A grudging feeling of admiration filled Alex's mind. She didn't blame Caroline one bit for brushing off the obnoxious Father Price. Nor for getting a life that was far beyond what one might expect from the image of her in the photographs. She wasn't that bad, either, Alex thought indignantly, however scathing Gary had been of her appearance. With a bit of make-up and a different hair-style she could be at least what people would call *handsome* . . . even striking.

She moved slowly about the cottage, trying to absorb Caroline's aura once more. Trying to be Caroline, and totally failing. How did a deaf person tick? How did she ever conduct a business successfully? And just how successful was she? Maybe the anonymous M was a pimp, and she really *was* a high-class call-girl. There were plenty of weirdos who would pay big money for any kind of deviation from the norm. A woman who couldn't hear the depths of their crudeness would appeal to some. Especially one who couldn't answer, or scream. . . .

It was a skin-crawling thought, and Alex bristled on Caroline's behalf. She wasn't dumb, and it was only the dregs of humanity who considered a deaf girl an oddity. People were more enlightened these days . . . except that she knew damn well that there was a huge section who didn't give a monkey's for political correctness, so who was she kidding?

She went into Caroline's bedroom again, and gazed through the tiny window at the surrounding countryside. Was this where she entertained her lover, the mysterious M? Did she watch for him to come to her from this window, where you couldn't even see the road except for the lane leading to the cottage? It was so secluded it was all too easy to think yourself into another world here. Isolated, lonely, alone . . . vulnerable . . . all the negative words floated through Alex's mind.

She drew back from the window with a gasp, her heart thudding. The sunlight dazzled, and the breeze rustling through the trees threw strange shadows, even in daylight. She had seen nothing of any substance, just a shadowy movement that had caught her eye. But all her instincts told her it was no prowling cat, or unseasonally early shedding of leaves.

Her gut feeling told her it was a human shadow. Someone was out there, watching her. Some local busybody, perhaps, wondering what she was doing here. Or kids, trying to scare her, or the kidnapper, if kidnapper there was. Knowing of Caroline's expected inheritance, and anticipating what could be at stake for Father Price if he didn't get his hands on it, the likelihood of kidnapping was high on Alex's agenda now. Yet there had been no ransom demand. . . .

'Calm down, you idiot,' she muttered, feeling her back against the wall, literally. 'What kind of a private di— eye – are you, for God's sake? Danger is meant to be your business. Courage is your middle name.'

She heard the hollow words come out of her dry lips. Saying them aloud was meant to be a mantra, a comfort, a confidence-booster. It didn't work. It never worked. Alex told herself she intended to write a coda to that bloody self-help manual on detective work she had bought, to remind foolish, wannabe 'tecs to go try something easier, like brain surgery.

She dragged her swooning thoughts together. *Swooning*? Now

she was thinking like some Victorian maiden, just because her nerves were reacting that way. And it was only a shadow, for God's sake. There was probably nobody there at all. She glanced out of the window again. In those few minutes the breeze had dropped and all was still. Silent. Tranquil. She forced the more positive words to her mind and called herself an idiot all over again.

Even so, she thought angrily, there was nothing in any bloody manual that said a private eye couldn't get as scared as the next person when it came to being threatened. Her breath caught in her throat, knowing it had better be mantra time again. Silent. Tranquil. Peaceful. All as before.

But once the panic had set in, she knew it was time to get out of there. She'd go for a stroll around the village like the tourist she was meant to be, then come back here later when her mind was fresher. And this time she might even force that desk drawer open. *Courage, man*, she thought, using some of Gary's jargon.

The old men were gathered together on the village green now, sitting on the circular seat around the ancient oak tree as if they never moved, creating a rural tableau especially for the benefit of snap-happy tourists. The image was compounded by the wreathes of blue smoke that surrounded them from their foul-smelling pipes.

'Good-afternoon,' she called out. 'Do you mind if I join you? I believe I saw some of you in the pub earlier.'

Actually, she didn't have a clue if they were the same ones. They all looked the same to her, anyway. Creased and jowled cheeks, sparse to non-existent hair, crumpled jackets or knitted pullovers, and baggy work trousers. They shuffled around to make room for her, and she stifled the urge to cough as the strong tobacco smoke reached her lungs.

Having glimpsed the village churchyard with its ancient granite tombstones, the epitaph *death from passive smoking* didn't escape her thoughts, but she ignored that too.

'It's a hot day today,' she said encouragingly when nobody spoke.

' 'Tis summer, see, miss? That explains it,' someone eventually replied, while the others either sniggered or grunted at this condescension to her city ignorance.

'The village is a bit out of the way for tourists. Do you get many here?' she asked next.

They looked at her vacantly. There were six of them, and none of them seemed willing to be the chief spokesman. Maybe she would have done better to wait until they had a jar of ale in their hands after all.

'I'm staying at the inn. Perhaps we'll meet there later. It's more fun talking over a pint, I always think.'

She stood up, aware that the gnarled faces had brightened a little, but deciding not to push her luck right now. Then another one spoke.

'Had another vis'tor passing through recently,' he mused. 'Fair gen'rous he was too. Most of 'em just think we be quaint old codgers, but this 'un wanted to know things.'

'Oh really?' Alex sat down again.

The man didn't elaborate on the visitor's generosity, but he didn't need to. Pints of beer were obviously looming large in the consciousness now.

'What kind of things?' she said casually.

The old man rubbed the stubble on his chin that had the appearance and texture of wire wool.

'Can't recall none of it, what with me throat being so dry. It'll mebbe come to me later, miss.'

They all agreed silently like so many nodding donkeys. She was right then. She'd get nothing out of them without showing the colour of her money.

'Right then. I'll see you all later. Is it a date?'

'Oh ah. 'Tis a date all right,' he chuckled, while one of his cronies made a gesture that could only be considered obscene. Dirty old sods, thought Alex as she sauntered on her way, well aware that their eyes were following her movements, and thankful that she wasn't wearing a short skirt.

Even so, her rear end was well outlined in her tight jeans, and she tried desperately to squeeze her thighs together as she heard a sudden raucous burst of laughter coming from the direction of the oak tree behind her. Though why the hell should she care? The resolve to take dieting more seriously flitted in and out of her head with its usual Concorde speed. Life was too short.

But the encounter with these good ol' boys had calmed her

down. Taking fright at a shadow outside the cottage was absurd, and she spent another lazy hour touring the village.

She took several photographs of the church, and on meeting the vicar in the churchyard, she casually asked him about newcomers to the village, with no joy. Caroline clearly wasn't a churchgoer to be welcomed with open clerical arms.

'I regret to say that most parishes are suffering the way ours is, miss,' he told her, ready with a hobby-horse sermon especially for Alex. 'Modern people simply won't spare the time for worship these days, except when something happens to disrupt their busy lives, of course. It's always convenient to turn to the church then. From the highest to the lowest in the land, they expect God to instantly forgive and forget any misdemeanours, and to give them some indication of what they should do next—'

'I thought that was God's role – to forgive and forget, I mean,' Alex murmured, not sure whether this statement was blasphemy or not, but quickly tiring of his pomposity.

The vicar stared at her coldly. 'I think you're missing the point here, Miss— Miss—?'

'Best,' she said. *A la* George, Your Reverendship. At the thought she was caught by a long memory. Her dad never used to miss watching a match when Bestie was playing . . . but she doubted that this guy knew anything about football.

She began to feel slightly hysterical. Solemn and ponderous folk like this one always reduced her to the inane. She couldn't take them seriously, which was just awful, considering the place where she was standing now, and with the graves of so many Wilsingham generations mouldering away beneath her feet. Without thinking, she stepped back a pace.

'I'm sorry,' she added. 'It's just that I'm trying to trace a – a friend of mine, and I seem to remember she mentioned this village once, and said something about maybe buying a property here, since old buildings are so pretty,' she invented.

Her voice trailed away as the vicar shook his head, his voice a mixture of sad and severe.

'That's the way of things, isn't it? People can be interested in the buildings, when they forget the true structure and foundation of the church itself. The Holy Trinity,' he added, when Alex stared at him blankly.

'Oh – yes. Yes, of course. Well, thank you very much for your time, Vicar.'

She backed away quickly, before he could expound still more. She was done with his stultifying talk.

And besides, she identified all too readily with something he had said. She, too, resorted to asking God for guidance when all else failed, even if it wasn't quite in the way the vicar had meant it. She switched her mind to the more annoying frustration of not properly seeking his assistance, which she had now virtually rejected.

But she could have told him Caroline's name. She could have mentioned the name of the cottage specifically. Weren't vicars meant to call on new parishioners to check them out or something? And wasn't she supposed to be the probing private eye, pursuing every lead? But she had her own methods, and so far she hadn't mentioned Caroline's name to anyone.

There was also a more personal reason for not enlisting the vicar's help: she simply didn't like him. She doubted that even God expected you to like every one of His stuffed shirts.

She felt more cheerful as she went back to the Little Harp Inn, deciding not to return to the cottage until tomorrow. She was at her sharpest in the morning, and it was already early evening now, and later she would interrogate the locals.

Some bright psychoanalyst had once told her she was a morning person, which presumably meant that she could shut up shop and sleep for the rest of the day once it struck noon, she had said breezily . . . but not if she wanted that winter cruise that Father Price's fat fee would bring her, she reminded herself keenly.

Which was why she found herself buying a hefty round of drinks for the good ol' boys with their foul-smelling pipes later on that evening. And surely there were more of them now than there had been earlier? Word had evidently got around, and anyone who assumed that village folk were simpletons had better think again. This lot, at any rate, were pretty cute.

'So come on, guys, tell me about this visitor who was asking questions recently,' she began, softening her best Sloaney voice in the interests of friendliness. 'Was he doing some kind of witch hunt, or something? I bet there have been plenty of old witch-craft tales down here in the past.'

And why the hell did she say such a daft thing, when such tales always scared the hell out of her?

'You don't want to listen to none o' that nonsense, miss,' one of them said, poker-faced and clearly taking her seriously. 'And they that tell it should be careful what they say an' all.'

Alex stared. The nodding donkeys were off again, and she'd only said it in passing. She didn't want to know about witch-craft, anyway, and had always tried to keep well clear of any of that caper.

'Don't get 'em started on all that, Miss Best,' the landlady said as she brought the tray of pint jugs to the table. No tame glasses for these hardies, Alex noted. 'You'll never sleep easy in your bed if they do.'

'Then I don't want to hear it,' Alex said, thinking there must be more than meets the eye in this sleepy little corner of the world that looked so sweet and so normal.

But they were just the places where you never *expected* any-thing sinister to happen, and she should be professional enough to know that by now. DI Nick Frobisher had told her some spine-tingling tales about covens and pagan rituals and gruesome animal sacrifices taking place in the most innocent-looking sur-roundings.

Such things had occasionally been uncovered during his own mundane police enquiries, and had turned up far more bizarre practices than any of them had bargained for.

For a moment Alex wished desperately that he was here now, with his big, comforting presence and his no-nonsense ways. Despite the sometimes unpredictability of his work, Nick could always be relied on to bring things down to earth. While here she was, letting her imagination run away with her before she had learned a single bloody thing. She drew a deep breath.

'I was only wondering about any recent visitors to the area. I'm trying to catch up with an old friend of mine,' she said, remembering what she had told the vicar. 'So was your visitor a lady?'

Come on, her logical thoughts nagged them silently. Surely you know I mean Caroline Price? The recluse who lives in Greenwell Cottage?

But since Caroline had been living here for some time, they probably wouldn't even class her as a visitor now, just an outsider who happened to live among them, but chose to keep herself to herself, as the saying went.

She decided to try another tack, but before she could speak, one of the old men spoke again, wiping the foam from his upper lip with his sleeve, then smacking his lips together in a perfectly disgusting manner before he belched loudly.

' 'Twere a man. Poncey-lookin' feller an' all.'

'An older man?' Alex said casually, thinking that for all their supposed verbosity, this was like pulling teeth. She took bets now that the man asking questions had been Norman Price. She certainly wouldn't have called him poncey-looking, but these disreputable-looking guys might. If so, the news was disappointing. She already knew he came here occasionally.

'Not old, nor ancient, like we. 'Bout your age, I dare say,' another one said, his head cocked on one side like a bird as he considered.

This was different. 'Was he looking to buy some property down here? My friend was interested in moving out of London, and he might have been here on her behalf.'

She was floundering now and she knew it. She could only hope that they didn't guess. There was no hurrying their replies, but Alex couldn't believe the speed with which the pints of beer disappeared. Within seconds the landlady had put another trayful down on the table, and she had nodded her agreement to put the cost of it all on her bill. At this rate, she'd be putting in a hefty expenses bill to Norman Price.

'Never said.'

'Did you talk to the man then?' she asked quickly.

'Only when he asked the way to Greenwell Cottage.'

At last! If the stranger had asked the way to Greenwell Cottage by name, then he had been looking for Caroline. Bingo.

'Is the cottage for sale then?' she asked.

The earlier spokesman from the village green guffawed.

'Not unless the cuckoo dame who lives there be thinking of moving out. And she never lets on about nothing.'

'Well, just in case the cottage *is* for sale, perhaps you can tell me a little more,' Alex persisted. 'Is the owner an elderly lady – or ill – or something?'

The old men stared her out. Just as if they could see right through the lies. Just as if they had second sight, the way certain strange village folk in isolated communities were reputed to have.

The smoke-charged atmosphere of the old inn was more thick and cloying by the minute – hadn't they ever heard of a smoke-free area in this place? – or was it just in her imagination as the rheumy old eyes seemed to mesmerize her for a few breath-holding moments?

And now she was *really* letting this hint of witchcraft get under her skin, Alex thought crossly, and immediately wondered how Nick would have handled this. Nick, with his refreshingly prosaic, plodding logic, that was suddenly and so blessedly *normal*. She cleared her throat as nobody seemed inclined to give her any more information.

'I've talked enough,' she murmured. 'It's late, and you'll excuse me, I'm sure.'

She got to her feet, and one of the men put a scrawny hand on her arm. She just resisted the urge to fling it away.

'Folk don't see much of the woman in Greenwell Cottage. Don't want to, neither. It always had a bad reputation.'

Alex managed a short laugh. 'What nonsense. As if a cottage could have a bad reputation.'

But as she almost flounced out, she could hear them whispering behind her, and she practically fled to her room. They were mad, the lot of them, she raged. It was all an act, anyway. Proving that for all the so-called sophistication of townies, country folk could still get the better of them in a macabre game of wits. And it worked, damn it. It *worked*.

Moments later, she jumped at the knock on her door. She answered it to find the landlady there with a steaming mug of cocoa in her hands.

'I thought you'd appreciate a hot drink to help you sleep, Miss Best, and you musn't pay any mind to their old teasing. They were just baiting you, that's all.'

'Thank you,' Alex murmured. 'You're very kind. And perhaps I was being too nosy after all.'

'Well, nobody likes to feel they're oddities, do they? That's the way a lot of city folk see us, and the old 'uns play up to it. We get a coachload of Americans coming here from time to time, and you should see some of the wicked old tricks they get up to then!'

'So they were just teasing about Greenwell Cottage having a bad reputation, were they? Just to get me going, was it?'

'Oh, I dare say that's all it was,' the landlady said soothingly, and it was only a long while afterwards, when she had lain sleepless for hours, ignoring the cocoa, that Alex realized she hadn't denied it either.

Maybe Caroline Price didn't react to atmosphere in a place, but Alex certainly did. She shivered. But she still intended to go back there tomorrow morning.

Maybe she should have drunk the cocoa after all. It was three in the morning when she decided she'd had enough tossing and turning in the lumpy bed, and did something she always vowed she wouldn't. She punched out Nick Frobisher's number on her mobile phone.

It was part of her researches to know when he was on nights, and with his usual caring concern for her, he had told her she was to call him any time, day or night, if she had a problem. She knew very well he didn't necessarily mean a professional problem. He almost certainly *didn't*, and she knew he'd prefer it to be a personal problem that he would willingly solve.

'DI Frobisher,' she heard his voice say abruptly.

Her own voice stuck in her throat. Why on earth had she called, and what the hell was she going to say to him, when she didn't even want him involved in her case?

'Say what you want to say, because I'm hanging up in three seconds from now,' she heard him say next.

'Nick,' she croaked. 'Nick, it's me. Alex.'

She heard the change in his voice at once, and knew he had recognized the desperation in hers.

'Where are you? Are you in trouble? Give me the address and I'll get there as soon as I can.'

'No. No, I'm not in trouble.'

God, he was so sweet. He was big and brash and *hopeless* at times, but right now, he was the only sane voice in a world that for Alex seemed to be tilting sideways. Before she could say anything else, she seemed to hear Gary Hollis's mocking voice in her head.

'Are you sure you're in the right business?'

And no, she damn well wasn't sure. But she wasn't giving up now, either. She pressed her mobile closer to her ear and made herself speak more moderately. If she could pick up the nuance of a telephone voice, so could Nick.

'I just fancied a call to an old friend, that's all—'

'At three in the morning? Pull the other one, Alex. What's up? Are you on a stake-out and feeling the need for company? Unless it's business and you want to call us in, I can't really oblige, darling, much as I'd like to—'

He gave her an unwitting lead. 'I didn't think you could, which is why I'm calling,' she said lightly. 'I just wanted to hear a friendly voice, that's all.'

There was silence at the other end, and then: 'If I didn't know you better, I'd say you were in danger of becoming a teaser, Alex, and it's not your style.'

She bit her lip, knowing the way he meant it. It wasn't his style, either. They teased one another, but they never went over the top. If something had to be said, it was said, and there were no hidden agendas.

'So what's really up?' he said, more gently. 'I know you're on a case. Are there problems?'

'None that I can't handle. Honestly. And I don't have any real problems. I was a bit uneasy earlier this evening, but hearing your nice solid voice makes me feel better.'

'Thanks – I think. Whatever happened to sexy?'

For a minute she thought he was referring to Gary, until she realized he didn't know about him.

'Sexy?'

'Me,' he replied. 'Good God, Alex, if my only male credentials are for having a nice solid voice, it doesn't exactly put me in the front line for sexy, does it?'

'You're fishing, Nick,' she said, a smile in her voice. 'And of course you're sexy.'

She felt an odd stirring as she said it. But he *was* sexy. She never denied it. She just didn't want the complications that a relationship with him might provoke. He could be the marrying kind, and she wasn't.

She didn't totally rule it out, of course, but she wasn't ready for any long-term commitment. Not yet, anyway.

'Good. Then unless you've got anything else to say, I'm afraid I have to go,' he said, suddenly more official. 'And we'll continue this line of questioning another time.'

Alex was still smiling as she switched off her mobile. He always had the power to calm her, she reflected. He was good for her. A good friend. And always there when she needed one. She turned over in bed and fell asleep instantly.

She awoke with a start. It was barely light and there was a hideous noise somewhere outside. It took a few seconds to identify it, and to remember where she was. Then she groaned. She was in the country, and while she could cheerfully sleep through any amount of London traffic noise, she hadn't been woken by the arrogant screech of crowing cockerels since her childhood.

She buried her head beneath her pillow and tried to resume her dream. She had been somewhere in the Mediterranean, sipping cocktails on a luxury cruise ship, and being attended by the dishiest of deck stewards. . . .

She was completely awake now. Remembering where she was and why she was here. And the cruise would never become a reality unless she did what she was being paid to do. Find Caroline Price and return her to the bosom of her family, however cold and inhospitable a place that seemed to Alex.

But one thing was for sure. The demons of last night had left her, and she could put everything the old village locals had intimated into its rightful place. They had just been baiting her, as the landlady had said.

She used her shower, gasping at the lack of really hot water and dressed quickly. The smell of bacon and eggs was already wafting upstairs, and if there was no other choice for breakfast, so be it. Her mouth was watering so much, she knew she was going to throw caution to the winds, and indulge herself for once, anyway. To hell with thighs.

Far more replete than she knew she should be, and still in her tourist guise, Alex eventually made her way back to Greenwell Cottage. It was another glorious day, and summer was truly lingering, for once. It had to break soon, of course. This was England, not the Mediterranean.

She noted again how surprisingly easy it was to reach the cot-

tage without being detected, either from the rest of the village or
the main road. It was completely secluded, a place where
anyone could truly get away from it all.

She also conceded that Caroline must be a pretty strong-
nerved woman. Alex's background meant that she had been well
used to the various country sounds that were so unnerving to
city dwellers. The quiet of the country was all a myth – and
hadn't she proved that herself by reacting so violently to the
squawking of the cockerel dawn chorus!

Country living was a long way back for her now, and she
didn't regret the move to London for one single minute, she
thought fervently. She pushed open the gate of the cottage and
searched for the front door key.

Her mild curse when she couldn't find it immediately seemed
to hang in the air.

Despite the brilliance of the sunlight in the clear blue sky,
there was an oppressiveness about the air that morning, and as
if to mock her renewed sense of equilibrium she realized the
birds had stopped their singing.

All was silent. All was serene. . . .

The small creak of the front door on its hinges made her heart
leap. She saw at once that it was already slightly ajar. Her
thoughts hurled ahead. She didn't need a key, therefore someone
else was here. Or had been here. Or was here now.

She made herself calm down. This was no way for an investigator to behave. Think logically. Step by step. So someone was
already here in the cottage. Maybe it was Caroline and the search
would be over. There was no ostentatious car, so it wasn't the
father. It had to be Caroline.

Tentatively, she knocked on the door, and then realized how
futile that was. Caroline was deaf. If she were here, she wouldn't
hear a feeble knock, nor a belting one.

Very cautiously, Alex pushed open the door. She wouldn't
want to startle the woman, nor let her think that she was an
intruder. She had more than a brief sympathy with how Caroline
might feel, once she learned that her father had instigated this
search for her. Caroline might have been off on an exotic holiday
with her lover, for all any of them knew.

And how would she feel when she discovered that her diary
was missing, and of the intrusion into her private life, and that

someone else was aware of all her intimate secrets?

Whenever Alex analysed some of the things she was obliged to do, that was the part of her job that she found pretty distasteful, easily imagining how she would feel if it happened to her . . . but it had to be done, since there was always the chance that nothing was as clear-cut and innocent as it seemed.

For a moment Alex blinked in the dimness of the room, adjusting her eyes to it, compared with the brightness outside. And then she gasped.

The entire room had been vandalized and ransacked. The desk, that Alex had so carefully avoided wrenching open, was now torn apart, with papers everywhere. Caroline's crossword grids, so neatly stacked before, were flung about the room, together with books and documents.

'Oh, Caroline.' Alex whispered aloud. 'Who could have done this? Who *would* have done it?'

Her heart hammered madly, knowing that whoever had done it might still be here. Might be upstairs, crouching on the tiny landing, watching, and waiting to pounce on her. Her mouth was as dry as dust, but as she forced her thoughts to clarify, one thing was certain: it sure as hell hadn't been Caroline herself who had done this. No one who was so proud and protective of their work would have scattered their precious research books and private papers about for someone else to find.

And it wasn't your usual brand of street vandals either. The computer, printer and photocopier, and all Caroline's other equipment, were untouched. Whoever had been here hadn't come on a thieving spree intending to sell the expensive stuff on at some market stall.

Whoever had been here had been looking for something specific. Something he – or she – hoped to find in Caroline's locked desk, or among her papers or books. But who? And what did they expect to find? What was there here that could be incriminating about a woman who minded her own business to the extent of paranoia?

Unless, of course, any incriminating documents wouldn't concern Caroline herself, but someone else. Her father? The mysterious M, with whom she had been having such a torrid affair? Or was all that simply in the woman's vivid imagination?

Solitude did strange things to people. Right now, Alex's own nerves were jumping, and she had to get out of there before she got completely claustrophobic and the walls started closing in.

'Hello!' she heard a voice call sharply from outside. 'Is there anyone there?'

'*Christ*, what now!' she croaked, immediately realizing she was in a very compromising position here, and could be accused of doing the business herself.

Nobody knew who she really was. She was simply a nosy parker tourist, and she had automatically picked up several chairs and straightened them. Her natural instincts hadn't prevented her looking through the chaos that the thief had so conveniently provided.

And a couple of bank statements proved that Caroline was no pauper. But in pocketing them, she knew she had done the unforgivable, and amateur had to be her middle name.

It was the first rule of detection, she thought, remembering the manual far too late in the day. Don't touch anything. Fingerprint evidence can be useful and damning.

She had successfully forgotten it all. Some detective she was turning out to be . . . but all that guff was applicable when the police were to be involved – and they weren't.

Someone called again, and heart in her mouth now, she peered through the window and saw the vicar standing by the cottage gate. For one wild, disorientated moment, she thought about falling to her knees and beseeching him to come inside and exorcize the demons inhabiting this cottage.

Then she saw the frown on his face as he began to move forward, and she collected her senses. She went outside quickly, and closed the door behind her.

'Oh, it's you, miss,' he said in surprise.

'Good morning, Vicar,' she said, as calmly as possible. 'I've just been enquiring about the cottage on behalf of my friend, but it's not for sale. I was given false information, and the occupant wasn't at all happy at being disturbed.'

She crossed her fingers at the blatant lies she was obliged to make – and to a man of the cloth and all – did that put a black mark against her with St Peter? She dismissed the thought, and prayed that the vicar didn't intend making a tardy visit to the occupant of the cottage.

'Ah,' he said slowly. 'Then allow me to escort you back to the village. It's easy to get lost in the lanes.'

'Thank you, but I can find my own way back. I'd like a little more country air before I go back to London.'

She looked at him pointedly. She didn't want his company, and besides she had something urgent still to do, and she certainly didn't want him around while she did it.

He stalked off in a huff, and she wondered briefly how such an insensitive and pompous man could ever be considered such a man of God. He was of the old Fear and Damnation brigade, and compassion wouldn't seem to be in his make-up.

But once he was well out of earshot, she immediately forgot him and called Norman Price on her mobile phone. His reply was less than cordial when he recognized her voice, which made her more curt than she intended.

'There's been a break-in at the cottage. I think you should get down here and assess the damage before we get on to the police—' Reluctantly, she knew it really was time.

'I told you. I want no police involvement, woman!' He yelled so loudly she had to hold the phone away from her ear.

'Mr Price, I'm afraid I do feel that this should be reported officially. It's beginning to look more serious than your daughter simply going off for a few days' holiday.'

And she wasn't prepared to handle it alone any more.

'Stay put until I get there, and meanwhile do nothing, understand? You're answerable to me, not the bloody police.'

'Yes, sir,' Alex snapped, resisting the urge to snap her heels and give a Heil Hitler salute as the line went dead.

Chapter 5

Alex decided that the idea of Caroline's disappearance being a conspiracy was something too ridiculous to consider. Even so, she couldn't quite get it out of her mind as she waited for Father Price to arrive. It was part of the job to consider everything, no matter how bizarre.

Killing time, she let her thoughts revolve around the scenario, just for the heck of it.

Maybe the village folk had got together and kidnapped Caroline, knowing of her inheritance. Maybe the vicar himself was involved. Stranger things had happened. Maybe these old locals were not so innocent as they seemed. Maybe the landlady was in on it as well. Maybe Alex's cocoa had been drugged and they had whisked Caroline away in the night while she had supposedly been in a stupor.

Well, that idea was out, since she hadn't even drunk the cocoa, and she had been sleepless for so long she would certainly have heard movements. It had been her reassuring call to Nick Frobisher at three in the morning that had finally allowed her to sleep, but after that, she had been dead to the world until cockcrow.

She shivered. Since calling Norman Price that morning she hadn't loitered around the cottage waiting for him or anyone else who might appear, but she hadn't realized she had already reached the village green again until she heard the concerned voice at her side.

'Are you all right, my dear? You look a mite off-colour, and I'd say you've been out in the sun too long.'

The landlady of the Little Harp Inn took her arm and steered her towards the hostelry. Alex felt briefly like a leaf in the wind, going nowhere, except where she was blown.

'I'm really quite well, thank you,' she said.

'Well, you don't look it. Come on inside or you'll be in no fit state to drive back to London later on. Unless you're thinking of staying another day or so?'

'Would that bother you?' Alex said, without thinking.

The woman laughed. 'Glory be, no. I'm in business to cater for guests, so you'd be quite welcome.'

'Thanks, but it won't be necessary. I have to get back to town for my work.'

'And what work would that be?'

Alex knew she had two choices. Either bluff her way out of it with some fictitious job, or come clean and see the reaction. She chickened out.

'I'm doing some research,' she said. Which was true enough. Researching into Caroline Price's secret life.

'My word. But I thought you'd be doing something clever. An educated girl like you, with beauty as well as brains.'

'Right. Yes. Thank you.'

There didn't seem anything more to say. Inside the inn it was cool, and a glass of medicinal brandy was pushed in front of Alex. She didn't want it, but she drank it dutifully and as soon as she could she said she felt better and needed some fresh air again.

Even to herself it sounded as if she had a butterfly mind and couldn't settle to anything. But who cared what the landlady thought? She had to be at the cottage to wait for Norman Price and to face his wrath at her suggestion of calling the police.

The thought of it sobered her. Just why was he so damned resistant to calling the police? What did he have to hide? It was an interesting thought, and no matter what the outcome of this day, she intended asking Nick to run a check on him. Just in case. She felt better for having thought of it.

First of all though, she went to the village shop that sold everything and bought some apples. The woman behind the counter was ready to chat.

'Staying long, are you, miss? I seen you coming out of the inn this morning, and I said to myself there's a city girl needing a bit of a change if I ever saw one.'

'Full marks,' Alex said with a smile. 'Unfortunately I have to leave this afternoon.'

She looked around admiringly. 'You certainly sell everything here. I suppose you supply the whole village – even the out-of-the-way cottages? Do you deliver?'

She groaned at her own corny question. It was so obvious, but only if you were looking for the obvious.

'Bless you, no, we don't deliver. Folk come in for a chat mostly, 'cept for them who think themselves too superior to pass the time of day.' Her sniff was eloquent.

Alex smiled sympathetically. 'I don't suppose you have many of them. Most people here seem friendly.'

'Not all of 'em. Strangers passing through are all right, like yourself, but them that move in and live among us, they can be the worst.'

Alex laughed. It was all too easy. She bought a bag of dough-nuts – in the cause of research – just to keep the woman sweet and talkative.

'Are there many like that?'

'There's one,' the woman said darkly. 'I don't know if she's simple or what, but she don't say much. I reckon she's one of those arty folk from the look of her clothes and her plain face. Just comes and picks up some groceries now and then and goes off again as if she don't have time to scratch her nose. She don't buy much, and from the looks of her, she don't eat enough to feed a sparrow, but it takes all sorts, I dare say.'

'I dare say it does,' Alex said cheerfully, deciding not to press her any further. The description was clearly that of Caroline, and it fitted her image perfectly.

She said goodbye to the woman and went back to her room at the inn to make some notes and to study Caroline's bank state-ments more closely. There was no clue as to where any money from her crosswords came in, but there was a substantial and regular payment from an unknown source.

And she might as well ask for the moon as ask a bank to tell her anything. Rightly so, of course. Alex wouldn't want anyone probing into her own financial affairs, whatever they were like.

'Somebody certainly meant business,' Norman Price snapped, once he had assessed the damage at the cottage.

'Yes, but what kind of business?' Alex asked. 'They didn't take anything of any value. The computer and all the other equipment is still here. We could be dealing with a lunatic, Mr Price, and your daughter could be in real danger.'

'Why? Because some idiots broke in and had a field day with a few papers? It was probably kids who were interrupted and made off after playing about. I think you're overreacting, Miss Best.'

God, he was unbelievable. What kind of father was he, to be so dismissive of the thought of any harm coming to Caroline? Unless he was quite certain she wasn't in any danger, because he knew very well where she was. She took a chance and stared at him unblinkingly.

'Do you know the penalty for kidnapping, Mr Price? I assure you it's a very serious offence, and anyone knowing anything – and I mean *anything* – about it at all, is classed as an accessory, and the penalty is just as severe.'

He wasn't slow to catch on and his voice was icy. 'Are you threatening me, Miss Best? Do you seriously think I had anything to do with Caroline's disappearance? Or that I would be so ludicrous as to call you in to investigate it?'

'You might, if there was something in it for you. In my business, Mr Price, you realize that anything is possible.'

She knew she was probably throwing away all chance of the winter cruise now. But a woman's safety was more important. Even a woman she didn't know. Caroline was still a living, breathing person – she hoped – with feelings and emotions similar to her own. They were all sisters under the skin, Alex thought, momentarily caught up in some latterday sense of being one of Mrs Pankhurst's young ladies. Standing shoulder to shoulder, and all that.

'I merely want my daughter back, Miss Best,' Price said now, his voice low and full of sincerity. Whether or not it was genuine, she honestly couldn't tell at that moment.

'Why?' she asked bluntly, using the shock effect. It didn't work this time.

'Why would any father want to know his daughter was safe?' he said indignantly, and Alex realized he was growing in confidence now. 'I'm paying you to find her, and that's really all you need to know.'

'Aren't you in the least bit curious to know what was taken here? Hasn't it crossed your mind that someone might have broken in to look for something specific? Letters, or documents, or something of that kind?'

She realized she was asking him the kind of questions he should be asking her. If he truly wanted to know that Caroline was safe, it was on his own account. She was sure of that. The bloody inheritance was at the root of it. He needed that money, and he needed it fast.

'I've already told you Caroline wouldn't thank me for any interference into her private life,' he said.

'But she did *have* a private life, Mr Price.' Alex knew it was time to open his eyes, however disloyal it might be to Caroline, and however shocked he might be.

'What do you mean by that? She kept to herself—'

'She had a very strong relationship with a male friend. There is some very fetching underwear in her bedroom and exotic toiletries in the bathroom. Do I need to elaborate?'

Price laughed harshly. 'I'm beginning to think I've *hired* the lunatic! You should stick to reading trashy romances if that's the way you're thinking. Caroline and a man? Don't make me puke!'

Bastard! Alex thought.

'Why is it so impossible?' she demanded, increasingly defensive of Caroline.

'You've seen her photos,' he said with a shrug. 'No, lass, you're off with the fairies if that's what you think. So if you're going to suggest she's gone on some holiday with this male friend, think again.'

'Where is she then?'

'How the hell should I know? I'm paying you to find out.'

This was getting nowhere. Alex switched tactics. 'Would you mind telling me how Caroline lives down here? Does she have independent means?'

She didn't dare let on that she had seen the bank statements in case he wasn't aware of his daughter's finances. He glared at her.

'She was offered voluntary redundancy when she got ill, and she gets a good pension. Apart from that, she has an allowance from me, and whatever she earns from her piddling little cross-words.'

Alex wouldn't mind betting that Caroline hated him as much

77

as she herself did. No wonder there was so little communication between them. She gave up.

'Well, I've already said I think it's a matter for the police now,' she said curtly.

'*No*, blast your eyes. How many more times? No police. And if you want to earn your keep properly, I suggest you clear up all this mess and let me get back to work.'

Alex felt her cheeks burn. 'I'm not paid to be a skivvy, Mr Price—'

'You're paid to do whatever I ask you to do,' he said coarsely. 'And while you're doing it, start looking for clues, since that's supposed to be your business.'

He stormed out while Alex was still deciding whether or not to throw something at him. He was a pig, and she loathed him. The sooner she got out of here and back to the land of the living, the better.

But the very intimation that this might be a house of the non-living, calmed her down. It would be hell for Caroline to come back and find the place in such a mess. On the assumption that she would be returning, then as a sister under the skin, the least Alex could do was to tidy the place. She'd probably mucked up any chance of the police finding fingerprints, anyway. Hers and Father Price's were already over everything. But apart from the bank statements there was little of any real use. Except. . . .

By the time she got back to her flat that evening it was dusk. She quickly took a shower to rid herself of the dust in the cottage and the misery of driving back to town in the rush hour. But she was triumphant. The cottage was almost back to its pristine state, barring the ruined desk drawers, and although there had been no useful letters or documents or anything else, a sudden thought had produced dividends.

She knew she should have thought of it before, but even the best of detectives knew there was always a lot of spadework to be done before you turned up anything significant. She comforted herself with that thought.

First, though, she checked the half-dozen messages on her answering machine. Three of them were from Gary, and the last one was the important one.

'God knows where you are, Alex, but if you want to get in

touch, you can reach me on my mobile. And if you don't, I'll know it's bye-bye.'

As he reeled off the number, Alex scribbled it down and called immediately.

'Gary. It's me, Alex.'

'Where the hell have you been? I've been trying to get in touch with you—'

'I know. I had to go out of town, but I'm back now.'

There was a short pause and then: 'Was it anything to do with the case of the missing millions?'

She laughed, her green eyes sparkling. 'I don't want to talk about it over the phone, but if you want to come round any time—'

'Can a duck swim? I'll be there in about an hour. Be ready for me, doll.'

She hung up. She was still smiling, but she was beginning to tire of his way of thinking, and of his arrogance. They hardly knew one another, at least in terms of time, yet he was so sure of her. He expected her to be ready and waiting ... and she still wasn't totally happy with the way he had come into her life so fortuitously. But you had to trust some time. So she decided to trust him.

After the necessary hugs and kisses and his inevitable manoeu-vring towards the bedroom, she held him off.

'Later,' she promised. 'I've made progress—'

'Do you know what it does to a guy when you keep him waiting?' He pushed her hand down to the evidence in his leathers. 'It can do real harm, sweetheart.'

'And I wasn't born yesterday to believe in that old chestnut,' she said crisply. 'I didn't ask you round here just for sex, Gary—'

'I'll go then,' he said, starting to get up.

She caught at his hand. 'Please don't go all stroppy on me. I thought you'd got as interested in finding the missing Caroline as I have. I need your help.'

'In what way? And what's in it for me?'

She remembered just why she had brushed him off the first time she saw him at the Rainbow Club. He was great in many ways, but he was also brash and crude – not really her type at all – whatever that was.

He also had an ego the size of Everest. and she wasn't just referring to what was in his jeans either. His first love would always be himself. Oddly enough, she was somewhat relieved to know it. It meant he would always be ready to turn to some other adoring female whenever he got the push.

'*So?*' he persisted.

'You don't want me to *pay* you, do you?'

He grinned. 'Only in kind, darling. Do we have a deal?'

'You're a slag, Gary, and before you say it takes one to know one, shut up and listen to what I found at Caroline's cottage.'

'So that's where you've been.'

'I found the cousin's address. Or at least, I found the name of his theatre. It's out of town. I accessed Caroline's address file on her computer and there it was. She didn't have anything much on there, though. It might have given us more clues, but she obviously didn't – doesn't – keep in touch with people. It was quite sad.'

'Can you afford to get sentimental over your clients?'

'I can identify with them,' she retorted, 'which is quite a different thing.'

'So the next move is to contact the cousin, is it?'

'That's where you come in. Or rather, both of us,' Alex said carefully.

'No way!' Gary said emphatically. 'I'm not into classical music, and I can think of better things to do than sit through a whole evening of it. *Much* better things to do—'

'You can stay the night afterwards,' she said recklessly. 'Please Gary, do this for me. I can hardly ask—'

She almost said she could hardly ask Nick Frobisher to accompany her. He wasn't into classical music, either, any more than she was herself, she admitted, but Nick would start getting curious, and she wouldn't be able to worm her way into Jeremy Laver's confidence in the way she intended. Whereas with Gary. . . .

'I can hardly ask Caroline's father to go with me, can I?' she amended.

'And I can stay the night?' Gary asked, still one-track.

'After we've been to the concert.'

She stared him out, bloody well determined not to let sex get in the way. She had work to do, and so far she was getting nowhere fast. The thought that Caroline Price might be in real danger was becoming ever more alarming to her now. The damage to the cottage had seen to that.

She was sure it hadn't been the work of kids. It was too deliberately targeted towards the contents of the desk. Whoever had done it knew exactly what he was looking for, and where to find it. She was also sure in her mind that it was a man. And just as sure now that her brainstorm notion of the villagers conspiring against a newcomer in their midst was no more than a fantasy. She'd got too caught up in the Stepford Wives syndrome – and she could thank Nick for that, whether he knew it or not.

Gary finally saw that she meant business. 'When is this bloody concert?'

'A week next Friday. I looked it up in the *Entertainment Weekly*. It's mentioned in the tiniest print, so I don't think our Jeremy's exactly on the world stage yet. Which means he'll be open to flattery.'

'Go on.'

'So I'm going to call him and ask for tickets because I've heard good reports of his music.'

'He's hardly going to give them away to somebody he doesn't know. And I'm not paying to hear that godawful tuneless rubbish.'

Alex grinned, assuming a drawling, Midwest American accent. 'He will when I tell him I'm an American arts reporter interested in featuring new musical talent.'

Gary laughed, his fingers nuzzling the back of her neck. 'I still don't think he'll bite – but you're pretty devious on the quiet, aren't you, Miss Best?'

'You have to be in my business,' she said, and then gave up all thoughts of business for one evening. The phonecall could go on hold until morning, and there were other ways of celebrating a brilliant idea.

'I'm sorry. Do I know you?'

The voice on the phone was strong and pleasing. Alex spoke quickly in the drawling American accent.

'You don't, Mr Laver. I'm with a small American arts magazine based in Ohio, and I'm here because we're interested in doing features on up-and-coming British artistes. There's no money in it, I'm afraid, just a certain amount of exposure. I can't even promise that my editor would use it, but I'd do my best for you,' she added, giving herself an out.

She could almost see him preen. Play to their vanity and it always got results.

'Well, it so happens that you're in luck. Miss—'

'Barnes.' She reverted to her real name, just in case.

'Well, Miss Barnes, I'm holding a concert on the 18th. I'll gladly send you a couple of complimentary tickets.'

'That will be just darling. Let me give you my post office box number and I'll look forward to it.'

'And you'll come to the green-room for drinks after the performance, of course. You'll want an interview.'

'Of course,' she said sweetly.

She grinned at Gary as she put down the phone.

'Told you. Like taking candy from a baby.'

Jeremy Laver's passion was the violin. He was the leading instrumentalist in the small ensemble of musicians who considered themselves far better than some of the big boys, and who were never going to get anywhere beyond playing to small select audiences. He knew that, but it didn't stop the ambition seething beneath the surface.

And if this American woman was going to be the catalyst to making his dreams come true, he was going to welcome her with open arms. Even so, he knew to his cost that working your way to the top took time. And time was something he didn't have. Not if he wanted to save his theatre.

The lease on it was up in three months' time, and there was no way he could raise the money to buy it outright, even if a recording deal fell straight into his lap. This magazine feature didn't sound exactly big-time though, and his brief feeling of elation was fading fast, the way it usually did.

He was a pessimist by nature. He seemed to live on a diet of highs and lows – mostly lows. It went with the territory. Musicians were meant to be tortured souls, and he certainly fell into that category.

In fact, the only thing stopping him from throwing himself into the Thames was the thought that there was one way to do everything he ever wanted, however distasteful it still seemed to him.

He had always quite liked his cousin Caroline. He still did. He'd always been scared of her bombastic father though, and kept his distance from him except when it was vitally necessary. But he and Caroline had rubbed along quite well as children. The fact that she was about to come into money while he was not wasn't something to be held against her.

He would never get personally involved in anything unpleasant regarding her . . . Jeremy wasn't into violence himself, and always managed to vindicate his own actions by telling himself as much. In fact, in what he knew would be his Uncle Norman's words, he thought, you delegated.

Nick Frobisher was worried about Alex. He always knew that one day she was going to bite off more than she could chew. Not that he doubted her ability in detection. There was a doggedness about her that he admired. She would never give in on a case until she got a result. Just like himself.

It was a pity she couldn't see how alike they were. They would make a great team, in more ways than one. But he admired her self-discipline too. If she needed his help she would ask for it, and not before. But this time . . . well, she wasn't the only one who got gut feelings, despite her lofty assertion that her woman's intuition was as good as any man's logic.

When it came to feelings, he had plenty for her, and not only in his gut. And it was so unlike her to call him at three in the morning from God knows where, that his concern for her overcame his reluctance to interfere. He called at her office a few days later, thankful to find her there – and in one delicious piece – without really knowing why he should feel such relief.

'Alex, how goes it?' he said breezily, noting the way she quickly slid a file over something on her desk.

'Fine. And you? Is this a social call, or what?'

He perched easily on the edge of the desk, large and hunky, and managing to look as if he filled the room.

'Social. Any coffee going, or do I have to fix it myself as usual? And a biscuit or two wouldn't go amiss. I know you've got some stashed away.'

She laughed. She was already planning how she would conduct the inteview with Jeremy Laver. It was her next project. It was giving her a buzz, and she could afford to play the little woman for now.

'Haven't you had any breakfast?' she said, rummaging in a cupboard for the tin of biscuits she kept out of sight in the forlorn hope that it would deter her from eating too many.

'I did, but it was so long ago my stomach's forgotten what it was.'

He swivelled idly around on the desk, ostensibly to watch her curvaceous rear as she bent down to the cupboard where she hoarded forbidden snacks, and in reality to slide the file across from what she had so deftly kept out of sight. His practised eyes quickly took in the details of the two poorly made theatre tickets before he slid the file over them again.

'Have you quite recovered from your stake-out, Alex?' he said casually.

'What stake-out? Oh, you mean the other night. It wasn't a stake-out. I was just feeling lonely, that's all, and I shouldn't have called you. It was stupid—'

'It wasn't stupid at all. I was flattered that you should think of me when you were feeling lonely. I wish you'd think of me more often in the middle of the night.'

Alex dumped the two mugs of coffee on the desk and pushed the tin of biscuits towards him.

'Well, don't get too excited about it. I'm not thinking of involving you in anything. I can't,' she added abruptly.

'Why not? Is that client confidentiality – or client's insistence?'

'You see too much, and sometimes you see things that aren't there,' Alex told him. 'I'm just dealing with a domestic case and it doesn't concern you.'

'Unless it becomes ugly,' he suggested.

'Unless it becomes – became ugly – which it won't.'

'As long as you're sure,' he said, drinking the coffee with a speed that suggested he had a cast-iron stomach. He had already wolfed down two chocolate biscuits to her one.

But she could make up for that later.

'Look, I do appreciate your concern, Nick,' she said, knowing that his feelings were genuine, but I really can take care of myself.'

'That's what they all say. I'll see you around then.'

He blew her a kiss and sauntered out. Too late, she remembered she was going to ask him to do a check on Norman Price, but she'd get around to that later, too.

She moved the file away from the two theatre tickets and smiled. She was on to something. She was sure of it. And apart from the fact that Gary was coming to the concert with her, she was perfectly capable of handling it without involving him. But she knew his unlikely presence at a classical concert would divert any unnecessary attention from herself, and that was something she was depending on.

Nick Frobisher had a photographic memory. He could picture the two theatre tickets as if he had them in front of him. He had quickly noted down the details, and once back in his office he started checking out a few things.

The theatre in question wasn't in the West End – far from it – and the name of the ensemble wasn't a familiar one. His thoughts followed their usual logical trail.

Alex liked middle-of-the-road music, same as himself. Radio Two wasn't a dirty word in his language, nor in hers. So why would anyone send her two tickets to a classical concert and, more significantly, why had she been careful to conceal them from him?

It had to be something to do with this case she was on, and she definitely intended going to the concert, otherwise the tickets would have quickly found their way to her waste-paper bin. He didn't trouble to query who she might be going with. It wasn't him, that was for sure.

He called in his WPC assistant.

'Mary, do a check for me, will you? See if there's anything on a Jeremy Laver. A musician, I gather.'

'Will do,' she said, and Nick sat back with his hands behind his head, awaiting results. It was amazing what files could turn up these days. Information from various sources passed around the network and spread like butter, and he was pretty sure he'd soon get the picture as far as this Jeremy Laver was concerned. What he was going to do with it once he got it was another matter.

'Well, well,' he said slowly, a long while later, when he had studied the papers in front of him. 'So young Jeremy gave a charmer called Norman Price as a reference on a theatre lease, did he? Now, there's an interesting connection.'

'Is it?' the WPC said. 'Who's Norman Price then?'

Nick was thoughtful. 'It's a name that's cropped up a few times in the past. Nothing major, mostly piddling motoring offences. But the manner of his responses leave nothing in the way of civility. Thinks himself above the law, does that one. I seem to remember he owned some factory or other. Do a check on him as well, Mary. Just to humour me.'

Nick burst into Alex's office that afternoon.

'What's going on?'

She screamed back at him, 'What the hell do you mean, what's going on? I'm going to give that doorman a piece of my mind, letting you in here as if you own the bloody place and frightening the life out of me again—'

'What's your connection with Norman Price of Price Chemicals?'

She flinched. 'I don't know what you mean.'

'You bloody well do know what I mean.'

He stared her out coldly. He was bluffing, but she didn't have to know that. It was part of the cat-and-mouse game they all played. And he was banking on her inexperience to cave in.

'If your little domestic case is going to ruin a police investigation, I'll have your licence taken away so fast you'll wonder what hit you.'

'Nick, stop it!' Alex stood up, her back rigid, fists on the desk, her knuckles white. The reference to her little domestic case had momentarily enraged her, but there was too much at stake to mess about with bruised egos.

'Well?' he said.

'I don't know anything about any police investigation, but nothing would surprise me,' she said wildly. 'I do know he's a nasty piece of work – and he's probably up to something. His kind usually are. So what have you got on him?'

He gave a sudden grin. 'Nothing – yet. So why don't you tell me everything you know, especially if there's anything *I* should know.'

Alex stared at him, her eyes blazing.

'You – you bastard! You tricked me.'

He came around the desk and pulled her into his arms.

'God, you're beautiful when you're angry.'

'And that's the corniest line I've heard in years.'

'Who said it was a line?' Before she could struggle out of his iron-hard embrace, his mouth had come down on hers, silencing her fury in a savage kiss.

He had kissed her before. Sometimes enthusiastic, New-Year's-Eve kind of kisses; sometimes brotherly, comforting kind of kisses; but never like this: savagely possessive to begin with, and slowly melting into the erotic. One hand was caressing the softness of her hair, while the other held her as tightly to him as if he owned her. . . .

'I mean it, you know,' he said, still a whisper away from her lips. 'You're the most beautiful woman on earth, and you should be sitting at home knitting bootees instead of getting involved in a world you know nothing about—'

She pushed him away from her so fast he almost lost his balance. 'That's just the kind of sexist remark I might have expected from a copper,' she said furiously.

All the same, she had to sit down again, because his erotic onslaught had affected her far more than she was prepared to let on. He was a *mate*, damn him, not a potential lover, or so she had always believed. Business and pleasure should be kept strictly apart. Now, she wasn't so sure what she thought.

He sat on the chair on the other side of her desk and folded his arms, clearly not prepared to move. As immovable as the bloody Sphinx, Alex found herself thinking.

'So are we going to compare notes?' he said calmly, just as if the fact that she had just been so deliciously and seductively held in his arms hadn't affected him at all, when his raging libido was telling him something very different.

'Why should we?'

'Because, my dear sweet and lovely Miss Best, it's time. I don't know what you're up to yet. but your little charade of calling me up at three in the morning just for a friendly chat doesn't wash any more. I know when there's desperation in somebody's voice and I heard it in yours. Trust me, Alex.'

If she hadn't felt so emotional she could almost have laughed. She was trusting Gary and she didn't know whether she should do so or not.

By her personal knowledge of Nick's code of ethics – give or take the deviousness which went with both their jobs – she knew she could trust him. But she still wasn't sure if there was any benefit in doing so.

Chapter 6

'So just what do *you* know about Norman Price?'

She might have known he wouldn't give up easily, and Alex's nerves twitched again at the question. She didn't want to give him the satisfaction of knowing she had been rumbled, to use the telly jargon. He didn't know if there was any real connection between herself and Norman Price yet – and she didn't know what *his* connection was, either.

She had been going to ask him to do a check on the man but his own question had effectively blocked the way for that, if she wanted to keep her case to herself. Which she did. She most emphatically did.

'All right. I know he owns a chemical factory out of town,' she recited, as if thinking about it. 'It's pretty run-down from the look of the outside, but I've never been inside the place. Why do you want to know, anyway?'

That was better. Throw the questioning back at him while she got her thoughts together. That was technique.

'Just a passing interest. No more.'

Oh yes? Tell that to the birds. For a certain person's name to crop up for both of them had to make it more than a passing interest. She would dearly like to be more probing but she knew very well it would only rebound on her.

'What's he done?' Nick pressed on.

'You tell me. You started this, remember?' she said coolly and on the upper hand. He'd obviously got wind of something to do with Price, but he'd bluffed her once and she wasn't going to let it happen again. She guessed there was no official police investigation going on, and Price himself had been so adamant about no police involvement regarding Caroline that she was determined to observe his wishes. Client respect went with the job. Even for a client like Price. . . .

She airily overlooked the fact that she'd been nearly as adamant in *wanting* Nick in when the cottage had been ransacked and she had got so jittery about it. But that was then, and this was now, and she no longer wanted him in.

She had Jeremy in her sights now. She was gut-sure – almost – that he was somehow involved in Caroline's disappearance, and providing she could prove it she was intent on solving the mystery herself. One-upmanship wasn't confined to the guys.

She stared at Nick unblinkingly, resisting the thought that that kiss had been spectacularly erotic, and that he really was superlooking when he got that intense look in his eyes that wasn't wholly to do with police-work.

She waited for the next bit of questioning, sure that he hadn't done with her regarding Norman Price yet. Cat-and-mouse-like as ever, he'd come up with something else. Baiting her. Waiting to pounce. But the silence went on too long, making her nervous. And when she was nervous, she talked.

'I really don't know anything more about him,' she said quickly. 'Nothing of importance, anyway.'

The moment she said it, she knew she'd given herself away. Now he would know she was on to something. Or that she was investigating Price. But he still didn't know the nature of her case, and she was damned if she was going to tell him. She waited for him to seize on her words.

'What are you doing a week next Friday?' he said casually.

Alex visibly jumped, and prayed that he wouldn't see it. Even if he did, he couldn't possibly know the reason for it.

'Why?'

'I've got two free tickets—'

She felt her heart begin to pound, and she was literally holding her breath. He didn't – he *couldn't* know anything about Jeremy Laver.

'—for that new film at the Odeon. Do you fancy it?'

Alex let out her breath without realizing she had been holding it in so tightly. Her chest ached with the effort.

'Nick, I can't,' she said. 'I've got something else on. I'm sorry, truly. It would have been nice—'

'What is it?'

'What?'

'Where you're going on the 18th?'

'Oh. Nowhere very interesting,' she said cagily.

He gave a short laugh. 'Well, that puts me in my place, doesn't it? "Nowhere very interesting" is obviously far more interesting than coming out with me.'

'I didn't mean it like that at all and you know it. It's just something that I can't put off. But if you've got free tickets to the cinema you can always take somebody else. Why not ask that nice WPC in your office? Mary, isn't it?'

Even as she said it, she felt a sliver of unreasonable jealousy shoot through her. Mary was small and blonde and a cute little compact package – according to some of Nick's more moronic colleagues. And why should she care about Mary snuggling up to Nick in a warm, darkened cinema, anyway?

'Mary's getting married at the end of the year, and I don't imagine her hunk of a fiancé would appreciate my asking her out. It doesn't matter. Another time maybe.'

To Alex's relief he finally turned to go. She liked his company, but now wasn't the time. She had work to do.

And she brushed aside the thought that maybe in a year or two Mary would be content to be knitting bootees the way Nick had described it earlier, all cosy and wifey. Alex had no argument with that, if it was what Mary wanted. Not that she had a clue whether she did or not. Some women wanted nothing more than the homely life, others didn't.

She might even fancy it herself in a few years' time, Alex mused, letting her work-concentration waver for a moment. There was a sweet domesticity about the thought, though for the life of her, she couldn't visualize herself pushing a pram in the park. Someday maybe. Maybe not. And certainly not now.

She put the idea out of her mind and concentrated on the reasons behind Nick's visit. He was curious about Norman Price, but she realized he had given away nothing about his interest. He was a clever devil all right. But he hadn't mentioned Jeremy Laver. He had no idea of the connection there – at least, she had to presume that he didn't. With Frobisher, you just never knew.

For the briefest moment, she wished he wasn't so bloody

devious. And then she grinned, because she knew very well he thought exactly the same about her.

She gave up worrying about it. The 18th was still more than a week away and she prayed that Gary wasn't going to lose his nerve about going to the concert with her. His kind of inverted snobbery said that if something was beyond his comprehension he simply sneered at it and called it rubbish.

She wasn't a snob or particularly well read, but she was fairly liberal regarding other people's morals and lifestyles, which was what made her good at her job, in her opinion. An investigator had to see the world through other people's eyes, and not through her own blinkered ones.

Hey, that was pretty good, she thought. Maybe, I was a philosopher in another life.

The phone rang, making her jump, and her hand reached out for it automatically.

'Alexandra Best—'

'I need your help on a sexual matter, Miss Best,' she heard the husky voice say. 'Can you meet me at midnight at Westminster Bridge, wearing something black and slinky—'

'Get off the line, Gary,' she snapped, recognizing the disguised voice with ease. 'I've got work to do and I can't waste time playing games.'

He was petulant at once. 'All right, keep your knickers on – though I'd much rather have 'em off.'

He gave his characteristic whistle as she sent an expressive oath down the line, and then chuckled.

'You've no idea how such language turns me on, coming from a classy lady like you. But we'll forget that for the moment. I'm on business too. I've got another package to deliver to Price Chemicals. Do you want to come along?'

But despite the chuckle, she could tell that he was ruffled now. He was a boy, for all his macho biker image and his manly attributes – and they were quite something. He'd always be the leader of the gang, if he had a gang, but she wasn't the type to comply with every changing mood of a boy.

'I don't, thanks,' she said. 'There's no point, and I've got other leads to follow. Price isn't one of them.'

'Oh yes? What's new then?'

There was that eagerness again, the nosiness she still didn't quite trust. She sighed, wishing that she did. Wishing she didn't always have to suspect every word, every tone of voice. But that was what she *did*, damn it. It was part of the role she had given herself. The Job.

'Nothing too clever if you must know,' she admitted.

That was true. What other leads did she have to follow? Nothing. *Nada.* Zilch. And time was moving on. Caroline had to be found if she was to claim her inheritance and thwart her father. And maybe Jeremy Laver too.

'See you later then?' Gary went on.

'No. Leave it for now, Gary. I've got to go out of town for a few days, so I'll see you the day of the concert. OK?'

She hung up before he could argue, and then switched her phone to answering machine. Then she stared at Caroline Price's file on the desk in front of her. It looked pathetically slim. So far she was doing a pretty poor job.

Sherlock would have been well on to the case by now, and she had practically nothing to show. Nothing to follow up until she met Jeremy Laver a week on Friday and began a careful quizzing of the cousin.

Except . . . maybe she hadn't followed through the crossword angle seriously enough. Once she had eliminated every possibility of agenting or publishing, she had got precisely nowhere. But Caroline must sell the damn things or why would she continue doing them? It wasn't being done for fun. Alex was sure of that. Some of the clues were cryptic to the point of being far too obscure for the casual solver to work out.

No, the crosswords must go somewhere, and from the professional appearance of her work desk at the cottage they had to be a huge part of Caroline's life – the central part, if you ignored the erotic association with the mysterious M.

Crossword compiling would seem to be all she did: refusing all communication with the outside world, even the locals in whose midst she had become the odd recluse; cutting her father out of her life as much as possible – and Alex didn't blame her one bit for that; just sitting at that bloody computer all day long and figuring out words and clues and filling in the grids.

It sounded hideously boring to somebody who led a normal life – whatever a normal life was.

Much against her will, she tried to think how Nick Frobisher would tackle the problem. She could almost hear his voice in her head.

'If you've tried all the bigger angles and the more obvious ones, then try the smaller ones. The ones nobody would consider. That's often where the clues are.'

She stared sightlessly into the far wall of her office. The smaller angles. What were they? She couldn't even bring to mind the bigger ones, for God's sake. She pulled her thoughts around to the two things she knew for certain. One was that Caroline was missing. The other was that her crosswords presumably – probably – appeared in some adult newspaper or magazine. The crosswords were definitely too sophisticated for kids' comic-book stuff.

She had tried all the major media. She drew in her breath, her eyes coming back into focus.

'Freebies!' she said out loud.

Her thoughts were racing now. Caroline obviously didn't need money from her work. She had plenty to live on. She'd be paid something for her contributions, of course, but the money didn't have to be great – and Alex still hadn't worked out how she received it. That could come later. If Caroline was compiling crosswords for a freebie, then it was the work that kept her mind stimulated, and maybe that was all she needed. After all, she had M to stimulate another part of her. . . .

Alex was elated. She was on to something at last. She was sure of it. For the moment, she could overlook the fact that there were probably dozens of free newspapers and magazines in central London alone.

Everyone was in on it, making a buck where they could. Smaller ones probably wouldn't even be registered as newspapers, just supplying a small area and keeping their publishing heads above water, small press stuff, even desk-top publishing at home. Church magazines and club magazines of every description, stuff like that.

Who was to say that Caroline's outlet was in London, anyway? Even as the elation hit her, Alex was fast realizing that there was a huge downside to the freebie idea, but she was determined to ignore the downside for now. The important thing was that she had something to work on.

But even as the excitement of the chase grew bigger in her

mind, Alex was struck by something she should have thought of before. Something that sent her spirits plummeting again.

Whoever said she was cut out for this? she thought dismally. Did the big boys ever go through such backtracking and self-deprecation? Just when she thought she was on the right road she remembered something to put her right back at the beginning again.

Wouldn't anyone doing such intricate and exacting work keep copies of their published work? Maybe Caroline wasn't in it for the ego trip of seeing her work in print, but Alex couldn't imagine that she wouldn't keep a single published copy. She had seen nothing at all at the cottage, and until this moment it hadn't occurred to her to look for any special type of publications.

In any case, the cottage had been bereft of any kind of magazine or newspaper except for those used for research purposes, but any private eye worth their salt would surely have checked out such a thing. What an *idiot* she was!

Did Caroline even submit her crosswords anywhere at all? That was the next thing to occur. Maybe she didn't. But if not, what a waste of a logical brain, and Alex couldn't credit that one at all. The crosswords had to go somewhere, and were presumably mailed to the freebie or whatever. Simply slipped through a village letterbox, perhaps, as anonymously as they were compiled.

'Caroline, you're not exactly helping,' Alex muttered aggressively. 'Don't you want to be found?'

She stared at the file in front of her. That could be it, of course. Maybe Caroline didn't want to be found, either before or after her birthday. She was a mature woman, and she could go where she pleased, especially with M. Her diary indicated the importance of the special birthday, with that one word FREEDOM written so prominently. But with no indication of its real meaning.

It was so bloody frustrating. For all Alex knew, there was no mystery at all. Caroline had simply gone off somewhere without telling her father. She clearly felt no obligation to inform him of what she did. She wasn't friendly enough with anyone in the village for them to know her movements. And even the break-in at the cottage could have been simply the work of vandals, finding the place empty.

There was always the possibility that all these things had a perfectly simple explanation and not a sinister one. Except that vandals would surely have stolen the valuable computer and printer items, and not merely ransacked a desk. Unless they had been looking for money, and had been scared off before they could finish their work, hearing cars in the distance, or a dog barking. There were just too many possibilities.

But, determined as ever, she spent the next week trailing round every possible small freebie newspaper and magazine in a wide area until her feet throbbed and her brain buzzed, and she drew continual blanks.

With her fingers crossed, she made her weekly report to Norman Price that she was hoping to have news for him soon, and then had to hold the phone away from her head while he ranted on at her for not producing results.

And for all his professed wish to find his daughter, she hated him all over again for his uncaring attitude. Whatever his true reasons for finding her, there was no paternal feeling for Caroline in him at all. No love. He was a pig.

'I keep trying to get inside Caroline's mind, and getting nowhere,' she said to Gary by the time they were finally *en route* to Jeremy Laver's concert. 'As soon as I think I'm on to something, I think of something else to counter it. I mean, we *know* her birthday has to be important, but why? Why was the word FREEDOM written so big?'

'Wouldn't you think it important if you were going to inherit a fortune on that day?' Gary asked, allowing her to drive for once, since he'd got all togged up, as he called it. Which simply meant he had left off his bike helmet.

'Yes, but is she interested in money? I hardly think so from the way she lives. She's not into material things at all, except for the necessary equipment for her work, and the expensive underwear in the bedroom. And that's only for M's benefit. If he wasn't on the scene, I bet she'd be perfectly content to be the plain Jane that she is.'

'So where does she buy them?' Gary said lazily. 'Have you checked that out?'

'No, because I get the feeling that it wouldn't help. There were no recognizable labels on anything. They were just sexy garments. Thanks for the suggestion, anyway.'

'All part of the service, honey,' Gary said, letting his hand slide over her thigh in her black silk evening skirt.

She slapped his hand away. 'Leave it, Gary, unless you want us to be another statistic in the London traffic.'

'All right,' he sulked. 'But remember that you owe me, Alex. I'm doing this concert as a favour to you, and you promised I could stay the night.'

'So I did.'

She clamped her lips together, manoeuvring her way between the evening glut of taxis, and mouthing back a matching obscenity to the guy on her right as she slid smoothly into the inside lane in front of him.

'*Asshole*,' Gary supplied for her.

When they reached the theatre, parking was predictably difficult even this far out of town, but Alex finally found a space in the road and squeezed the car into it.

It was obvious that it wasn't a theatre of any importance. It was small and tucked away in a side street, and the dour frontage was in need of care and attention. But Alex let out her breath with a sigh of relief at finding it at all, and the certainty in her mind that whatever else Jeremy Laver was about, he was probably in need of money.

She turned to Gary. 'Now remember the story. I'm an American journalist with a small arts magazine based in Ohio, and we're interested in doing features on up-and-coming British musicians. You're just a friend. Oh – and my name is Audrey Barnes.'

'Christ, couldn't you have thought of something snazzier than that?' he hooted.

She looked at him coldly. 'It happens to be my real name. But if you can't handle it—'

'I can handle anything,' he said with a smirk, and she gave another sigh, wondering why the hell she had let him into her life at all. Sometimes he irritated her so much. And sometimes she wondered if she was getting too tunnel-visioned about this case to even joke any more. But tonight wasn't for joking. Tonight she was on business and Gary had better believe it.

'Let's go inside,' she said.

'Is there a bar where we can have a drink first? If I've got to sit through an evening of caterwauling, the least you can do is buy me a drink. We *are* on expenses, aren't we – Miss Barnes?'

'Of course,' Alex said.

A drink might help to stop her jitters too. She admitted that she had some. She didn't forget for a moment that she was here to observe and talk with Jeremy Laver, and to try to assess his character. There was a close family relationship with the Prices and he was the one who stood to gain by Caroline's disappearance. It didn't always follow that he was going to be the villain. But she also knew well enough that anyone could resort to crime if the right incentive was there.

Money was a very strong incentive. The cousin could be a potential kidnapper, even murderer. There was always the possibility that Caroline Price might even now be mouldering somewhere in a murky makeshift grave, on his account.

Her eyes glazed for a moment. Suddenly, her earlier calming thoughts that Caroline had merely gone away without telling anyone, seemed childish in the extreme. Surely there was too much at stake. The coincidence of the timing was too great. The inheritance was too large. And Norman Price's need for cash, if her instincts were right, was too desperate. What could be easier than a plan for the two men to share it, if Caroline wasn't around to claim it on the due date? But if those suspicions were to be proved right, then what the hell had they done with her?

'Come on, before the crush at the bar gets too much,' she heard Gary say, while her thoughts raced on haphazardly.

His voice was brash and arrogant now, and Alex could see it was because he was perfectly aware of the withering glances he was attracting in his leather gear. Despite the undoubted seediness of the place, most of the men were in lounge suits, their female companions generally wearing long skirts or dark dresses. There were also a number of bohemian long-hairs who looked as if they were hard put to find the price of a ticket.

It didn't bother Alex to be seen with Gary. Having an eccentric companion at her side only added to her persona of crazy American journalist. She moved towards the bar with him now, ignoring her last few traumatic thoughts.

As she did so, she caught sight of someone at the back of the bar area. Someone who caused her to draw in her breath in fury as he raised his glass to her slightly, and then turned away, as if to acknowledge the fact that neither of them would wish to greet the other in public.

'What's up?' Gary said, hearing her indrawn breath. 'Is there someone you know who's going to blow your cover?'

She forced a smile, giving herself time to think . . . to breathe.

'Sometimes, Gary,' she said, 'I think you should be the one in this game, not me. You've got all the lingo, and you obviously watch too many American cop shows on television.'

The barman asked him for his order then, and she could cool down while she praised herself for neatly fending off his question, while still fuming at the thought that not six feet away from her was DI Nick Frobisher.

What the hell was he doing here, and on this particular evening? He was supposed to be at the cinema with two free tickets and somebody to replace herself or WPC Mary . . . and even as she remembered his invitation, she knew it had been just a ploy.

Everything clicked into place as she recalled his visit to her office. He must have seen the concert tickets on her desk, and even if he didn't know why she was here, he knew she didn't care for classical music – and neither did he. So he must have known there was something in it. She could follow his reasoning, because it would have been hers too.

'Is that your man?' Gary said, nodding towards the large publicity blow-ups of a slender, long-haired musician in evening dress, his image all over the walls of the bar.

Where the pictures were of the whole ensemble, he always dominated them, and the other musicians were always in the background. Jeremy Laver was clearly the most important.

'I imagine so.'

She studied the face. It was darkly attractive, with a kind of haunted, Romany look in the eyes. And, oh God, she was in danger of succumbing to the stereotypical image of a serious musician . . . but he fitted it so perfectly it was difficult to do anything else. Jeremy Laver was handsome in the gaunt, hollow-faced way that made younger women lust for him, and older women want to mother him.

But was it the face of a kidnapper – or a murderer? Alex

chided herself for the thought, well aware that criminals didn't come ready-stamped like something in Sainsbury's. There was no way anybody could tell by appearances, and it was a complete fallacy to think that they could.

The five-minute bell sounded, and people started moving towards the inner door of the theatre. She glimpsed Nick Frobisher with a glamorous female companion who wasn't his WPC Mary, and told herself it was nothing to do with her. But she hoped he was going to hate the concert more than she did. She hoped he would *really* hate it, then it would serve him right for following her.

As it turned out, the music wasn't too heavy after all. If it had been solemn chamber music, she was sure Gary would have walked out, but he merely fidgeted from time to time, and caused the people behind to tut-tut at such ill manners.

But a couple of hours later it was all over, and people began filing out of the auditorium. She was relieved to see the back of Nick and his companion moving towards the street exit, while she and Gary had to socialize.

'Here we go,' she murmured, as they presented themselves to a flunkey and said they were to be guests of Mr Laver in the green-room.

'I'm Audrey Barnes from the Ohio arts magazine; Mr Laver is expecting me,' she said, in her drawling American Midwest accent.

'Oh, that's right. Miss Barnes,' the man said, giving Gary a dubious look until Alex tucked her arm inside his and included him in the invitation. 'Follow me, please.'

Alex felt a sliver of shame about what she was about to do to Jeremy Laver. The theatre was so obviously on its last legs unless it got a real injection of money, and it was wrong to boost the guy's hopes in this way. But it was all in the interests of finding Caroline, she reminded herself, and it had to be done. All was fair in love and detection.

They weren't the only guests. The green-room was buzzing with noise, the musicians obviously hyped up to the eyeballs now that the concert was over, and there were plenty of sycophants at their metaphorical feet. Wine was flowing freely, and glasses were being filled as soon as they were emptied. At this rate, she'd have to be careful how much she drank, thought Alex, or she'd lapse into her plummy voice or even her native Yorkshirese and give herself away.

Someone murmured her name to Jeremy and he came forward at once, his hand outstretched to shake hers. She was prepared not to be impressed by the effusiveness of the greeting. She could see the green light behind the eyes at this appearance of an American arts feature writer, wondering just what was in it for him. And why wouldn't he?

But he had charisma, she thought. He most definitely did. She could see how the photographer of the publicity shots had seen him. All the others faded into the background once Jeremy got you in his sights; it was as if you could only focus on him. It was reciprocal, Alex realized. He fixed his gaze on you as if there was no one else in the room. It might be a practised affectation, but it was an instant aphrodisiac. She swallowed, and moved swiftly into journalist mode.

'I'm delighted to meet you, Mr Laver—'

'Jeremy. Please call me Jeremy, Audrey. Everyone's quite informal here.'

'Jeremy it is then,' she murmured. 'And this is Gary, a friend of mine—'

She looked around for him, but he had already moved away from her side, and was surrounded by a small bevy of women.

'Shall we find a quiet corner?' Jeremy said.

She laughed. 'Is there such a thing here?'

'Oh, we'll find a seat somewhere, and I'm quite sure you're used to working in difficult situations in your job. Do you want to take notes?'

'Of course,' she said quickly. She got out her notebook and followed him to a small sofa at the back of the room. Seating was sparse, but when Jeremy needed to sit down, the way was made for him. Besides, she guessed that the other musicians knew very well why she was here.

'Would you like some nibbles?' he asked, and her heart leapt at the look in his eyes. But she shook her head at the plates of crisps and miniscule sandwiches that were being passed around now. She didn't want to eat, and she had better not drink too much since she needed to keep her head clear. She dredged up the usual journalistic questions.

'So tell me something about yourself, Mr— Jeremy. How long have you been working in this theatre?'

'Eighteen months, give or take a concert,' he said. 'We like it here, although it's not in the best area of London as I'm sure you realize. But we have a loyal following, and we can get into more adventurous musical outlets than the norm. We're progressive, though that's a word more usually applied to jazz than classical music.'

'And you obviously love the work that you do.'

'Of course. Don't you? You have to love your work in order to be a success at it.'

His mesmeric gaze held hers for a moment. Starry success wouldn't seem to be a very high rating here, she thought. Although she agreed that success in a small pond was preferable to struggling to survive in a large one. And the theatre had certainly been full of devotees tonight.

'Have you never wanted to move into better premises then? Forgive me. I don't mean to be rude, but certainly in America image is everything these days—'

'Have you any idea of the cost of property in London, Audrey? Unfortunately the lease here will soon be up, and we'll have to look for other premises. We don't want to split up and take gigs around the country. That's not what classical music is all about. If I could find the money to buy it and revamp it, I would rename it the Jeremy Laver Theatre, and hopefully get a publicity package going that would allow it to receive more attention. We all love this place, and we want to keep it if it's humanly possible.'

He wasn't lacking in ego, Alex thought, busily scribbling in her notebook as he rambled on. And he had the motive for needing money, and needing it quickly. Caroline's money would make all his dreams come true.

'And you obviously love the violin. You really made it sing tonight, and I must compliment you on your performance, by the way. I've been neglectful in not doing so already—'

His hand closed over hers for a second. 'Please don't apologize. The fact that you're here is compliment enough.'

Oh yes, he had charisma all right. And ego. And style.

'And what about your background, Jeremy?' she went on determinedly, after a quick slurp of wine. 'Your family, for

102

instance. Do you come from a musical background?'

He gave a short laugh. 'Hardly. My parents were shopkeepers in Kent. I have very few relatives left, in fact. There was a wealthy and eccentric great-aunt some years back, a feminist before they were fashionable, but she's long gone. There's nothing in my family remotely interesting. No aristocratic ghosts, or skeletons in the cupboard to excite your American readers, I'm afraid.'

Maybe not, but there was plenty to interest Alex Best, Private Investigator. He had given her enough to feed on. Caroline was almost certainly due to inherit her money from the wealthy feminist great-aunt, and Jeremy Laver's intense eyes had glittered with an almost obsessive anger the moment he spoke of her.

She could almost read his mind. He resented the fact that the aunt had left the money to Caroline, and he wanted it. How far he would go to get it, was something else. But the fact that Caroline was missing at this critical time was more than interesting. . . .

'I'm sure my readers will be very interested in all of this, Jeremy. Most of them are Anglophiles. You'll be sure to give me a photograph, won't you?'

'Of course.'

Predictably, he had a selection, taken from different angles and in different moods. She asked for several and got them. You never knew. Nick might want one for his collection eventually, when she had nailed him. Or his rogues' gallery.

'What do you like to do when you're not performing or rehearsing?' she asked next. 'Our readers are always intrigued by a person's pastimes and hobbies.'

'I don't have time for hobbies.'

As Alex waited, he went on, 'Oh well, sometimes I get out of town and go down to a friend's place in the country for a break, but he's not there right now.'

'Oh? On holiday, is he?' she said conversationally.

'Something like that. We don't keep tabs on each other. but I find it a useful retreat occasionally.'

And why did she have the strongest feeling that he was talking about Caroline's cottage, and that he was making all this up as he went along, just to give her some copy for her imaginary magazine?

'It sounds just darling,' she said. 'So rural and olde worlde English.'

She had to resist from cringing as she said it. Gary was hovering nearby now, and he'd be just as likely to laugh out loud at her gushing voice. She snapped her notebook shut.

'Well, I think I've got all I need for now, Jeremy. If I think of anything else, I'll be sure to contact you again.'

'And you'll let me see the piece when you've written it, won't you? For the archives,' he said with a smile.

Self-satisfied berk, Alex thought. She smiled back sweetly. 'Of course I will. It will be my pleasure.'

It would also be her pleasure to see him behind bars if he'd done anything to harm Caroline, she thought savagely.

Chapter 7

Norman Price phoned again a few days later, aggressive as ever. Alex forestalled him before he could launch into an angry tirade about why she hadn't found his daughter yet.

'I wanted to talk to you, Mr Price. Do you have any idea where Caroline sends her crosswords, please? It's important that I find out.'

Whether it was or not was immaterial at that moment. She just wanted to catch him off guard.

'Why the devil should it be so important?'

'Because she may deliver the work herself, and if so, the people concerned may have some idea of her movements. The editor would know her, certainly, and so far I haven't been able to trace anyone. She may well have a confidante at the magazine or newspaper office concerned. She may even have gone on holiday with a friend and isn't missing at all. I presume you've considered that.'

She heard him curse as she elaborated recklessly.

'Haven't you been listening to a word I've told you these past weeks, woman? Caroline doesn't make friends, and I don't know where she sends the piddling crosswords. If you think it's important to know, then it's your job to find out.'

She winced as he slammed down the phone, obviously having forgotten why he'd called in the first place. But it prevented her from having to make further conversation with him, and admitting that she had really hit a block in her investigations.

It was one thing to be convinced that Jeremy Laver might have something to do with his cousin's vanishing act; it was something else to be able to prove it – and even more so, to find out what he had done with her.

*

She was still puzzling over all the possibilities when she went home that evening and closed the door of her flat with a sigh of relief. Some days were good, and others were not, and this was definitely one of the baddies.

She was getting jittery again, and she knew it. Aspects of her job were dangerous, and she tried never to dwell on the thought for too long, otherwise she might really take fright and take up something simpler, like computer technology.

But there was always the chance that she could be on the trail of a potential killer. If that were so, then everything could backfire on her, and she could be the one who was killed.

She had forced herself to think seriously about it since meeting Jeremy at the theatre. She had a sixth sense that there was a ruthless personality hidden behind the rather laid-back look of the musician. But did that mean he was capable of a crime? She tried to be analytical as she studied the various photographs he had given her.

That lean, hungry look was extremely sensual, but it could be menacing too. Some women liked a hint of danger and excitement in their men, and he had it in abundance. One look from those mesmeric eyes could make any woman go weak-kneed.

She ignored the sudden rush of adrenalin in her veins, and concentrated on checking off what he might have done to keep Caroline out of the way until her birthday came and went. There were only four – maybe five – that made any sense.

He could have killed her.
He could have paid someone else to kill her.
He could have kidnapped her and hidden her.
He could have paid someone else to kidnap her.
He was in cahoots with somebody else anyway.

Alex thought hard about the choices, and didn't want to believe the first two. She knew she had got ridiculously fond and protective of a woman she didn't even know, and wanted to find her safe and well, but she honestly didn't think Jeremy would have killed Caroline. And she preferred to keep an open mind about him employing a hitman to do the job.

He was an artiste, passionate and exciting in many ways, but still fastidious. She sensed that even being remotely involved in anything as distasteful as a murder would offend him. His fingers were long and sensitive, the fingernails beautifully kept, and his hands were so smooth they had to be regularly creamed because they were on show so much.

He was vain all right, but Alex didn't condemn him for that. He played the violin with all the finesse of caressing a woman, and his smile was whiter than white. He was a man who took care of himself. She didn't think for a moment that he was homosexual, and nor did she think he'd have the stomach for murder.

The other possibilities were more likely, but there was a big flaw in the first one. She didn't know how close the relationship was between himself and Caroline, but she was his cousin, and therefore they must know one another well. Even if they didn't meet frequently now, they would recognize one another physically. How could he possibly get away with kidnapping her and hiding her away himself, knowing of all the repercussions that would follow?

Of course, she could have been blindfolded and gagged and hidden away in some dark place all this time . . . and since she was deaf, she wouldn't have recognized a familiar voice. . . .

The visual horror of this wasn't lost on Alex. She hated dark places herself, and the fact that Caroline wouldn't be able to hear anything if she was in captivity and in the dark, horrified her even more. Not even the scuttling of rats . . . the silent world of the deaf must be even more terrible in such circumstances.

Squeamishly Alex pushed the image away, and hurriedly thought of choice number four. This seemed the most likely one of all, except for the perfectly reasonable one of Caroline simply disappearing on a whim of her own. She was strong-willed and independent, and Alex admired her for that, considering what she had for a father.

There was a sidebar to the last choice. Jeremy and an accomplice, in it for mutual gain. Jeremy and Norman Price, perhaps? Now that she had met them both, Alex didn't think so. They were poles apart in temperament, even if they did both hope to gain from Caroline's inheritance.

But in different ways. Norman wanted her found in order to manipulate her, if Alex's theories were right. He needed his factory to succeed for his own prestige. She wasn't sure that Caroline was the type to be manipulated, but there were always ways for a father to persuade a daughter to go in with him in business matters. False accounts . . . pleading illness in order to pass the business on . . . there were ways.

And then there was Jeremy. He needed the inheritance to fund his theatre and make a name for himself. He might brag about the theatre being his life and not being ambitious in any razzmatazz way, but Alex made a pretty shrewd guess that he was as aspirational as the next man given the chance – and the money. Her head throbbed with the complexity of it all. It had seemed relatively simple at first, but there were always twists and turns that sent you up wrong alleys.

She finally gave up all thoughts of any more work for the evening, and took a long leisurely bath to relax her instead of a shower, and then turned on the television. Even an inane game show was preferable to letting her mind go round and round in endless circles and getting nowhere.

Jeremy Laver's dark basement flat was in one of those tall houses in an outer London suburb that would have once housed a moderately affluent family with servants of the *Upstairs Downstairs* variety. Iron railings that hadn't gone to the Second World War effort flanked every house on the square, and there was a minimum amount of space between the steps leading down to the flat and the street above.

Nowadays the narrow entry space merely held the obligatory dustbin and a tacked-on letterbox on the outside of the door to the flat. The basement occupants could only see the feet of passers-by, if they bothered to look up through the window, and the whole place would be claustrophobic for anyone so inclined.

Fortunately Jeremy wasn't. The flat suited him admirably. He wasn't a pauper, but he certainly wasn't rich, and it pandered to his artistic mind to think that he lived in a style that artistes such as Beethoven and Mozart might have approved. One part of him accepted that it was good for the soul for a creative man to suffer for his art.

While the other, the more acquisitive side of him, said that if he had the money to buy his theatre he'd have no objection at all to seeing his name in neon lights and living the good life.

He was contemplating whether or not to go out for a late Chinese takeway that evening or settle for whatever he had in his refrigerator, when he heard the footsteps come down the stone steps outside his flat, then heard the rap on his door.

Frowning, and not wanting or expecting company, he opened it a chink, and then swore an oath as he saw his visitor.

'What the hell are you doing here, Daneman?' he hissed. 'We agreed not to make any kind of contact unless it was absolutely necessary.'

'I needed to get away for a few hours, that's what,' the swarthy man said with a scowl. 'The company's not all that it might be and I ain't sticking around all night to be abused.'

'You didn't object to the company in the past as far as I recall. Tired of it already, are you?'

'*Already*? Man, I was tired of it before we began this caper. Now it's got this bloody bee in its bonnet about needing some work to do because it's bored.'

Jeremy grinned. That sounded about right. It was Caroline to a T. He felt briefly sorry for her, knowing of old how much she hated to be idle, but the sympathy soon faded as he quizzed Daneman some more.

'You've made everything secure, I hope. It's madness to leave her alone. I thought you had more sense—'

'You stick to your fiddling, and leave me to know my own business, Laver,' Daneman said coldly. 'A few pills slipped into its drink and it'll be out cold for the rest of the night. And everything's completely secure. In fact, it'll be so peaceful there for a change, I'd probably have done better to stay behind. Its perpetual whinging is enough to drive a man to drink. It don't like the surroundings—'

'No details, remember?' Jeremy said sharply. 'That's your end of it. I don't want to know where she is – as long as you're not – well, you know. . . .'

'Sticking a knife in its guts?' Daneman taunted as he saw the other man wince. 'Don't worry, pansy-boy, it'll not come to harm, providing it don't drive me nuts in the meantime.'

He despised Laver, for all their collusion. Laver wanted the dibbs, but he didn't want to get involved. He didn't even want to know where Daneman had taken his cousin.

'I wish you wouldn't keep referring to her as *it*,' Jeremy

109

snapped. 'She has a name, damn it. And you weren't so averse to her in the beginning. You said it was a treat to convert a drudge of a woman to a sex bomb, if I recall the choice words you used,' he added, wishing he hadn't managed to produce such vivid imagery of Caroline and this oaf, and feeling briefly sorry for her.

'That was all part of the job. If you don't like my methods you should have got somebody else. It's not too late now, if you want to pay me off.'

'You know I can't. Not yet.'

'Then keep your trap shut and listen to me. I didn't come all this way just to make small talk,' Daneman snapped back.

Jeremy eyed him with real dislike, but their plotting had tied them inexorably together now. He was slightly built and Daneman was a bull of a man. He supposed the local police would refer to them as unlikely partners in crime. Not that he considered this a real crime.

He was just getting what he thought he deserved and, but for an accident of birth or fate, he'd be getting the old trout's money instead of his cousin. The fact that his great-aunt had decided a woman was the only fit person to inherit her money, only incensed him more, since he considered himself far more worthy than a female who spent her days doing crosswords for a pastime. The skill of it completely escaped him. He could only see the unfairness of it all, and it was something that had festered inside him all his adult life.

'It sent me to the cottage a while back to get more of those bloody grids that it calls them,' Daneman went on. 'I only agreed to do it to stop it screeching all day long.'

'Go on,' Jeremy said, knowing there must be more to come.

'There was somebody there—'

'What?'

'Somebody was standing near the bedroom window, so I got away pretty damn quick. I didn't go back until the next day, then I trashed it to make it look like a break-in, just in case. I saw the woman come back though. I didn't think much of it at the time, but I thought you might want to know.'

'What woman?' Jeremy snarled. 'Are you sure it wasn't just a cleaning woman or something?'

Daneman grinned for the first time. He had thick fleshy lips and a face that some would liken to an unmade bed. Jeremy supposed that certain women would find him sexy. Amazingly, Caroline had.

'Did you ever see a slinky cleaning woman dressed all in black, with great tits and big hips, and flaming red hair long enough to claw through while you were on the job?'

Any other time his graphic description and thrusting gestures would have made Jeremy sick, but not now, when he could visualize the woman so clearly in his mind it was almost as if she was sitting beside him, notebook in hand while she flicked back that stunning, pike-straight red hair.

'Made you horny, have I?' Daneman said with a leer, when his companion seemed too dumbstruck to respond for the moment.

'Red hair?' Jeremy said hoarsely. 'And in her mid-twenties, would you say? Green eyes?'

'Christ almighty, I never got close enough to see her eyes. The age would be about right. Why? What is she to you?'

He finally caught on that Jeremy had gone a sickly colour and was pouring himself a stiff brandy that he downed in one swallow. Since it didn't look as if he was going to be offered one, Daneman strode over to the decanter and poured one for himself, sinking it as fast as Jeremy had.

'All right, so talk,' he said, sprawling out on the sofa. 'But I warn you, if things are going wrong at this stage I'm out of here.'

'I don't know,' Jeremy said agitatedly. 'A journalist called me out of the blue recently, saying she was doing a feature for some American magazine and wanted to interview me. I sent her two concert tickets, and she fits the description you've given me exactly.'

'And you didn't think to query a stranger wanting to do an interview on you?' Daneman yelled.

'It's not unheard of,' Jeremy said angrily, mortified at the implication that he wasn't newsworthy. 'But I'll let that pass for now. What's more to the point is that if it's the same person, what was she was doing at Caroline's cottage?'

'*If* the woman was a journalist,' Daneman said.

They looked at each other and Daneman's voice became vitriolic. 'Somebody's on to us. God knows how, but it looks as if this woman's got wind of the operation. Maybe she's after a cut. She may need to be silenced—'

Jeremy shuddered. 'Can't you stop talking like some American gangster for one minute? We need to think. And we're not silencing anybody. That wasn't part of the deal.'

'All right, Einstein. Then think.' Daneman clamped his lips together and put his hands behind his head.

As his body odour wafted across the room, Jeremy visibly moved back a fraction. How on earth could Caroline have ever fancied him. . . ?

She had always been so fastidious and reserved, even before she became deaf. But from the way Daneman had once described their bedroom activities so lasciviously to him, it would seem as if that had changed drastically, at least as far as the affair with Daneman was concerned.

'You do still have her, I suppose? She is still *safe*?' he persisted, but still not wanting to know more.

He had been adamant about not being personally involved. Now, far too late, he realized he only had Daneman's word for everything. He *said* she wanted to work, but even that could be lies on Daneman's part.

Jeremy cursed himself for having had to bring Daneman into the plan, and even more so that he had only been to the cottage once himself, just to check that it was empty when she had gone off with her lover. It hadn't been a proper kidnapping anyway, Jeremy had excused himself at the time, since she had gone so willingly.

And on his one visit to check, the cottage had certainly looked deserted, but he should have checked again.

Daneman gave him a withering look.

'Don't be a bloody fool. Of course I've got her, and I've got the scars to prove it.' He turned his head sideways to show the fingernail scratches on his neck.

'So let's get practical. If this woman's no journalist, who is she?' he went on curtly.

'Well, for a start I'll lay odds that her name's not Audrey Barnes,' Jeremy said, remembering.

'Try it. Look her up in the phone book.'

After checking through pages of people called Barnes, they phoned more than a dozen with varying responses, some irate, some slamming down the phone at once.

'You've probably got a few women on the skids now, their

husbands demanding to know who's calling them so late at night,' Daneman said with a leer. 'This is pointless, anyway. Didn't she give you a business card, for Christ's sake?'

'No she didn't. Just a post office box number where I could send the concert tickets.'

Jeremy was getting more incensed by the minute at what he considered this toe-rag's censure. How was he supposed to know the woman wasn't genuine? People were always trying to get free tickets for concerts, and he admitted that it had played to his vanity when the woman called.

'That's it then!' Daneman said. 'We send her an anonymous note asking her to meet you at the cottage if she wants to hear something to her advantage.'

'And you think she'll bite, do you?'

'Why not? She had to be there for a reason in the first place, and we need to find out what it was. You don't give the exact address of the place or say who you are, dummy. You just say the cottage. If she's not a journalist she'll know where to go. She won't be expecting the writer to be you, and you'll take her off guard the minute she recognises you. And you'd better get on to it pretty damn quick. Call me on my mobile when it's done.'

'Are you mad? You don't actually expect me to go there and confront her, do you? What am I supposed to do when she recognizes me, since she has no idea of my connection with Caroline?'

He panicked at once, completely out of his depth at the prospect, and by the cunning way Daneman's mind worked. He couldn't even follow it properly. He'd be well used to this sort of thing; Jeremy wasn't.

'That's up to you. Pay her off. Silence her if you have to. Do your own thinking for once.'

He left the flat, and Jeremy splurged air freshener about the place. His innards were turning to water, and he'd give anything not to have to follow this through. But the more he thought about it the more he knew Daneman was right. They had to know who the woman was. Catching her off guard was the only way to do it. But what the hell he was going to say to explain himself was completely beyond him.

Alex didn't check her post office box number every day. Most of the time there was nothing in it anyway. But this time, along with several other items, there was a long brown envelope written in handwriting that she knew at once was clumsily disguised. She'd been in the business too long not to know when a slanting, every-which-way scrawl wasn't genuine.

She didn't open it until she got back to her office. It could be from a client not wanting their name to be known, or a threat to '*do you in, missus*', as had happened more than once. Or a note sent with a lurid and unsavoury description of what the person intended doing to her, like several she'd had previously, and which had found their way to the waste-paper bin pretty smartly. You didn't want to waste time pondering over whether or not such messages might be from kids mucking about, or worse.

The other letters were merely circulars. Alex made herself some coffee and decided that a doughnut wouldn't do any harm. Then she slit open the last envelope, anticipating some tacky correspondence, but since you could never be sure . . . and then she sat up quickly, her heart thumping.

Far from being intimidated – and knowing that was a feeling that would come later – her eyes sparkled as she scanned the pathetically worded message.

'How corny can you get, meatball?' she addressed the letter. 'Cutting letters out of newspapers went out with the Ark. Though I suppose it would have been scratchings on tablets of stone in those days—'

She realized she was babbling out loud. Not that there was anyone to hear. Still . . . first sign of madness, so they said . . . she looked at the letter again.

MEET ME AT THE COTTAGE SUNDAY, the haphazard letters said. IT WILL BE WORTH YOUR WHILE.

She calmed down still more as her thoughts raced. There was only one cottage on her immediate horizon. Caroline's. This *thing* had to refer to Greenwell Cottage, since they hadn't bothered to specify the address or give any further details. But somebody knew she had been there. She felt a sudden deep suspicion.

It wasn't that effing Gary, was it? She wouldn't completely rule it out. She'd held him off a bit lately, and it was just the kind of trick he'd enjoy, getting her down there on their own in that idyllic little cottage. . .

Against her will, Alex didn't find the thought of it exactly unexciting. He was a vigorous lover, she'd say that for him, and she knew he was still hot for her. His favourite comment was that he relished screwing a classy dame.

And if it was him, why not play along? Her hormones were working overtime now. Why bloody not? Take time out. Pretend this was for real, go down there and find him there, waiting . . . except that he didn't know the address of the place.

'Slow down, girl,' she admonished herself severely. 'This is no time for fantasies. What if it *is* real? What if the guy who sent the letter knows where Caroline is, and really does have some information? He must know I'm looking for her.'

Despite her shivery reaction to the alternative possibility that she might well be in danger herself, she smiled ruefully as the melodramatics took over. She was getting nowhere at all. But *he* – if it was a he – didn't know that. Apparently.

She thought fast. Sunday was nearly a week away, so the guy had evidently given her time to check her post office box. She wasn't sure whether or not Gary knew she didn't do it too often. She knew he was aware of the number, because he would have seen the envelope with Jeremy Laver's concert tickets in it. It had to be him. Didn't it?

Half of her hoped that it was, and the other half didn't. Because if it wasn't Gary, someone had genuine information about Caroline, and whatever the risk to herself, it could be a breakthrough at last. She couldn't pass up the chance of following this through. It was what PIs did, whatever the danger – and however sleazy the method of communication.

Anyway, she was seeing Gary that evening, and she'd soon damn well find out if it *was* him. They were going to the cinema and he'd expect to be invited back to her flat afterwards. Her part of the bargain for a good night out. . .

Around midnight, Gary raised his head from the depths of her bedclothes, leaned on his elbows and looked down at her voluptuous body, glistening in the light from the bedside lamp. Sex was a healthy and energetic form of exercise to him, and it beat going to the gym every time. Alex normally participated fully. But not tonight.

'You've got something on your mind, babe,' he complained at

115

her failure to respond with her usual squeals.

She pulled his mouth down to hers, tasting herself on his lips, contrite (and somewhat surprised) that she had allowed her thoughts to go elsewhere than on achieving orgasm.

'Maybe I'm impatient for the real thing to begin,' she whispered seductively, her hand moving downwards obligingly.

After a few seconds scrutinizing her flushed cheeks, Gary moved over, and lay flat on his back beside her.

'Nah. Anyway, I've lost the urge now – and before you say that's a first, it's only temporary. So tell me what's up.'

Well, not you, that's for sure, Alex almost said, but knowing he'd take it as a slur on his manly ability, she managed to resist it.

'It's this missing woman case. I can't seem to get her out of my mind,' she said at last.

He was instantly offended. 'Well, that's just great. Three in a bed was never my style, lady, even in thought, and I don't appreciate the idea of that stuffy dame being here between us—'

'Stuffy? I told you about the sexy underwear Caroline had in her bedroom. There was nothing stuffy about that!'

'All the same, let's leave her out. Unless you've got something particular to tell me.'

She hesitated. 'Not really. But I shan't be able to see you on Sunday like we arranged, Gary.'

He swivelled his dark head around to watch her face. She was watching him too, wondering if he would give himself away, or if there was anything to *give* away.

She gave a tiny sigh. This job certainly had its exciting moments, but sometimes it was just too frustrating. You never knew who to trust and who was about to betray you. Just like poor Caroline. If you couldn't trust your own father – and possibly your own cousin – then who could you trust?

'Why not?'

'Why not what?' she murmured, still caught up in Caroline's predicament.

'Why can't you see me on Sunday? If you're going somewhere to do with the case, can't I come? I'm not doing anything – then or now,' he added with a grin.

'Do you want to see the cottage?' she said, watching him unblinkingly. There wasn't a flicker in his eyes.

116

He whistled. 'Darlin', when you look at me like that with those green dazzlers, I'd go with you anywhere,' he said.

'Sunday then. Around nine o'clock. I'll drive,' she said in a strangled voice, because she could tell that he was getting randy again. Very randy. And she was in no mood to resist now that the question of Caroline was out of the way.

But later, she knew she had to show him the anonymous letter. Since he was agreeing to go to the cottage with her, it seemed the polite thing to do after they had just spent a glorious couple of hours thrashing about in her bed and then showering together. There was no point in pretending the proposed visit to Wilsingham was just a female whim.

They sat in companionable closeness on the sofa in towelling bathrobes now, and she handed him the envelope.

'What's this?' he grinned. 'Are you paying me now?'

'It's the reason we're going to Caroline's cottage on Sunday,' she said, wishing he wouldn't turn everything into a sexual innuendo. 'Read it, Gary.'

He opened the envelope and stared at the ill-fitting newsprint letters that made up the message. Once he had read it, his voice was full of derision.

'Good God, this is straight out of an Agatha Christie novel. You're not taking it seriously!'

'I have to,' Alex said. 'I need to know who sent it. And since I don't think it was you—'

She gave a sudden cry as he gripped her wrist, and her coffee spilled, making a dark stain on the white towelling bathrobe. She resisted the thought that in an Agatha Christie novel it would be likened to blood. An omen.

'*Did* you think it was me? What kind of a game do you think I'm playing, Alex?'

She scrubbed furiously at the coffee stain with a tissue.

'I didn't – well, only for a second – I just wondered if it was a trick to get me down there – you know, on our own—'

'For sex? I don't need to lure you out of town to get you to drop your knickers, babe,' he said crudely.

She ignored that. 'It's my job to be suspicious, that's all. And it *could* have been you.'

'Well, it wasn't. So that leaves who?'

117

'That's what I've got to find out. But I do want you to come with me,' she said in a rush now. 'I'm scared, if you must know. If somebody has kidnapped Caroline, then that somebody must also know that I'm looking for her.'

'She's a bit old for kidnapping, isn't she?'

But Alex could see he was mollified at the thought of her being scared. The little woman and all that, while he was the big strong minder ... the hell of it was that if she thought about it for long enough, she knew she was good and scared at the thought of whoever might be lying in wait for her at the cottage.

'He didn't say what time Sunday,' Gary said.

'That's why we'll get there early. I want to be there first so I can see him coming. And before you make any crude remarks about that, just tell me you'll support me in this, Gary, please.'

To her relief he only said that nine o'clock on Sunday sounded more like the crack of dawn to him. But at least he agreed, and she had to be thankful for that.

He arrived at the flat sharp on time on Sunday morning, but Alex had been ready for ages. She hadn't been able to sleep since six. Despite her preference for working alone, she had involved Gary now, but she would dearly have liked it to be Nick Frobisher instead. He had the solidity of the police force behind him, and you never knew when you needed it.

But she dare not do it. For one thing it would incense Norman Price and kill off her retainer and therefore her chance of the winter cruise; for another it would alert the stranger at the cottage if he got the slightest whiff that the police were around.

More seriously – and something that should have got first priority in her mind, she thought shamefacedly – it might well put Caroline's life in danger as well as her own.

As it was, she knew she had to keep Gary out of sight until the opportune moment. When that moment would arrive she didn't have the faintest idea. She was simply going on instinct, leaning on him as her insurance, her safety-net.

They reached Wilsingham right after lunch, after having a bite to eat at a pub along the way. It wouldn't have been wise to go to the Little Harp Inn, and anyway, she doubted that they did food on a Sunday, or if they opened at all until the evening. It was that kind of sleepy-town place.

Alex clenched her teeth together as Gary whistled loudly while they cruised through the village and neared the cottage. His voice was anything but complimentary when they reached it.

'Gawd, this is real Hansel and Gretel stuff. The kind of place that would drive you to drink within a week. I'd have thought your bird would be glad to be out of it.'

'Sometimes Gary, you can be so bloody insensitive,' Alex snapped, thankful that the village seemed as quiet as death compared to London on a Sunday morning.

But she had to agree. And wasn't it W.C. Fields who said that Philadelphia was half as big as New York cemetery and twice as dead? Or something like it, anyway. He could just as well have been thinking of Wilsingham at the time.

They had reached the cottage without seeing a soul, and Alex parked the car in the lane. It hardly mattered that it would be seen by anyone coming here. The stranger who supposedly had information would expect to see a vehicle.

The place was so familiar to her now. The white picket fence and the creaking gate; the garden that looked so sadly neglected with the encroaching weeds; and the quaintness of the cottage itself. She stood outside for a moment, breathing in the sweet scent of the overblown roses.

She could just imagine how a private person like Caroline loved the isolation of it all, and she felt a huge sense of pity for her in being deprived of her chosen place of freedom.

'Have you got a key then, or are we going to stand here like idiots all day?' Gary said. breaking her concentration. 'I want to see where this nympho lived.'

Alex fumbled in her bag, feeling the sting of tears in her eyes. It was so bloody, bloody unfair. Caroline had had a life here, and it had been snatched away from her by God knew who, and this miserable sodding moron couldn't wait to get inside to poke around her personal things.

She pushed the key in the lock and turned it, and they went inside. The usual stale smell of unlived-in property rose to their nostrils, and Gary sniffed audibly as he looked around and then walked over to Caroline's desk.

'So this is where she did her crossword stuff, is it?'

'Leave it, Gary,' Alex said sharply, as he started to shuffle papers around. 'She'll want to find everything the same as before when she comes home.'

She avoided his eyes as she spoke. The insidious dread that Caroline might not come home at all was starting to fester in her mind. She didn't want to consider it, but the thought wouldn't go away. She wanted to find Caroline safe and well. She already thought of her as a friend, even though it was fatal to get so involved with someone she didn't even know. She must be going mad.

But there was just so much against Caroline – her loveless background that Alex could identify with so well; her obnoxious father; her strange cousin; and whoever had decided to deprive her of her freedom; and presumably of the one great love in her life: M, the unknown quantity.

Try as she might to ignore it, that damn word FREEDOM kept coming into Alex's mind. The word Caroline herself set such store by in her diary. The one thing she no longer had. Might never have.

'What the hell's wrong with you?' Gary said, shaking her as her eyes blurred. 'You're not going to pass out on me, are you? You're as pasty as an uncooked tart.'

'Thanks,' she said, starting to laugh. 'I needed that to make me feel really attractive!'

He grinned. 'You'll always be beautiful to me, doll. So why don't you show me these sexy kecks of Caroline's? If they really exist, that is.'

'Why wouldn't they? Come on then.'

He followed her upstairs, his hands cupping her backside, and she couldn't be bothered to tell him to stop it. Just moments ago she had had such a weird presentiment of doom, that it was reassuring just to know that she was living and breathing. and that a man found her desirable, and alive.

And it would be far better to spend their time in the bedroom, where they could see who was coming down the lane from the window – as long as Gary didn't get the wrong idea about it, of course.

Just imagine being found in a compromising position with her lover in Caroline Price's bed. It would put her at a distinct disadvantage, she thought, with a nervous giggle. And that must be the biggest understatement of the year.

Chapter 8

Watching and waiting was always a tedious part of the job. Alex knew it, and accepted it. Gary didn't. Nearing the end of the afternoon he fingered the pile of soft satin lingerie for the umpteenth time, and finally threw it on the bed in a sulk when Alex flatly refused to model it for him.

His voice was truculent. 'Why the hell not? This is a bloody good waste of a day, if you ask me.'

'Give it a rest, Gary, and put those things away before somebody comes – oh, let me do it,' she said, bundling them back in the dressing-table drawer when he didn't move.

There was something stuck at the back. Maybe it was another diary, she thought hopefully, with even more clarifying material, but it was merely a small bundle of papers in a plastic wrapper. She couldn't afford to miss anything, especially something stuffed in the back of a drawer, so she pushed them in her bag to study later.

'Nobody's coming here today, including—'

'Oh, do shut up, Gary. It's getting boring, and I'm jittery enough without you keeping on. We are *not* going to bed and that's final.'

'Why not? If anybody did turn up, it would probably give them a thrill to watch.'

Alex glared at him. After today she was going to be *very* unavailable as far as he was concerned, she told herself. He had outdone his usefulness, and she wasn't apologizing to anyone for thinking that way.

He was boorish, and he only ever had one thing on his mind. It might be great – *was* great – but it didn't have to be top priority every minute they were together. Whatever happened to conversation?

'I brought a bottle of wine, and I suppose you're not interested in that either,' he sulked.

But Alex was no longer listening to anything he had to say. Conversation was the last thing an her mind now as she saw the man walking very cautiously down the lane towards the cottage. He was keeping well in to the hedgerow as if trying to keep out of sight until his presence was unavoidable.

But it was a man she recognized all too well. A man with gaunt Romany features, mesmeric eyes and collar-length hair. Jeremy Laver – Caroline's cousin.

She turned to Gary in a panic, her throat like chaff.

'Do you still want to go to bed?'

'Hey, is it my birthday or something?'

Her words fell over themselves as she tried to get her thoughts in order, and to force him to follow them.

'Shut up and listen. Jeremy Laver's out there, so either he's here quite innocently, which I don't believe for a minute – or he sent the letter. God knows why, but there's no time to think about that now. He has to keep believing I'm Audrey Barnes from Ohio, and we have to pretend we know Caroline and that we assume she's on holiday, so we're having a bit of a ding-dong down here, right?'

The words raced as fast as her thoughts. If this was thinking on her feet, she knew damn well it was better to be seen on her back. She groaned, knowing it all sounded so bloody feeble – and so humiliating. Would Jeremy even go for it? Would anybody with half an ounce of intelligence? But that depended on what the other person had to hide as well. She counted on it. And she knew she could count on Gary.

'Get on the bed and start kissing me,' she hissed, as she heard the front door open.

'Anything to oblige, lady,' Gary said with a grin.

He pinned her down beneath him and slid his hand up her skirt as she kicked off her shoes and let them slip silently to the carpet.

A few minutes later they heard someone prowling about in the rooms below, and then footsteps coming up the stairs. Alex held her breath and pulled Gary more closely to her, winding her legs around him as if they were in the throes of foreplay.

'What the hell's going on in here?' they heard Jeremy's out-raged voice say a moment later. He couldn't immediately recognize the two bodies so thoroughly intertwined. And then:

'Who – good God – what do you think you're doing?'

Alex struggled up. It was almost comical to see the flickering thoughts and emotions passing over Jeremy Laver's face. They were transparent to her in those moments. She was sure he had sent the anonymous letter. He'd never admit it without incrimi-nating himself though, so how was he going to get out of this one? But he certainly hadn't expected to find her here like this, *in flagrante delicto*, so to speak.

Presumably he would have drummed up some good reason to confront her here, and she knew she'd been right in trusting her instincts one hundred per cent in bringing Gary along. Her insurance. Her safety-net, she thought fervently again.

But the next second she had to give Laver every credit for being so quick-witted.

'I don't know what the devil you're doing here, Miss Barnes. This cottage belongs to my cousin. While she's away I make it my business to check it out for her now and then. The police reported a break-in recently, and I just hope you've got a good explanation for being here with your . . . friend.'

Oh, he was good, thought Alex. If he hadn't pre-planned this defensive attitude on his cousin's behalf, then he was very resourceful, and there was no way he was letting on that he'd sent her an anonymous letter.

He had just the right amount of indignation and suspicion in his voice – and the reference to a break-in recently was inter-esting, especially the police being informed, which Alex knew was a downright lie.

But how did he know about the break-in unless he had done it, or knew who did? She sat up quickly and managed to look suitably aghast at being caught like this.

'This is really awful, Jeremy,' she said, remembering the Midwest accent. 'I know Miss Price slightly through some mag-azine features, but I had no idea of any connection between you and her. Gary and I thought we'd call to surprise her, but as you rightly say, she's not here. We shouldn't have taken advantage of

123

her absence, but it's such a darling little place, we couldn't resist it. We'll tidy up in here and leave at once.'

He fixed her with that penetrating gaze as she surged on. She didn't have a clue whether or not he believed her; it was all a double bluff, anyway. He had sent the letter to her post office box number, so he must have suspected her of something, but what? And now that she was here, he must know she had picked it up and knew of Greenwell Cottage.

If he had nothing to do with Caroline's disappearance, and just had an inkling that something was wrong here, he might even think Alex was a villain. It was totally unfeasible that he had come here on the off-chance on this day of all days. No, he had to have sent the letter, but he evidently didn't intend to give himself away, nor could she think what he had hoped to achieve by luring her here. If he *hadn't* sent it, and this really was just a hideous coincidence, then somebody else was probably lurking in the hedgerows by now ... her wretched imagination was soaring in leaps and bounds, and her head was throbbing fit to burst.

'So just who are you really, Miss all-American Barnes? And don't give me that guff about doing a feature on me for some rag. There's more to it than that—' he said at last.

'Why the hell should there be?' Gary spoke aggressively now. 'We just came to see this friend of – uh, Audrey's, and decided not to waste the afternoon. Do you have a problem with that ... *mate*? Or is it out of your range of activities?'

Laver would know it wasn't the case. But it seemed that he wasn't prepared to pursue it with Gary here, ultra-macho now at being disturbed in his little love-nest. Thank God for Gary, Alex thought, brushing aside her previous uncharitable thoughts about him. She had done right to follow her instincts in making him her insurance, her safety-net. She couldn't get the words out of her head now. If he hadn't been here, things might have been very different. She moved closer towards him, making them a complete unit. And it was pretty obvious that whatever else Jeremy Laver was, he was no match for a powerfully made younger man. He wouldn't want to get his precious features roughed up, and especially not his hands.

She pressed on, with that thought very much in mind. She was off the bed now, and smoothing down the rumpled covers.

'Look. I've already apologized, Jeremy, and now we're leaving, OK? I can't do more. But I assure you we haven't touched anything of Miss Price's. You can check, if you like.'

'That won't be necessary,' he said coldly. 'But in England we go about things differently, and we don't enter other people's houses without their permission.'

He was so pompous and self-righteous now it wasn't true. What was *he* doing, if he wasn't entering Caroline's house without her permission? But Alex wasn't waiting to find out. All she wanted was to get out of there and assess the situation back home as quickly as possible.

Thank God he didn't know who she really was, and after Gary's aggression he hadn't pursued his questions. But when he had time to think about it, his pride and ego would probably be mortally offended that she wasn't going to write him up after all. Write him off, would be more like it. But unfortunately she couldn't do that either.

Jeremy Laver was not the brightest of men. Despite his passion for his theatre and his creative talent, he was oddly lacking in any other kind of perception. He was not susceptible to atmosphere in buildings or picking up nuances. He called a spade a spade.

Or, in more modern jargon, What You See Is What You Get. And what he had seen was the red-haired tart who called herself an acquaintance of his cousin's, making out with that greasy lout she called her friend. He ignored his affronted reaction to that for the moment.

But he was also completely averse to doing anything nasty, unlike Daneman, who he was sure wouldn't hesitate in slitting someone's throat if he was threatened.

Jeremy preferred to take the easy way out. To believe that Audrey Barnes *was* who she said she was, and had met Caroline at some time. She may even have heard about himself through Caroline. His ego wouldn't quite be squashed on that score, though there wasn't much chance of the woman writing him up in her American rag now. He'd killed that for good and all, he thought with a scowl.

But for all Daneman's suspicions in seeing her at the cottage once before, he supposed it was reasonable that she had come to Wilsingham expecting to visit Caroline then too.

Rather than have to do anything at all that was unpleasant, Jeremy put his own interpretation on the fact that Audrey Barnes had responded to his anonymous letter. It was just the kind of thing journalists did, for God's sake. They had a nose for everything, and she wouldn't have been able to resist. She may even have thought it was Caroline playing a trick – not that he could ever remember his cousin playing many tricks. He let that pass.

No, the more he thought about it, the more obvious it became. There was no funny business going on here. Audrey Barnes was just a slick American, from her sleek red hair down to her toes and everything in between. Daneman had got it all wrong, and he would call him on his mobile as soon as he returned to London, and tell him everything was sorted. He could always manage to sound more forceful on the phone. Trusting that Daneman wouldn't ask for details, he closed the cottage door behind him with a sense of relief. He was in it up to his neck in what he called their little collusion, but the less he was physically involved, the better he liked it. That had been part of the deal.

'Are you all right?' Gary asked Alex, as she drove away from the village far too fast and crunched the gears every time she changed up or down.

Her voice was clipped. 'I will be when I get home and take a shower and have a gallon of coffee and *think*.'

'In that order?'

'In that order. I just don't know why he wanted to get me down there at all. It doesn't make sense.'

'Perhaps he fancied you, and he sure as hell didn't expect to see me there, so it put him off.' He cracked his knuckles in a pseudo-mafioso gesture.

Alex glared at him. 'You would think that, of course. I'm glad you *were* there, as it happens, but maybe I'd have got to the bottom of it if I'd been on my own.'

She shivered, knowing she hadn't wanted to take that chance. She might have been at the bottom of a deep ditch by now. Some private eye she was turning out to be. It was part of the job to take chances, and she knew she'd flunked it. It was depressing her more by the second.

126

'Do you want company for the rest of the day, or do I take it that you'd prefer to be alone for this thinking process?' Gary asked, with more insight than usual.

'Alone – if you don't mind.'

She didn't need to apologize, but everything seemed so topsy-turvy today. In fact, the only *sane* thing was Gary, who hadn't sent the letter, and hadn't let her down when she needed him. She put her hand on his arm.

'I do appreciate what you did today, Gary. I mean it. But I need to get my head together on this one, and I can't do it with anyone else around.'

'OK, doll,' he said. 'You know how to find me when you want me.'

By the time she closed the door to her flat, it was early evening, and Alex felt as if she'd been driving for ever. It had rained steadily all the way back, making the journey slower than usual with the Sunday nose-to-tail traffic into London. The gloom of the sky and the incessant swishing of the windscreen wipers only added to her downbeat mood.

But, thankfully, Gary had respected her need to be alone. Instead of the promised shower she took a long soak in the bath, hoping it would help her unwind, then wrapped herself in her towelling dressing-gown for comfort, put on the kettle for the coffee she hoped would revive her spirits, and refused to answer the persistent ringing on her doorbell.

If it was Mormons or Jehovah's Witnesses she didn't want to know, she thought savagely. And who else would come calling on a wet Sunday night without an invitation?

'I know you're in there, Alex,' she eventually heard a disembodied voice say through her letter-box. 'I've got some news that may interest you.'

She certainly didn't want to talk to Nick Frobisher. In her present mood she was in danger of blabbing everything, just for the comfort of having someone else take this whole Caroline business off her shoulders.

And IT WOULD NOT DO. The self-help detective manual continually told her so in large letters.

Once you started on a case, you had to see it through. Once you took on your client's problems, you had a duty to him or her to respect their privacy and their confidences. She could recite it almost word for word, blast it.

But the longing to confide in *someone* was sometimes very strong, and the puffed-up author of the manual hadn't taken any account of that feeling. In fact, she doubted if the author had any normal feelings at all or else he/she/it was just a robot. That would be it. A robot had rattled off the necessary rules and instructions . . . she was getting more light-headed by the minute.

'It's to do with our mutual friend at the factory, Alex. Let me in and I'll tell you more.'

Her hand froze over the kettle, knowing that Nick had to be talking about Norman Price. And he couldn't have said anything more likely to entice her to open the door. She did so suspiciously.

'Are you sure this isn't just a trick to get a free cup of coffee while you're in the area doing the business—'

He put one hand over hers. His large, comforting, brotherly hand that had the instant effect of reducing her to infuriating tears. She was so blinded by them for a moment that she was almost unaware that he was coming inside the flat, closing the door behind him, and holding her fast to his chest. His voice was low and caring. She could feel its deep vibration against her body.

'Hey, what's wrong. sweetheart? This isn't like you at all. Where's my tough girl?'

She snuffled, knowing she was dampening his rough jacket. She was overcome by his concern, and even though his words would be thought sexist and patronizing in some quarters – including her at any other time – they were exactly what she needed to hear right now.

'I'm not feeling very tough at this moment,' she mumbled against him, 'and I've got the mother and father of all headaches.'

He steered her towards her sofa and sat down beside her, his arms around her so that she leaned back against him.

Without another word, his fingers began to caress her temples – those fingers that could seize a villain around the throat when necessary, and almost – but not quite – choke the life out of him.

Large, gentle fingers that were doing the most amazing job of soothing and relaxing and easing away the tension that had been gripping her so viciously for so long.

'That's good,' she whispered. 'That's so good.'

'All part of the service, ma'am,' he said, causing her to react by sitting up swiftly, simply because they were the same words that Gary sometimes used.

She didn't want to compare the two of them: there was no comparison. But the mood was broken, however sensual and emotive it had been, or might have been leading up to. And Alex didn't want to examine that too closely either.

'I was making coffee,' she said, her voice cracking now. 'I know you'll never say no to that. Then you can tell me what you're doing here on this awful night.'

Thoughtfully, Nick watched her go into the tiny kitchen, wondering if she had any idea how bloody seductive she looked with that ghastly white dressing-gown curving around her buttocks and revealing their delicious shape, the cord holding in her waist so tightly, as if to ward off all-comers. Including him. Especially him, he thought ruefully.

He held himself in check. He had things to say, and it had already confused the issue in his mind by finding her tearful and vulnerable for once. So much the woman he knew she was, underneath all the slickness of her job.

She brought back two mugs of coffee, and sat on the sofa with her legs tucked beneath her, bare toes sticking out beneath the voluminous dressing-gown. As innocent as a child, and as bloody seductive as a Mata Hari, Nick thought again.

The lack of make-up did nothing to detract from the classic shape of her face, and it only made those gorgeous green eyes more luminously beautiful; if anything . . . he was in danger of turning into a ruddy poet if he wasn't careful, which was not the way for a hard-nosed copper to be.

'So?' Alex encouraged. 'What is it that I might find so interesting to know?'

By now, she had got herself together. He had mentioned the factory friend, who was obviously Norman Price. He didn't know she had any real connection with him, but the fact that his name had even cropped up between them was something he wouldn't let go. She gazed at him with a vacant look, although all her senses were alert, warning her not to give anything away that she didn't want to.

'It's our charmer, the factory king.'

'So you said. What about him?' she said.

'He's in hospital.'

Alex paused with her coffee mug halfway to her lips, praying that the shock of Nick's statement wouldn't make her spill even more on the already stained dressing-gown she hadn't had time to sponge properly.

'Oh? What happened? Heart attack or something?' she said, trying not to sound too keen to know.

Nick laughed. 'Nothing so ordinary, my clever little sleuth, and that wide-eyed innocent look won't work with me. I know you're interested, and *damned* interested, if my guess is right.'

She put her mug down on a side table. 'All right, so tell me why he's in hospital – if you must. Honestly, Nick, you can be so infuriating.'

'He was mugged late on Friday night near his factory. Presumably he was working very late, and they jumped him. He was shoved into some bushes and wasn't discovered until an old chap walking his dog found him next morning. Or rather the dog did. The old boy thought it was just a bundle of rags from the state that Price was in. Shook him up pretty badly.'

Alex was too stunned to interrupt. This was not good news at all. Apart from her instant sympathy for anyone who got mugged – and she had seen enough of those poor devils – she wondered just how much her obligation to Norman Price's need for privacy went now.

And with the thought came another one: if Jeremy Laver was involved in Caroline's disappearance on account of her inheritance, had he organized this mugging too? Was there more behind that bland, if haunted, exterior than she believed? She seriously thought him too wimpish to do anything violent himself – but he could always delegate. . . .

'I wonder—' she said involuntarily, and Nick noticed the flickering of her eyes at once.

'What?'

'Nothing. Nothing at all.'

For an instant she had been in danger of blurting out the second thing on her mind: whoever the muggers were – and for whatever reason they had duffed up Norman Price – they might also have been the ones who ransacked the cottage. And Alex had been down there at the time. She might have suffered the same fate as Price . . . and who would have found *her*?

'Well? Do we put our cards on the table now, Alex?'

Suddenly chilled and knowing that her eyes had glazed, she flinched as his voice softened. It was a well-known technique to catch the other person off guard, but she didn't want to recognize his methods right now. It was one thing for her to question her own need for client-confidentiality; it was something else when DI Frobisher questioned her with all the subtlety of an alligator.

Despite the softening of his voice, she knew that ruthless, unwavering look he was giving her. He was gut-sure she knew something about the man who was mugged, and he wanted in on it. She thought swiftly.

'Look, I really don't know anything about the guy. I saw him at a club where he was making an idiot of himself over some girl. My friend mentioned his name and said a middle-aged businessman should have had more sense.'

'You're a lousy liar. And if the friend in question is the jerk who was with you at Jeremy Laver's concert the other week, what would he know about businessmen and their habits?'

'He knows about Norman Price. He delivers stuff to his factory sometimes.'

Too late, she knew she had said too much. Now he'd know there was a connection between herself and Gary and Price, however tenuous.

'Did you know Jeremy Laver once gave Norman Price's name as a reference?' Nick went on lazily.

'No. Why should I?' *Damn* his ferrety nose, she thought furiously, while trying to sound completely uninterested.

'And that Price is seriously in debt to several casino owners and other creditors?'

'You have been a busy boy, haven't you? Look, I really am very tired, Nick, and I honestly don't see what all this has to do with me.'

She faked a successful yawn and looked at him pointedly.

'I'm going to drop in at the hospital to see if our man has come round and is able to talk, and I wondered if you'd care to come along,' he went on.

131

'No, I would not!' she said, and he pounced at once.

'Why not? Afraid he wouldn't be too pleased for the police to be seen in your company?'

Alex closed her eyes. He was a good guesser, she'd give him that. At that moment it was very tempting to tell him everything. Almost too tempting to resist. . . .

But this was still her case and, as yet, it seemed that Nick didn't have a clue about Norman Price's missing daughter. The only thing he'd be interested in was finding the people who had mugged Price. It didn't take a genius to know that it was probably some heavies from the casinos or Price's other creditors. It was hardly Jeremy Laver's style.

'I just want to go to bed, Nick. I'm sorry Mr Price has been mugged, and I hope it's not too serious, but it really doesn't have anything to do with me.'

He got the message at last. She was never averse to his company when they weren't on opposite sides, and she liked him enormously, but there was just too much at stake now for her to be comfortable with him.

She wouldn't have dared go to visit Norman Price in hospital anyway, not with the police hovering over him to get a description of the muggers as soon as possible. But once she was alone she looked up the number of the hospital that was nearest to the factory, assuming it would be the one where he'd been taken. She dialled the number and struck lucky.

'Are you a close relative?' the she-dragon at the other end replied when she finally got through to the ward where Norman Price was detained.

'No. Just a friend,' she lied. 'Though I'm calling on behalf of a – a relative – his daughter.'

'Oh, then I suppose it's all right. Mr Price is very poorly. His injuries weren't life-threatening, but he's badly bruised and is still sedated. If you'd like to speak to the constable on duty—'

Alex put down the phone quickly. That was the last thing she wanted. She shouldn't have mentioned the daughter, either. The nurse would undoubtedly report to the constable sitting beside Norman's bedside and since Nick was about to call at the hospital, he'd have a pretty good idea who had called in so soon after he had left Alex's flat. And so far she didn't think he knew about any daughter, missing or otherwise.

132

Right at that moment she dearly wished she had the nerve to shove her passport into her bag, drive down to Gatwick and take a plane to anywhere. Just out of here.

And now she was getting desolate again, knowing she was doing everything wrong. Giving herself away at every turn, and finding Nick Frobisher much too clever for her. Even Jeremy Laver may have seen through her by now. Gary was as shallow as they come, and only wanted her for her body . . . right now she could wish the entire male population at the bottom of a deep dark pit.

She fumbled in her large tote bag for some tissues to mop up her streaming eyes, and encountered the large plastic wrapper she'd found at the cottage, the one at the back of Caroline's underwear drawer. Tired as she was, she knew she wasn't going to sleep yet. She opened the wrapper instead.

The duty nurse at the hospital was efficient. She didn't like the phone being slammed down on her. You got some strange customers in accident and emergency these days, and muggers frequently checked on the state of their victims. It wasn't unknown for them to turn up at the hospital on the pretext of being concerned friends, in order to finish off the job. And she didn't like messiness either.

Just to be on the safe side, the nurse dialled 1471 to get the number of the caller, then reported it to the duty constable. When the DI arrived, he passed on the message, and Nick stared at the number, recognizing it at once.

'Well, well,' he said thoughtfully. 'So our Alex isn't as innocent of information as she liked to pretend. And what's all this about a daughter?'

'Could be just the woman's way of getting information out of the nurse, sir,' the constable offered. 'They never give anything away unless they think you're a close relative.'

'True, Constable. So you'd have expected the caller to simply say she was the daughter, wouldn't you?'

He gave a self-satisfied smile. He was sure now that Alex was on to something. He didn't know what, but somehow this Norman Price, perhaps Jeremy Laver, and *perhaps* an unknown daughter were all involved.

He consulted the nurse. 'Has the patient talked yet?'

She looked at him with dislike. He was good-looking if you liked the husky type, but she didn't care for his brusque, arrogant attitude in her domain. In fact, having to deal with policemen was the part of her job she liked the least. She hadn't come into nursing to be interrogated.

'Well?' Nick said impatiently. 'Come on, woman, I've got my job to do.'

'And I've got mine, and Mr Price is still sedated. He's rambling a little, but when he comes round properly, you can see him— Here, where do you think you're going?'

Nick pushed open the door of the ward and strode over to Price's bed. The guy looked pretty much of a mess. Cuts and bruises were swelling and distorting his face. Being hooked up to various tubes and monitors didn't help his ugly features much either.

But a half-conscious guy who was rambling could often give more relevant information than one who was fully alert and watching what he was saying.

Nick tried the shock approach, knowing that the nurse would be organizing reinforcements by now to order him away, so he had to be quick. He leaned close to Price's face.

'Your daughter's worried about you, Norman,' he said quietly. He saw the man stir restlessly, but there was no verbal reaction. He tried again.

'She sends her love—'

The response was a guttural choking sound. It could almost have been a cynical laugh, though the guy was in no fit state for laughing. He reminded Nick of a gargoyle right now, like something out of *Ghostbusters*, he thought uncharitably. Then came a gasping thread of sound, so low that Nick wasn't even sure he'd heard right.

'Has she . . . found . . . her?'

Before he could say any more, the duty nurse swished into the ward with the second wave of defence. A buxom sister pushed Nick out of the way and leaned over the patient while the orderlies stood guard. Then she turned around, backing up to the bed as if to protect Price from the enemy.

'This man needs complete rest, Detective Inspector,' she snapped. 'You know the rules, and when he is capable of talking coherently, you'll be informed.'

'Thank you, Sister,' Nick said, apparently contrite. 'My apologies for intruding, of course.'

He went out of the ward and spoke rapidly to the constable, instructing him to let him know the instant Price recovered full consciousness and to note down everything he said in his ramblings, no matter how insignificant it seemed. He was also careful to let the nurse know that she was not to mention any daughter or enquirer, to her patient.

Not that he thought the constable would get anything more useful out of him than Nick had already got, but he didn't want Price alerted that his incoherent ramblings had told Nick something more than he already knew.

Once out of the hospital he sat in his car and mulled over the possibilities. His first reaction to the mugging had been that Price's creditors had beaten him up as a warning to pay up, or else.

But now there was a different and more serious scenario. The guy had a kid who was missing – a girl. The kid could just have gone off by herself, of course. It happened, and Price wasn't a choice piece of work to have for a father.

But supposing she'd been snatched? Maybe the kidnappers had no idea that Daddy had money troubles of his own. Maybe all they saw was a guy who owned a factory and could pay a hefty ransom to get his kid back. Unfortunately, as she hadn't actually been reported missing, there wasn't a whole lot he could do about it. He knew that too.

Once Alex had opened the plastic wrapper, she spread out the various items inside. She stared for some minutes at the newsprint, all her tiredness gone, the adrenalin pumping around in her veins again with a sense of triumph.

She knew Caroline had to have kept some record of where she sent her crosswords. There was no earthly reason for her not to do so, however humble the newspaper or magazine she contributed to. But these few issues of what was essentially a newsletter weren't bad in terms of quality of paper and print. The content was interesting and worthy, and the crossword in each issue may or may not have been Caroline's work. Or maybe seeing this freebie was where she got the idea from.

It didn't exactly look like something that was run on a shoestring. But the nature of it was something Alex might have thought of long ago. Right from the start. It was so true what Nick Frobisher always said. The more obvious the way ahead, the more obscure it became. You simply overlooked it.

But now she had something to work on. Somewhere to look. Providing she could find the place where the newsletter was produced. As she searched through the pages, she became more and more incredulous. It was a conspiracy. It was as if they didn't want to be found either. There was no editorial address or phone number on the heading. No e-mail hieroglyphics. All there was was a post office box number.

Alex had the craziest vision then of how communication might operate between herself and the editor. She would contact their box number, and give her own. Word would go back and forth robotically between the boxes . . . it wasn't exactly cyberspace stuff, but it was weird, all the same. And time-wasting. Far too time-wasting, she thought more soberly.

She couldn't waste that much time. She must give her own credentials and ask them to contact her as soon as possible. Too much cloak-and-dagger stuff would be totally undesirable. She needed to speed things things up, and to look for Caroline more urgently.

Her birthday was looming, and the longer she was missing, the more at risk her inheritance became. Alex saw no reason why she should be deprived of that as well as her liberty.

That was the important thing. Far more important than the thought of the retainer Alex may or may not get from Norman Price, she thought now. His mugging had shaken her up as much as seeing Jeremy at the cottage. Whatever was going on, she was getting really concerned for Caroline's safety now. And at last she had something to pursue.

But as if to thwart her. the adrenalin rush was draining away, and a sense of exhaustion was fast catching up with her again. It had been one hell of a day, and since she couldn't get a letter away until the morning, she might just as well try and get some sleep for what was left of the night – though she was almost surprised to find it was barely midnight.

But she would feel more alert in the morning, and more than ready to get to work. As Scarlett had said, with such amazingly non-tongue-in-cheek perception . . . tomorrow *was* another day.

Chapter 9

Nick Frobisher was not a happy man. Norman Price was recovering remarkably quickly, and bleating about getting out of hospital PDQ. And from the patient's belligerent attitude, Nick guessed that the nurses caring for him fervently agreed with the sentiment.

Despite all his questioning, Nick was getting nothing at all out of Norman Price. Either the man genuinely didn't know who had mugged him, or he was determined not to say. No matter how hard Nick tried, he kept getting the same old story.

'I've told you a hundred times. It was late at night and it was dark. God knows where the security man was. Sleeping it off somewhere, I dare say. That's what these buggers usually do. Anyway, I was about to get into my car when somebody jumped me from behind—'

'One man? Two?' Frobisher persisted.

'It could have been a dozen for all I know. When you're being bashed over the head and seeing stars you don't stop to count how many thugs are involved,' Price snarled. 'Anyway, I've already told you I'm not pressing charges. Waste of time. It happens all the time to management who stay on at their premises too late. Sitting targets, see?'

He paused for breath. His ribs were still sore where they'd kicked him, but he wasn't giving this bloody copper the satisfaction of letting on that he knew very well who the assailants were. The gambling estabishments he frequented had their own ways of dealing with welshers.

Besides which, he had no intention of letting outsiders start probing into his business dealings. There was just too much that didn't add up, and too many ways he could be done for fiddling the books. He didn't relish the thought of prison for fraud and Income Tax evasion.

If only that bloody detective woman would get on with it and do her stuff, then with a good bit of sob-stuff manipulation and persuasion on his part, however much it galled him. Caroline was going to solve all his troubles.

Unexpectedly, he felt a stab of remorse for the reason he wanted her found. He didn't want her hurt, damn it, just available . . . this lapse into a rare feeling of filial concern must have been to do with the fact that he was feeling bloody sorry for himself.

He realized Nick Frobisher wasn't finished with him yet.

'What about letting your family know? Is there a wife, or a son or daughter you'd like us to contact?' Nick said next.

The magnanimous feelings towards Caroline vanished at once. 'My family's my business, and there's nobody I want to get involved. I know my rights, and I don't want anybody prying into my private affairs, and that includes you.'

'Then if that's your last word, Mr Price, there's not a lot we can do to help you.'

'Thank God for that,' Price snapped.

He watched as the DI left the ward, and let out a long breath. He wasn't concerned about the mention of contacting anybody. It was routine stuff. The duty nurse had guardedly asked the same thing. They all thought you wanted family members hovering over you like vultures. And he wasn't about to mention Caroline's disappearance to the police at this stage of the game.

They wouldn't be too interested, he thought cynically. Missing persons didn't attract a great deal of interest to the plod unless they were under age or suspected of some crime.

He instantly forgot the lot of them and bellowed for the nurse to fetch him a bed-pan. Since they were insisting that he stayed in bed for a couple more days, they could bloody well do the jobs they were being paid to do.

Alex was secretly relieved to know that Norman Price was safely out of harm's way for a week. She was sorry he'd been mugged, of course. It was a horrible thing to happen to anybody, but at least he wouldn't be constantly calling her to know what progress she was making.

By the time he came out of hospital, she might have some real news for him. She crossed everything as she thought it.

The morning after her discovery of the freebies. she wrote a letter to the box number on the newsletter heading. The production wasn't bad, but some of the content was quite amateurish, with lots of bitty information, and various sketches that Alex could have done considerably better herself.

The editor obviously fancied him or herself as a desk-top publisher. Alex had seen a lot better. But as the content would have been specifically targeted to reach the readership for which it was intended, that was all that mattered.

She worded her letter carefully after the obligatory opening, not wanting to give too much away at this stage.

'I need to contact someone urgently, and I think you may be able to help. Rather than discuss it in writing, I would appreciate it if you could give me an address where I can come to see you. I would be grateful if you could contact me as soon as possible,' she ended.

She used her headed notepaper. There was no point in disguising the fact that there was some special reason in her request. There was a section in the freebie where readers could write in hoping to make contact with lost friends, or making new ones, and if the editor thought she was merely one of those people, her letter could be put on hold. It had to be seen to be official.

There was nothing more to do then, but wait to see if she got a reply. She prayed that the box was opened more frequently than hers. Since finding Jeremy's anonymous letter, she had been wary of opening her own, but nothing untoward had transpired since then.

Over the next few days, she realized Gary was leaving her strictly alone. Even more ominously, so was DI Nick Frobisher. She had half expected him to come storming into her office, demanding to know what she knew about any daughter of Norman Price's. But maybe the nurse hadn't had the gumption to mention it to him at all, and she was quite sure Price himself wouldn't have done so.

In any case, why would Nick think that Price's daughter was involved with whatever case she was on? Ostrich-like, Alex lulled herself into a false sense of security.

139

Three days after she had written the letter to the freebie, her phone rang mid-morning.

'Alexandra Best,' she said.

'Good morning, Miss Best,' a female voice replied. 'My name is Edwina Selby-Jones. You wrote to me a few days ago, and I understand you want to talk to me on an urgent matter.'

Alex's mind went blank for a moment. 'I'm sorry, but I don't recognize your name, Miss Selby—'

'That's all right. And it's Mrs, by the way. I'm the editor of the *See-All, Hear-All* newsletter.'

Alex wasn't often taken off guard. Nor did she normally reply so clumsily to a contact.

'Oh . . . but I didn't think . . . forgive me, but I didn't expect . . . I thought you'd be writing to me.'

There was a reassuring laugh at the other end.

'You thought I'd be aurally-challenged and unable to speak to you on the telephone, I dare say.'

'Well – yes. I suppose I did. And now I'm mortified to think I made such an assumption—'

'My dear lady, you musn't be. It's a mistake that people make all the time. Actually, I do have *some* degree of deafness, but not enough that a special piece of equipment on my telephone can't correct.'

'I see,' Alex said, feeling ridiculously humbled.

'And you simply supposed that because I'm the editor of a newsletter for the non-hearing community that I would be deaf too. Elementary, my dear Watson-Best!'

Alex warmed to her. 'You have a delicious sense of humour, if I may say so, Mrs Selby-Jones.'

'Certainly you may. Deafness doesn't exclude that facility,' came the reply, with just the hint of a barb in it now. 'So do you want to discuss your business over the phone, or would you still prefer to come and see me?'

'I'd definitely prefer a visit if you don't mind. And as soon as it's convenient for you.'

'How about tomorrow afternoon?'

'Perfect!'

She scribbled down the address of the house. As she had guessed, it wasn't business premises, nor in London. She wondered just what the distribution area could be, but that probably had no bearing on Caroline's contribution to the freebie. If it was her contribution. She still had to find that out for certain, but comparing the grids in the newsletter and the ones she had taken from the cottage on her first visit there, Alex was in little doubt about that.

Her spirits lifted. It was the first really positive lead she had got. Not to Caroline's whereabouts yet, of course, but at least this woman editor must know her and could possibly give her further information as to friends and acquaintances. For all that Norman Price was so sneering about the fact that she didn't make friends, everybody knew someone. Nobody could live in a complete vacuum.

The grandly styled Mrs Edwina Selby-Jones might even be Caroline's confidante, despite the distance between them. Edwina Selby-Jones might even know where she was right now. Caroline might actually be somewhere in the area, keeping out of sight for whatever reason. Out of Norman's way, perhaps. . . .

Alex was excited by the thought that she might be closing in on Caroline at last. And tomorrow she was going to drive down to Bournemouth and meet this Edwina Selby-Jones. It might be necessary to stay a couple of days. In fact, the more she thought about it, she knew darn well she was going to stay for a couple of days. A small break was justified, providing it coincided with work.

She didn't know Bournemouth, but a quick look through the A–Z told her there were plenty of hotels in the area. Being out of town had other advantages too. It would get her out of the way in case Nick came snooping around again. It would get Gary off her back – or her front, as the case might be.

By now, Alex's spirits were lifting by the minute. God bless Edwina Selby-Jones, whoever she was. Caroline must be acquainted with her, if only by post. Except that it was always possible that with Caroline being as introverted as she appeared to be, she always sent her crossword grids to the freebie's post office box number.

In that case she could be as anonymous as she liked. Except for payment. The accounts department had to send her payments somewhere. Bingo again.

No, however many points and counterpoints Alex thought there might be, she refused to let herself get downhearted. As her dad might have said, *she had a feeling in her water* that she was on the brink of discovering Caroline Price at last.

It was a long drive down to Bournemouth, but Alex allowed plenty of time, and once well on her way she relinquished the main roads and drove leisurely through the New Forest.

It was ironic that the glorious forested area reminded her so much of the Yorkshire Dales where she had grown up. In reality, she knew there wasn't the remotest similarity. except for the clean fresh air and the scent of the trees and foliage that was so lacking in smoky old London. The dales were softer in character than the moors, but there was still a grandeur and starkness about them. Much as she loved the city now, there were times when the old tug of nostalgia could still catch her unawares.

She didn't know what to expect when she first came in sight of the sea. Like most people who had always lived well away from the coast, it gave her a breathtaking sense of power and space. And she was exhilarated by the sight of the high cliffs coupled with the rippling waves on the beach.

She could just picture Caroline here, striding along the shore in those long Laura Ashley skirts of hers, head down against the wind, complete in her own company. Or maybe with M, she thought suddenly! Maybe this was one of their secret hideaways ... in some little love-nest well away from their everyday lives.

And who was letting herself get overly fanciful now? she chided herself, as an impatient motorist behind her began tooting his horn. She resisted the urge to give him a two-finger salute and speeded up along the coast road, and concentrated on finding the road where Mrs Selby-Jones lived.

The house gave her something of a shock. It stood well back from a wide, tree-lined avenue in elegant surroundings overlooking the sea. It was practically a mansion, and obviously belonged to someone with Money. It was hardly the place where Alex had expected to find someone dabbling in self-publishing a freebie for the aurally-challenged. She bit her lip, hating the phrase, and wishing it hadn't come into her mind, even though Mrs Selby-Jones had put it there.

Did the people concerned really like it or appreciate it, she wondered? She remembered an old blind man in the dales who would have spit blood had he been called *visually*-challenged.

Effing nonsense, he'd have called it. *I'm blind as a bat and there's nowt else to say about it – and I'll challenge any folk who say owt different*. Alex grinned, hearing the echo of his rich Yorkshire tones in her head.

Anyway, this was definitely the place. She drove into the curving driveway and parked her car outside the imposing double front doors alongside the spanking new Range Rover. She almost expected a flunkey to come rushing out and ask her what the hell she thought she was doing here.

Her nerve didn't often fail her, and she considered she could cope with any situation, but no job had ever sent her to a place of this splendour before.

'Come on, where's your sense of pride?' she muttered. 'They can't eat you, and you have a job to do, remember? Put on your professional face and stop gawping.'

And at least she could communicate with Mrs Edwina Selby-Jones. They had spoken on the phone, and she had seemed a perfectly pleasant woman. She knew what work Alex did, so she had better get on and do it before somebody inside those long mullioned windows thought she was some market researcher about to come canvassing, in which case she'd probably get short shrift from a snooty minion.

A housekeeper answered the door. Predictable. Now that she saw the house, she wouldn't have expected Mrs Edwina Selby-Jones to answer the door herself. Try as she might she could no longer get the woman's full title out of her head.

She handed the housekeeper her business card and smiled with more confidence than she felt.

'Would you please tell Mrs Selby-Jones I'm here? She's expecting me.'

'Follow me, please, miss.'

The woman stood aside for Alex to go inside and, as she followed her into a luxurious sitting-room, she noted that the interior was as splendid as the exterior promised. The carpets were of deep, luxurious pile, the furniture was ornate and richly decorated. and there were costly Chinese ornaments on every surface. Whoever lived here was clearly a collector and well travelled.

For one crazy second, Alex almost expected Loyd Grossman to appear and demand to know *'Who* lives in a house like *this*?'

The illusion – and the query – faded when a well-preserved elderly lady appeared in the room and held out her beringed hand to her. Those rings didn't come out of a Christmas cracker either, Alex thought inelegantly. She must be toting around several thousand pounds worth of diamonds on her fingers alone. Her dress was made of silk, her skin was carefully made-up, and her well-controlled, rigidly waved hair looked as if she had just come out of a top-class salon.

Talk about how the other half lived. To someone whose at-home attire consisted mostly of jeans and T-shirts, the vision of such obvious wealth threw Alex, leaving her momentarily tongue-tied.

'Good afternoon, Miss Best. I'm glad to see you're right on time. I do admire punctuality in a person, being hopelessly tardy at everything myself.'

Mrs Edwina Selby-Jones greeted her with the consummate ease of a rich woman who could probably get away with being late for her own funeral.

'May I offer you some refreshment? Tea or coffee?'

'Some coffee would be very welcome, thank you,' Alex murmured, quite sure that the Lady of the House wouldn't need to make it herself.

Seconds later, as if by magic, a maid appeared and received the instructions, and they made small talk – or rather, Mrs Edwina Selby-Jones made small talk – until the maid returned and served them with coffee and biscuits.

Almost too nervous to pick up the delicate bone china cup, Alex instantly saw herself as the unfortunately flummoxed neighbour in *Keeping Up Appearances*.

And she obviously watched far too much television, she told herself severely. But thankfully the idiotic memory dispelled the brief attack of nerves, and reminded her of who she was, and why she was here.

'Now then, Miss Best, what can I do for you?' Mrs Selby-Jones prompted. 'I understand it's a matter of some urgency.'

Alex assumed her professional pose. 'It is. I'm trying to trace someone, and I have a strong feeling that she may be the person who compiles the crosswords in your newsletter.'

'Oh dear.'

Alex felt her heart sink. She was totally unable to read anything in the woman's expression, or her intonation. But the starkness of the reply was ominous enough.

'I assure you that this is a legitimate and confidential enquiry, Mrs Selby-Jones. The person in question has done nothing wrong, but I do need to find her as soon as possible. Her name is Caroline Price, so I would be grateful for any information you can give me as to her whereabouts.'

There was total blankness on the lady's face.

'Do you recognize the name?' Alex persisted.

'I'm afraid I do not. But that's unsurprising in the circumstances.'

'What circumstances would those be, Mrs Selby-Jones – if you don't mind my asking?' Alex asked carefully, seeing all her carefully constructed answers to the mystery collapsing like a house of cards.

She had been so sure. *Was* still sure that the crosswords had Caroline's stamp on them. Every compiler had a personal work method. and used their own style of clues, whether it was cryptically impossible, or anagrammatical, or blatantly obvious. And this one was definitely Caroline's.

For one wild moment she wondered if there was something sinister in Mrs Edwina Selby-Jones's reluctance to admit to knowing Caroline. But the idea vanished at once. Whoever else wanted Caroline's inheritance it was a certainty that this woman didn't need it. The whole place oozed luxury, and wouldn't have disgraced royalty.

'I'm sorry to disappoint you, my dear,' Mrs Selby-Jones said more gently. 'But you see, we don't operate in the same way as regular newspapers or magazines. Any outside contributors remain anonymous. It's one of our peculiarities, if you like.'

'But they must send in their stuff to you. Caroline must send her crosswords – and receive payment – I presume. They all live somewhere, so you must have names and addresses, surely. It's business procedure.'

She was aware that she might be stepping on hallowed ground as far as probing into someone else's business methods went, but it seemed mighty suspicious to her. Everyone needed money to live, and payment for their work. Businesses had to account to tax inspectors and the like.

Mrs Selby-Jones gave a slight smile. 'You might care to see our

THICKER THAN WATER ·

operations room, Miss Best, and then you can see for yourself that everything is above board.'

'I'm quite sure it is, and I didn't mean to imply—'

She followed the lady meekly out of the room, feeling that she had been reprimanded, yet in so genteel a manner that it hadn't seemed like a reproof at all. But then, everything here seemed surreal. This lady obviously didn't need to run a business of any sort. She should be gracing coffee mornings and bridge parties – and who was being stereotypical now!

They entered a large room where three young women were busily at work on computers and lay-outs for the newsletter. It was so quiet in there you could have heard the proverbial pin drop, and none of them looked around when they entered. Alex and Mrs Selby-Jones stood silently for a moment, and then the hostess turned to her.

'Peaceful, isn't it? Have you caught on yet, Miss Best? That *is* the expression, I believe.'

One of the young women looked around then, and began gesticulating towards Mrs Selby-Jones, who immediately responded in hand signals, so rapid that Alex could never have followed them, even if she had the faintest idea what they meant. The lady moved across to the girl's computer, pointing out something that the girl immediately corrected.

'Are all these people deaf?' Alex said.

'Right again, Miss Best. And they all do a splendid job in producing the *See-All, Hear-All* newsletter that we distribute to all the deaf clubs in the country who request it. I don't do it for gain, only for love. Although, of course, my trusty staff here are well-remunerated for their skills. Does that answer some of your questions?'

'Not really—'

Mrs Selby-Jones sighed. 'Then let me explain. My husband was a very wealthy man, Miss Best. He was High Commissioner in an overseas government post until he lost his hearing due to a coup in that country blasted his eardrums, along with other injuries that I don't care to discuss.

'But it finished his career, and he had a painful time adjusting to a very different way of life. That was also when we discovered how the rest of the world views deafness. After he died I decided to do what little I could for the deaf community by starting this newsletter, and it's proved successful in its own small way.'

Alex was chastened by her frankness. 'But I notice that you don't give your contributors any credits or by-lines in the newsletter. Isn't that odd?'

'We *are* the contributors, Miss Best, apart from those who send in voluntary news items such as holiday reports, which we keep as upbeat and informative as possible. We're completely non-profit-making, and I do this in memory of my husband.'

'But what about the crossword compiler? Don't you pay her? She's not one of these people here, is she?' Alex said, a note of desperation in her voice. The woman stated the facts in such a matter-of-fact way, that it was obviously just as she said – a labour of love.

But none of these girls bore the remotest resemblance to the missing Caroline, so the faint hope that she might even be here, went right out of the window.

'The compiler sends them in in batches, and has never sent an invoice or a request for payment, nor given her name and address. If it *is* a she, of course.'

'Could I ask how and when she sends them?' Alex said, starting to feel as if she was going down a long dark tunnel from which there was never going to be any light. She had been so *sure* she had almost cracked it, and now it was all falling apart again.

Mrs Selby-Jones signed to one of the girls again, and she brought out a large brown envelope and handed it over. Alex tried not to register how weird the operations room was, compared with a normal office. The keyboards were virtually silent, there was no radio playing, and all communication between the girls and Mrs Edwina Selby-Jones was by these silent, explicit hand signals.

It was almost creepy ... but she was also filled with respect and admiration for the way they conducted their lives. To someone whose own life had always been filled with noise, it was sad – but she knew better than to say so, especially since the people here looked anything but sad.

Alex opened the proffered brown envelope and took out the batch of four crossword grids. She recognized them at once from those she had seen previously; and they were so obviously Caroline's work. There were the expected duplicates of each one, the blank grid with the clues, and the completed grid with the answers.

'And this is all that's ever sent to you?' she asked Mrs Selby-Jones.

'That's all.'

The postmark on the envelope was Bishop's Stortford, which was the nearest major town to Wilsingham. It confirmed the origin of the crosswords, and their compiler. Presumably a small village like Wilsingham would have a local pick-up for sorting at a main post-office depot.

'I'm sorry I can't help you any further, Miss Best,' Mrs Selby-Jones was saying now.

'You've been a great help already,' Alex assured her. 'But could you tell me when the last batch of crosswords arrived, and when will you be expecting the next ones?'

'They come in regularly. Our mystery compiler is very efficient, once a month we get the four that are required, and she never misses out on a fifth when it becomes necessary. Let me see now—' She asked one of the girls for the information, and once again, Alex was subjected to the amazing display of dexterity. She guessed that Mrs Selby-Jones would have learned it with her husband at the time he became deaf, and she was filled with admiration, and not a little envy, for what she perceived must have been a devoted couple.

'I just wanted to confirm it for you, Miss Best,' she was told now. 'We had the last batch three weeks ago, so the next ones should be arriving in about a week's time, or less.'

'Would it be a terrible inconvenience to you to call me and let me know when they arrive, just so I can be sure that everything is all right?'

'Of course.'

There was nothing else to say, and Alex was almost glad to get out of there. Despite the opulent surroundings, she had felt oddly stifled by the silence of it all. She got back in her car and turned on the radio full blast, relishing the raucous sounds of a Mick Jagger oldie on Radio Two.

She had checked into a small hotel just outside the main part of the town. Bournemouth was at the tail end of the summer holiday rush, but it was still bustling with tourists. and Alex guessed that the season wouldn't end for some while yet. As long as the weather held, the tourists would keep coming. And for now, she was going to join them.

She spent the evening making notes of everything she had learned that day, then having a lazy dinner in the hotel dining-room. There was still plenty of daylight and she took a short stroll along the sandy beach below the hotel. There were families everywhere, enjoying a late holiday, and occasionally a pair of lovers, their arms entwined, oblivious to everyone else.

It was a scene that did nothing but depress her. Finally, there seemed nothing else to do but go back to her room, take a shower and lie on her bed watching television. At this rate, she would be square-eyed, she thought, remembering the words her father had admonished her with years ago.

Those eyes smarted now, and not only with the drive down here and the tension of the day and the meeting with la Selby-Jones. Nor was it the residual sand in her eyes from her stroll along the beach; it was remembering her dad, and the love they had never been able to express to one another.

It would be the same with the Prices, she thought, yet there must have been love between them once. Alex only realized how much her own father had loved her when it was too late. And if there was one thing in this world she wished she could pass on, it would be to express love when you could, because once the chance was gone. it was gone for ever.

'And I'm turning into a pathetic lump of lard,' she muttered aloud.

All the same, there was a poignancy between her own paternal background, and Caroline's. It drew her to the other woman in a way that few other cases had done before. If ever she longed for a happy ending to a case, it was this one, Alex thought. And she obviously wasn't going to find it here.

The urge to stay a little longer in Bournemouth, pushing the case out of her mind for a while, was fast diminishing. She needed to be back in London, because if there was anything at all to report. it would be reported there. Mrs Selby-Jones had promised her that.

She was back in the city soon after lunch the next day, having called in at her office and picked up the mail, and checked the answering machine. There were no messages on it, but when she reached her flat the machine there was flashing. She pressed the play button and was told by the mechanical voice that there was one message, timed at late last night.

'Our man has done a bunk, Alex,' she heard Nick Frobisher's voice say. 'He's discharged himself from hospital and gone to ground somewhere. If you've any idea where that might be, give me a call.'

Alex played the message again to make sure she had heard it properly. It referred to Norman Price, of course, and knowing what she did about him, she wasn't at all surprised that he'd discharged himself. She didn't imagine the hospital staff would be too displeased to see the back of him either.

She guessed immediately where he would be. He would have gone to Wilsingham to Caroline's cottage. He could hide away in perfect secrecy until he felt able to face the world again, without the police breathing down his neck urging him to press charges against his attackers. He wouldn't want any of that, guessing that it would expose too much of his private life.

Nick Frobisher had no idea of the address of the cottage, or that it even existed. He had no idea that there even was a daughter, unless Norman had inadvertently blabbed about it. But Alex doubted that. Once he recovered his senses, he'd be far too cute to give anything away. His first priority in hiring her to find Caroline was that he hadn't wanted any police involvement.

So, disregarding Gary, who had only been to Greenwell Cottage once, and hadn't been interested enough to note the address – there was only Jeremy Laver who definitely knew of it. And unless Nick had worked on the connection between them there was no reason to suppose he would have contacted Jeremy to ask if he knew what Norman's movements might be.

It still niggled Alex that Nick was interested at all. He wasn't meant to be a part of this investigation, but somehow he had become involved, almost as a sideline. And if she didn't get back to him, he'd sure as hell follow up his phone message with another one, or come around to see what she knew. He wouldn't let it alone now.

But she had no intention of calling him. Before she could stop to think, she had switched on the answering machine again and was out of there, bundling her overnight bag back into her car and speeding out of town in the direction of the M25 and the maze of minor roads to Wilsingham.

When she reached the village she drove straight to Greenwell Cottage. Sure enough, there was the sleek, forest-green Mercedes parked in the secluded lane outside. She pulled up behind it and went up the path to the front door. She didn't want to alarm him, so even though she had a key, she knocked on the door and called his name quietly.

'Mr Price, it's Alexandra Best here, and I'm quite alone. May I come in, please?'

There was no reply, so she repeated the words again. She thought she heard something, but it sounded more like the low growl of a dog than a human voice. Her heart began to pound, but she couldn't leave things as they were, without knowing. She put her key in the lock and pushed open the door cautiously. Then she gasped.

Norman Price was lying on the sofa, his face grey and mottled, his eyes closed. For a ghastly moment Alex thought he was dead, until she saw his lips move feebly.

'Thank God. Get me some pain-killers, quick.'

'What on earth's happened? Has someone attacked you?'

She ignored his lack of manners. In the circumstances it was understandable. And she had just managed not to add the word 'again'. She wasn't supposed to know he'd been mugged. As far as Price was concerned, she didn't know DI Nick Frobisher.

'Never mind that. I need some bloody aspirins. I slipped and fell and nearly knocked myself out, face and all.'

Tell that to the marines, Alex thought. But there was no point in arguing with him. He looked terrible, and even though his facial swellings had gone down now, he was still rainbow-hued. Anyone with any gumption at all would know those bruises hadn't suddenly appeared.

'Stay where you are and I'll see what I can find in the bathroom cabinet,' she said.

'I wasn't thinking of going anywhere,' he snarled, savage with pain and exhaustion.

So far he hadn't asked what Alex was doing there, but it wasn't unreasonable that she would have come to check whether or not Caroline had returned. She found the pain-killers and gave him a couple with a glass of water, then put the kettle on for some tea. He wasn't totally coherent, and she wondered just how long he had been there without food. His injuries had obviously become more pronounced since driving himself all this way like the lunatic that he was.

'I thought she might have come back,' he muttered vaguely now, leaning back on the cushions. 'I hoped it might all have been a dream and she wasn't missing – or worse.'

Startled, Alex realized he was talking about Caroline. It was the first time she had heard anything like anxiety in his voice. It might even have been real anxiety, however fleeting, of the kind that a father might feel for a daughter, instead of the mercenary jerk she thought he was. Maybe he was human after all. But she wasn't totally convinced about that yet.

'I'm on the track, Mr Price,' she said carefully. 'I know time is getting short now—'

Immediately, she saw a different light in his eyes, and her sympathy for him vanished as quickly as his apparent anxiety for Caroline.

'You've found her?'

'I didn't say that. I said I'm on the track. These things take time, especially when someone may not want to be found. But there's no reason to suppose that she won't simply turn up in time to claim her inheritance, is there? She may just be, well, teasing you.'

He snorted. 'Caroline doesn't tease. We don't have that sort of relationship,' he said with a scowl, but again Alex wondered if she caught a glimpse of a vulnerability in him he wouldn't even admit, even to himself.

The hard-headed businessman couldn't be seen to care about a daughter who was too prickly-skinned to want sympathy, or love. That produced faults on both sides. It was also a childish, tit-for-tat situation.

You don't love me, so I won't love you. Yah boo sucks.

Alex guessed that much of the difficult relationship between them could well have stemmed from childhood. It took two to make a relationship, and if neither side was willing to make allowances, there was nothing left but stalemate.

'Well, if you've got nothing else to report, you'd best get out of here and leave me be,' he said now, wincing as he tried to haul himself up into a more comfortable position.

'Don't be ridiculous,' she said, coming to a decision. 'I'm starving, and I'm sure you are too. There's probably some food in the pantry and freezer. I'm not moving from here until I've made us a proper meal, and if I think it's advisable, I'm staying the night.'

'You fancy yourself as a nurse now, do you?'

'Why not? Now, are you going to accept my help, or not? And don't worry, I'll be putting all these extra services on my bill,' she added, knowing this was the kind of currency he would understand.

The poor sap really did look as if he needed looking after right now, though. He shouldn't have discharged himself from hospital before he was properly fit. And he certainly shouldn't have driven all this way on top of it. After a minute, he gave a distorted grimace.

'You've got a bossy kind of bedside manner, Miss Best, but since I don't have the energy to refuse, I suppose I'd better accept.' After a pause, he added, 'You do think she's all right, don't you?'

She reassured him non-committally. She didn't know any more than he did what had happened to Caroline, or if she was alive or dead. But it was the nearest he'd come yet to showing any sign of being worried sick about his daughter.

And finding a spark of humanity in Father Price was far more important to Alex than any thanks for staying here, even though she was well aware that she musn't confuse the issue.

Her own background wasn't in the least like Caroline's . . . but there was still too much of a parallel between two sets of fathers and daughters that made her feel a special kind of commitment to this particular pair.

Chapter 10

Jeremy Laver was rehearsing a particularly difficult violin passage for the tenth time that morning. As always when things weren't going well, the artistic temperament so gloatingly described by music critics as a character flaw, was burgeoning forth. In recollection of one of their favourite smug phrases, he knew he was *venting his spleen*, whatever the devil that was, both on himself and on his fellow musicians.

To his credit, he never spared himself when things were going wrong. This was one of those times when he despaired of anything in his life ever going right. And there were plenty of those. He knew he was one of life's pessimists. . . .

'Mr Laver? Can I have a word. please?'

His head jerked up from his instrument as he heard a voice he didn't recognize. He saw the heavily built man approaching through the centre aisle of the theatre, and anger flashed in his eyes, knowing he'd have words with the bloody doorman for letting in a stranger during rehearsal times. Some things were sacrosanct, and this was one of them.

'No you may not. I don't give interviews without a prior appointment,' he said arrogantly.

DI Frobisher kept right on walking towards the stage, with no intention of being put out by the reaction of this little snot. Temperamental poofter, he thought privately. But what the guy did in his spare time was no concern of his. It wasn't why he was here.

He waved his ID card under Laver's eyes and didn't miss the quick movement of the other man's Adam's apple as he swallowed involuntarily. It affected many people that way.

'In private, please sir,' Nick went on.

Jeremy turned to the waiting musicians, his voice curt.

'We'll continue rehearsals after lunch. Maybe we'll all be in a better humour by then, and more able to do justice to the piece.' He turned back to Nick. 'You'd better come to my dressing-room.'

Nick followed him. He wasn't offered a seat, nor did he want one. This wasn't exactly a social call, even though he admitted it wasn't an official one either. He was going on instinct, and in his own time.

Laver remained standing as well, leaning back against the counter strewn with make-up and the usual performer's props. Nick supposed it was all in the name of art, but privately, it made him want to puke, even though he came across all sorts in his line. It went with the job. He'd had dealings with transsexuals and all kinds of pervs, had been propositioned into the bargain. He didn't imagine this guy was in that league, but he'd never forgotten the encounter when he was a young and green copper.

'So what is it you want with me, Detective Inspector?' Jeremy said, becoming more and more nervous when the man didn't speak. His mind was in turmoil.

Surely Daneman hadn't been careless, he thought, with a rush of fear. Dear God, he hadn't actually *done* anything with Caroline, had he? Something unspeakable. . . ? His mouth went dry, and he found himself clutching the edge of the counter behind him, knocking over several bottles of lotion and not even being aware of it.

Nick was, but since he was here on a little mission of his own that wouldn't let him go, he put it on hold for now.

'I believe you once gave the name of a Mr Norman Price as a reference,' he said, his gaze unwavering.

Laver's eyes flickered. Then he gave a forced laugh.

'Uncle Norman? Good Lord, what's the old boy done?'

'You tell me. So he's your uncle, is he?'

Jeremy shrugged. He was starting to gain confidence. This was nothing to do with Caroline's disappearance, and he guessed it was more likely to be Norman dipping into the factory coffers. His uncle had always been a gambler, and it had been sure to get him into deep water eventually.

'We've never been a close family,' he told Nick. 'I can't remember the last time I saw him—'

'He has a daughter, I understand.'

Jeremy held himself in check with a huge effort. If his knuckles hadn't been turning a deathly shade of white, Nick would almost believe he had nothing to hide. As it was, he was damn sure that he did, even if he didn't have the faintest idea what it was as yet.

It wasn't even his case – and as yet, there *was* no case, he reminded himself. If there had been, he'd have sent someone lower down the pecking order to do the initial interrogating, even on a mugging enquiry. In his world, muggings were ten a penny nowadays, for God's sake. They had become a depressing fact of life, along with baby-snatching and rape.

But this particular attack was different. He didn't know the details, but somehow Alex Best had an interest, and that was what drew him. None of the pieces were fitting together in his mind yet, unless this luvvie was involved in the uncle's mugging. Which was what he was here to find out.

'Yes, there's a daughter.' Jeremy answered the question as calmly as he could. 'But I haven't seen her for years either. I doubt whether her father knows where she is. They never got on—'

'And her name would be?'

Jeremy replied quickly, the way people did when they were nervous. 'Caroline. But as I've already told you, I've no idea where she is.'

Shock tactics were as good a way as any to make people talk. Nick applied them now.

'Then since you're the nearest relative, I must inform you that Mr Norman Price was attacked a few nights ago.'

'What? Where? *How?*'

It had nothing to do with anything, Jeremy thought wildly, his senses reeling. The old fool was always at risk of being done over. He antagonized everybody who came in contact with him. Always had. Even Caroline. But God help Daneman if he'd done this mugging for whatever reason his twisted mind had devised. He wouldn't put anything past him.

'Your concern is touching, Mr Laver,' Nick said.

'Well, he *is* family, even if we don't keep in contact—' They hated one another's guts, he thought privately.

'And why is that? Any special reason?'

157

'None of your business,' Jeremy snapped. 'But if you think I had anything to do with him being attacked—'

Nick gave him a withering look that said he didn't think Jeremy capable of battering a flea. 'I don't. But if you could give me his daughter's address, I'll see that she's informed.'

'I don't know it. I've already told you we're not a close family. Why can't you ask him yourself?'

'Because he's disappeared. He discharged himself from hospital before he was fully recovered and he hasn't returned to his factory or his home address.'

Jeremy felt a sense of rising hysteria. So the old coot had disappeared as well now. That made two of them. But if he hadn't returned home – and he presumed the police were clever enough to figure out where home was – he sobered at once.

There was one place where Norman Price could have gone, and almost certainly *had* gone: Greenwell Cottage. The one place where Norman could go to ground and no attackers or creditors would ever find him. But he was sure as hell not telling this snooper about the cottage and having him go down there and start asking awkward questions around the village.

Jeremy was pretty sure that very few people knew of it. Caroline had become practically agoraphobic since her deafness, and didn't invite company. Besides herself, there was only his uncle and himself and Daneman ... and that bitch of an American journalist and her fancy-man.

Nick saw him pale. But whatever the guy was up to, Nick knew when to quit. Laver had that clammed-up look on his face he'd seen often enough before, both in suspects and witnesses.

It was that *I've said enough, and you aren't getting another bloody thing out of me* look.

'Well, thank you for your time, Mr Laver. This is only a routine matter, and nothing for you to worry about.

Oh no? And since when did detective bloody inspectors make it their business to check up on a discharged hospital patient with no good reason?

Jeremy wasn't born yesterday, and the minute Nick had left the premises, he punched out a series of numbers on his mobile phone. It seemed to take for ever before anybody answered and when they did he was almost frantic.

'Daneman?' he hissed. 'Don't talk. Just listen. My uncle has been mugged and he's discharged himself from hospital. The police have been sniffing around here, looking for him—'

'*Jesus Christ*, man, that's all we need.'

'Will you *shut* it a minute, and listen,' Jeremy snapped. 'You didn't have anything to do with it, did you?'

'Don't be bloody stupid.'

'All right, I had to ask. Everything's still all right at your end, then?'

'If you mean is it still driving me crazy with its whining, then yes it bloody well is,' Daneman stormed.

Jeremy ignored that for the moment. At least he knew Caroline was still safe – if safe was the word for it.

'Well listen up then,' he repeated. 'My uncle hasn't gone home, so he may have gone to the cottage instead. *Whatever you do, don't go there*. Got it?'

After a small silence, Daneman spoke vindictively.

'I'm warning you, Jeremy, if this whole thing is about to fall apart after I'd got it cut and dried—'

'It's not. I'm just guessing where my uncle's gone, that's all. But if he has, and you were to turn up there for any reason, like fetching more of her work stuff—'

'Don't worry, I ain't fetching and carrying for it any more than I need to,' Daneman snarled.

'Don't be—'

'What? Too hard on it? You stick to your fiddle-playing business, Jeremy-sweetie, and leave me to mine.'

Daneman stabbed at the off button on his mobile, and rammed it back into his pocket. He had been standing with his back to the woman all this time as he always did when talking on the mobile, just to be on the safe side.

Although she couldn't hear the discussion, he still found it unnerving to have her all-seeing, accusing eyes on him.

He heard her gasp now, and he looked up sharply. Reflected in the mirror in front of him he saw her ashen, disbelieving face from where she crouched on the bed.

Instantly, he knew he had been careless. She had seen his reflection in the mirror too, and had lip-read the one significant word he had spoken.

'Jeremy?' Caroline whispered. And then her voice rose to a scream. 'Did you say *Jeremy*?'

159

*

'That wasn't bad,' Norman Price grunted, when he had polished off the meal of tinned ham and baked beans Alex had hashed up, together with some reconstituted mashed potato powder.

From the ingredients she had found, it was clear that Caroline wasn't a *cordon bleu* cook, but the end result had been reasonable enough.

'I think I'll go down to the village and get some fresh groceries though. There's not much else here,' she said.

'No! You can't do that—'

'Yes I can. I've been here before, and if anyone recognizes me I'll just say I've rented a place for a few days so that I can work without being disturbed.'

'Worked it all out, have you?' Price said.

'More or less. Now then, are you sure you're quite comfortable?' she said, and then stopped. She had been on the point of plumping up the cushions behind his head, and she realized she was starting to act out the role of nurse or surrogate daughter – far too efficiently.

'I can manage,' he grunted, and she knew he had realized it too. 'But thanks. You didn't have to do any of this.'

'It's my job, remember?' she said briskly.

She left the cottage and walked towards the village. One or two people nodded at her, and then she came face to face with the vicar, his face as unwelcoming as ever. Whatever happened to good old-fashioned geniality – and wasn't the church supposed to be the be-all and end-all of turning cheeks and kissing my. . . .

'So you're here again, miss. What brings you back this time? Are you still looking for that friend of yours?'

'No. I'm just buying some groceries. I'm taking a sort of work-combined-holiday down here for a couple of days.'

She spoke glibly, thinking that even vicars must go on holiday sometimes, but she was willing to bet that this one didn't often bother. It would come into the category of Sodom and Gomorrah, the evils of the flesh and all that rot.

He didn't ask any more questions, and she went on her way, swinging her tote bag, and hoping he'd dismiss her from his mind as the city slicker beyond redemption.

The village shopkeeper was more interested, and Alex invented a rented cottage outside the village where she could get some much-needed peace and quiet to do some work.

'It's not easy to concentrate in London where everybody calls on you for business reasons,' she elaborated. 'This area is just perfect when you want to be left alone. People appreciate the need for privacy here, don't they?'

'Oh. they do that, miss,' the shopkeeper said, secretly agreeing that if the snooty piece didn't want to talk to folk, then that was up to her.

Alex left the shop with some meat, fruit and vegetables, bread and butter, and fresh milk. The basics, including powdered milk, which she detested, were already in the cottage. She daren't buy too much though, in case it seemed as if she was stocking up for a siege. And that would create curiosity in the village, which she didn't want.

In any case, she couldn't stay in Wilsingham very long, and with a few good meals inside him and his confidence restored, she guessed that Norman Price would be glad to get back home – wherever home was. It occurred to her that she didn't know that yet.

'Where *do* you live?' she asked him over a steaming cup of coffee some while later. 'I see no point in your holding out on me now that we've gone this far, do you?'

'Chelmsford. Not that it's relevant.'

'Would that be the family home, where Caroline grew up?'

'It would – and that's enough about that.'

Alex saw that he was immediately reverting to his old aggressiveness. He was presumably successful enough in business dealings, but his social graces were minimal and never lasted long. She wondered about a wife. There must have been one once, if there wasn't one now.

'Won't your wife be worried about what's happened to you?' she asked casually.

He snapped back, seeing through her at once. 'If you want to know if I've got a wife, why don't you just ask me?'

'Do you have a wife?'

'No. She died when Caroline was six.'

'Oh. I see.'

He glowered. 'No, you don't see. That's the kind of stupid

remark everybody makes, when they don't see anything at all. My wife died and I brought up Caroline alone with the unavoidable help of do-gooders and child-minders until she was old enough to fend for herself. Does that answer the rest of your damn-fool questions?'

She'd certainly got more than she had expected out of him now, Alex thought. She spoke more gently. 'I was merely trying to get the full picture, Mr Price. It may help—'

'It won't help you to find her, which is what I'm paying you for. And right now you can get me some more bloody pain-killers and let me get to bed. I've had enough chit-chat for one day. I'll take Caroline's room. If you're staying, you can take the other one.'

Oh yes, he was back on form all right, thought Alex. Just when she thought there was some good in him after all, he went and spoiled it. She might have known it.

Silently, she delivered the aspirins and a glass of water, and made no attempt to assist him up the stairs, despite the fact that his bruised ribs were clearly still troubling him. Sod him, she thought sourly. She deliberately turned on the TV and tried to forget him.

Next morning, after a night in an unfamiliar bed where she found it very difficult to sleep, and with her unwanted companion snoring his head off in his daughter's bedroom, she awoke to the raucous sounds of country birdsong.

'Do you want some tea?' she yelled outside the other bedroom door.

'And breakfast. Did you get any bacon and eggs?' he bawled back.

'I did not. You'll have toast and like it,' she snapped.

But she grinned, because for a moment she had gloried in scoring over him in such a small and unintentional way. She simply hadn't thought about breakfast food at the village shop, and anyway, there was a jar of marmalade in the pantry to go with the toast, and that would have to do.

By the time they both appeared downstairs, she could tell that he was feeling better. He had more normal colour in his face now, and the visible bruises were fading. She soon discovered that any softening on his part, towards Caroline, or anyone else, had gone just as quickly.

162

'I'll stay here one more day,' he announced. 'I don't want to leave those buggers meddling about at the factory for too long, but I don't want 'em to see me looking as if I've done ten rounds either. I'll phone in and tell 'em to expect me tomorrow. In any case I'm not cut out for country living.'

'Fine,' Alex said, after his grand speech, recognizing the dictatorial boss only too well. 'Then I'll leave at the same time, once I've outdone my usefulness.'

He didn't even notice the sarcasm.

'Right. You'll need to get back to town. You still haven't done what I'm paying you for.'

She counted to ten. 'I assure you I'm making progress. You must be aware that some people who disappear are never found at all, and at least I know where Caroline sends her crosswords—'

He gave an explicit oath. 'Is that all you've done so far? What the hell's the good of that?'

Alex looked at him coldly. 'It tells me that she's still alive, Mr Price, since she's still sending her work to the publication concerned. That is the most important thing to know, I would have thought.'

As far as she knew, the continuing work-submission angle may or may not be true. She wouldn't find that out until she heard back from Mrs Selby-Jones, but she certainly wasn't letting on to Price about that. He growled a reply.

'Of course it is. She's my daughter, isn't she?'

It was a bit late in the day for showing paternal feelings, Alex thought. But she supposed it was something that he remembered to mention them.

And she had been just as remiss in neglecting to ask one very pertinent question. She threw it at him now.

'You've never told me just how much money Caroline is due to inherit on her birthday, Mr Price, just that it's a substantial sum. Would you mind telling me?'

'I don't see that it has anything to do with anything, but if you must know, it's a quarter of a million.'

'Wow! And her cousin will get it if she doesn't claim it on her birthday – is that right?'

'That's right. But don't bother thinking he's your suspect. He's always got his head in the clouds with his music-making, and he's too much of a weakling to have done anything about it.'

That was a matter of opinion, thought Alex, remembering the way he'd accosted her and Gary at the cottage, together with the fact that he must have sent the anonymous note to get her there. Oh no, as far as she was concerned, Jeremy Laver wasn't out of the frame yet.

'How does she claim it?' she went on, knowing she should have checked on all this weeks ago, and hoping Price wouldn't question her incompetence. 'There must be a solicitor involved in the legalities. You don't just get a huge cheque like that through the post.'

'Oh aye. When the time comes she'll have to prise herself out of here and go to the offices in London.'

'Would the solicitor be acquainted with her cousin?'

Price gave a short laugh. 'I told you you're barking up the wrong tree there, girl. Laver's got no gumption in that department, and the firm of Walton, Walton and Bradbury is as solid as a rock, old school-tie partnership and all that.'

Alex's faint idea that Jeremy could be working in conjunction with a crooked solicitor vanished as fast as it had come. It had been a non-starter, anyway, but exploring any idea, however fanciful, was better than having none at all.

But she could see that her musings were only serving to make Norman more irritable than ever at what he apparently saw as just time-wasting, so she let it go.

There was just enough food to keep them going for one more day. For Alex, the time passed extremely tediously. Price was a tetchy patient, and that was putting it mildly. Mealtimes, when she could escape to the kitchen and get domestic, were the pathetic highlights of the day.

And just to keep out of his way for a while she pulled up a few weeds in the garden and dead-headed the roses, letting herself wallow in their heady sweetness.

While she was indoors she kept the television turned on, no matter what the programmes were, and ignored Price's scathing remarks about the inane game shows and American imports. However mind-clogging Alex found some of them, she wouldn't turn them off, since it effectively stopped her having to make conversation with this boor of a man.

On the second morning, she thankfully packed up the remaining food to take back to her flat. She'd paid for it anyway. Price left before her, still nagging her to get results and earn her money. She breathed a huge sigh of relief when she saw his car drive smoothly away – not that she had any intention of lingering.

But she couldn't leave without changing the bedsheets and cleaning the bathroom and kitchen. She couldn't let Caroline return and find that the place had been used so obviously. Being with Price for two days had depressed Alex, but this new thought was marginally uplifting.

By implication, restoring the cottage to tidiness for Caroline's return meant that she was definitely coming back. Alex bundled the used linen into her car to send to the laundry and made a mental reminder to put the charge on Price's bill.

The cottage was quaint and charming, and the type of place that many city-dwellers dreamed of retiring to. She presumed Caroline felt perfectly safe here. Alex didn't, not any more. It was strangely oppressive to her now, and had taken on an altogether sinister feel. She was thankful to get in her car and head back to London and the land of the living.

She had only been away from home for two nights – three, counting the night in Bournemouth, she reminded herself – but in some ways it seemed like a lifetime. She went straight to the flat for a shower and a welcome change of clothes. There were no calls on her answering machine, and she felt a surge of disappointment.

It would have been fantastic if Mrs Selby-Jones had been able to let her know that Caroline's next batch of work had been sent in. It would mean Caroline was still alive. still working, still capable of putting her skills into practice.

Alex swallowed, feeling the thickness in her throat, and knowing how much she longed for it to be true. She knew she had become too personally involved with this case, but it was difficult not to feel that way.

It had taken a long while before she recognized the similarity between herself and Caroline. On the surface they were poles apart, both physically and in personality, she guessed, but deep down, there was a fundamental similarity: they had both been deprived of a father's love.

And who was getting awash with sentiment now? Alex asked herself, blinking her blurry eyes. She hadn't been bothered by the fact for years, and it had taken this case, and in particular, her association with Father Price, to bring it all into the open again. There were times when she longed to put things right between them, and the chance would never come.

She wasn't some Sam Beckett in a *Quantum Leap* situation . . . *able to put right what once went wrong* . . . she was doing it again, damn it . . . absorbing too much television.

But even the most amateur psychologist would tell you that the past affected the present. You couldn't get away from it, because your own past made you what you were today. And she was letting herself get into a right old state of useless introspection, she thought savagely.

The phone rang, and she grabbed it quickly. Anything to get her mind off impossible scenarios, even if it turned out to be Gary being his normal brash self, asking her out, making her laugh, wanting her body. . . .

She mumbled her name into the receiver.

'Who is that, please?' a woman's voice said uncertainly.

For a moment she didn't recognize it, and the caller obviously hadn't recognized her muffled one either.

Then her heart leapt. 'Mrs Selby-Jones? I'm sorry, you caught me at a bad moment. This is Alexandra Best. Do you have any news for me?'

'I'm not sure if it's of any significance,' came the reply. 'The next batch of crosswords has arrived, but there's something a little different about them.'

'Yes?' Alex said, her breath catching in her throat.

'Well, as I told you, our compiler is normally very efficient, and we always receive two identical sets of grids for each crossword. One grid is blank with the clues alongside, and the second grid has the answers filled in. We always proof-check them, of course, and in one of the sets we've received this time, there's a lot of what I believe is called gobbledegook in the clues, and the completed grid is missing. Are you following me?'

'Of course. Please go on,' Alex said quickly.

'That's about it, really. It may have just been an oversight in leaving out the completed grid, and it was certainly an aberration regarding the strange clues, since many of them don't make sense. We wouldn't be able to use this particular crossword at all. I'm not sure if all this is of any use to you, Miss Best,' she added apologetically, 'but you did want to know when we heard anything.'

'I did indeed. I think this may be very important, and I need to see the grid as soon as possible. Could you fax it through to my office, Mrs Selby-Jones?'

'Oh dear. I'm afraid we don't have a fax machine. There's no need, you see?' she said, without explanation. 'I could arrange for someone to take it into the town to fax it if you wish, but we're very busy with our current issue at the moment, so it wouldn't be until later this afternoon.'

Alex made up her mind. 'Then it would be just as quick if I come down myself. I can be there soon after lunch. You do have a photocopier, I believe? If you could copy the two parts of this doubtful crossword for me to take away, Mrs Selby-Jones, I would appreciate it.'

She knew it would be just as quick to wait for the fax, but she simply couldn't sit about twiddling her thumbs for the rest of the day, knowing that there might be an answer in the badly prepared crossword grid.

'We could do that, but you may as well have the originals since they're of no use to us,' she was told. 'We'll be expecting you later in the day then.'

Alex put down the phone, aware that her heart was pounding. At last she was onto something, and she prayed that these missing answers weren't simply an oversight on Caroline's part. But she was sure they wouldn't be. By Mrs Selby-Jones's own account, and by her own observations at the cottage, Caroline was meticulous in her work.

She would never have sent out an unfinished set of grids without a good reason. Either she was being unavoidably prevented from doing a good job on the work, which Alex didn't want to consider – or this had been done deliberately, in the hope that someone who studied the crossword would find some significance in the answers that did make sense.

Looking at it from Caroline's viewpoint, it must be a very slim chance, thought Alex, with a huge rush of sympathy. Mrs Selby-Jones and the girls working for her would be the first people to see the crossword and try to work out what had gone wrong, but in any case there was no reason why they would be suspicious about any of the answers unless they were looking for anything specific.

Alex could imagine Caroline's desperation in doing this at all, but if these thoughts were correct, then it might have been her one chance of informing anyone of her whereabouts.

She found herself wondering what Nick Frobisher would make of all this, especially of the way Alex's imagination was soaring in leaps and bounds now. He'd say she was living in fantasy land, but she knew there was just as much logic in her feminine intuition as in his solidly analytical methods.

But he knew nothing about Caroline, nor her penchant for cryptic crossword-compiling. And when Alex was triumphant in producing the missing woman in time for her to claim her inheritance, she'd be able to tell Detective whizz-kid Inspector Frobisher a thing or two about detecting.

She switched on her answering machine again and left the flat. She didn't care to think that any psychic influences were at work here, and preferred to keep well away from any of that caper. But she had an uncanny feeling now, almost as if the missing woman was reaching out directly to her, and she felt more buoyant than she had in days, with a certainty that once she had cracked Caroline's clues, she'd be on the brink of finding her.

'Winter cruise here I come,' she thought. Though, with a little start of surprise she realized it had been the last thing on her mind lately. Caroline's safety was paramount.

Gary Hollis had some information he was sure Alex would be interested to know. He hadn't seen her for days. But even though he sensed she was going off him a bit he was still interested enough not to lot her go.

With his usual brand of arrogance, he was sure that being apart for a while would just have made her all the keener. She wasn't the only woman in his life, but it wasn't every day you got to sleep with a luscious goddess – not that sleeping was ever on his mind at such times.

He wasn't a forever kind of guy, but Alex was still the best thing on his horizon at present. And since she'd got so involved with this missing woman case of hers, he'd be able to tease her with a bit of useful knowledge and keep her sweet.

He called her flat that evening and scowled as he got her answering machine message.

'If you're there, doll, talk to me—'

She rushed across the room to grab the phone and switch off the machine.

'Is that you, Gary?' he heard her voice interrupt the message. Her bubbling, excited voice produced an immediate reaction in his jeans, but he soon realized that her excitement wasn't for the thought of his body.

'I've just got indoors this moment, and I was going to call you,' she went on in a rush. 'Can you come to the flat? I've come up with something very interesting and I could do with your help.'

'I've come up with something interesting too,' he said with a leer in his voice.

'We'll discuss that later,' Alex said, too wound up to discourage him. 'Get round here as soon as you can, OK?'

'I'll be there in about half an hour.'

She put down the phone. She had literally just arrived back from Bournemouth, and after all the dashing about of the past few days she would normally have felt drained. But not now. Not tonight, when she was sure she had a real lead at last. And knowing that she needed to share her exhilaration with somebody, Gary was just the one. There were times when being solitary didn't fit the mood.

She hadn't taken the time to study the crosswords properly when she picked them up from Mrs Selby-Jones, but she hadn't been able to resist a peek when she stopped in a lay-by on the way back to London. She didn't want to delay her journey home and she realized at once that if there were any hidden messages in the clues, they could be anywhere.

As Mrs Selby-Jones had said, so much of it was just gobbledegook, and the numbers given before and after the clues didn't always match the spaces in the empty grid. It definitely needed studying, because it seemed that Caroline had either been ultra-careless – or ultra-clever.

Alex had tried to get inside Caroline's mind, and guessed that any hidden message-clues would probably be dotted about.

Even so, one of them had leapt out at her after just a few moments. It wouldn't make sense to any ordinary readers; it only made sense if you were looking for something special, but it told her she was on the right track.

The clue was *Oral Cine – the start of the talkies*, and the number of spaces the answer took up was correctly given as eight. In one nail-biting instant, Alex knew that *Oral Cine* was an anagram, and that the word it spelled out was Caroline.

The adrenalin had surged around her veins at that point, and she had driven back to London with a reckless speed, almost as if Caroline was drawing her back.

'It's good to see you, babe. I've missed you.'

Gary swept her into his arms the minute he entered the flat. The essence of the night-time outdoors combined with the sensuous smell of his leathers enveloped Alex for a moment. His cheeks were cool and fresh, his stubble just tingly enough to be tantalizing, and she remembered why she had fallen for him in the first place. But that could wait.

When she could catch her breath, she opened her mouth to speak, but before she could say a word, he forestalled her.

'You'll never guess what I discovered today. Your bolshy bloke at Price Chemicals has been beaten up,' he announced. 'The factory was my last call this afternoon, and boy, was he in a state, ranting and raving all over the place, and giving everybody a piece of his mind. Even the warehouseman had plenty to say about him for once.'

'Like what?' Alex said, momentarily diverted.

'Oh, just that he always knew he had it coming to him, and it would never surprise him if old Pricey didn't end up in a ditch one of these dark nights with his throat cut.' He spoke with relish. 'Surprised you, have I?'

'Actually, you haven't,' Alex said, almost sorry she had to admit it from the disappointed look on his face.

'You mean you already knew? Bloody hell, Alex, you're cuter than I thought.'

'Never mind all that. I've got something far more interesting to tell you about than Father Price's mugging. I've tracked down the place where Caroline sends her crosswords, and we've got some solving to do. She's the cute one, and if my theory is correct I'm sure she's trying to tell somebody where she is.'

'You mean there's something more behind that plain Jane than meets the eye?' Gary said with a grin, and then pretended to back off as she glared at him. 'OK, she's not that bad, though I wouldn't go so far as to call her cute.'

'Shut up for a minute, and take a look at this.'

Not wanting the cosiness of the sofa to interfere with work, Alex took the crossword grid out of her bag and put it on the table so that they both had to sit on dining-chairs to study it.

'I was never much good at crosswords,' Gary said. 'Give me a code to crack and I'll do it. But crosswords, no.'

'You'll help me solve this one, or you'll be getting a crack on the head from me,' Alex told him. 'Now concentrate, and let me show you what I've found already.'

She marked the relevant clue and its answer with a yellow highlighter pen. Gary looked at it for a moment and said nothing. Then he began his tuneless whistle, while Alex told herself that however annoying it was, it was best not to interrupt whatever thinking processes went on in his mind at such times.

'Most of it doesn't make sense,' he said at last.

'I know. But assuming that some of it does, that's what we have to sort out.'

'Well, why don't you get a different colour highlighter and cross out the rubbishy bits?' Gary said, clearly caught up in the chase now.

'Brilliant,' Alex said.

She didn't want to admit that two brains were better than one, because they frequently weren't. They could often send people off in different directions with too many options. But this time, Gary had scored.

It took a fair time to eliminate everything that didn't make sense, because some of it was so nearly logical. Caroline obviously found it difficult and offensive to appear completely stupid, and she had been almost too devious in parts. But at last there were half-a-dozen clues that looked like possibles.

'This could be something,' Gary said, pointing. 'The number of blanks fit, anyway. Five and eight letters. There's nothing to help us from the first clue, though. She might have thought about that,' he grumbled.

171

'And she might have been too uptight to worry too much about connecting the clues,' Alex retorted. 'I don't know what it means though. Do you?'

She read it aloud. '*Not exactly onshore even offshore could be cat's whiskers*. Why cat's whiskers? Why not exactly onshore? I don't get it.'

'Read it slowly. Separate the words as if they're not connected. It's not a proper sentence, anyway.'

Alex did as she was told. Obviously her thought processes weren't working along the same lines that his were – if they were working at all.

'Not. Exactly. Onshore. Even. Offshore. Could. Be. Cat's. Whiskers.' It meant even less to Alex than before, and Gary began whistling, infuriating her all over again.

'This is no good—' she began in frustration, and then she jumped as he slapped his thigh hard.

'Cat's whiskers – do you know what that was?'

'Uh – something to do with early wireless, wasn't it?' she said, dredging it up in her mind.

'Yes, but think *radio*, instead of wireless. And radio not exactly onshore means that it may be *off*shore. The rest of it's probably a blind. What does that tell you?'

It was all a blind to her, but his brain cells were clearly galloping away faster than hers were now, Alex thought. She should be able to see what he was seeing, and she damn well couldn't.

'It's not telling me anything,' she said in annoyance.

'*Radio*, babe. Offshore radio. And the clue is five and eight letters. *Radio Caroline!*'

'Good God!' Alex said. 'So what does this tell us about where she is?'

After a minute he said, 'Precisely nothing, I'd say.'

'No? You don't think we're looking for her in some exotic place, like on a cruise-liner then? How about if her *M* had simply whisked her away for a romantic trip around the world and that I could follow her and claim it on expenses?'

Alex kept on talking, the rush of excitement fading fast as they stared at the mutilated crossword grid. There were only a few bits left that weren't highlighted now. And then she felt her heart began to beat faster again.

It was a long shot, and the nonsensical clue could mean nothing at all, but they were all nonsensical, and she had to question it.

'*Broad car needs assistance*,' she read slowly. 'Four letters. Such as *Help*, do you think? If you turn the words around, it could be Caroline needing aid. And this other clue about '*not exactly onshore*, – maybe there is a connection after all.'

She gasped, turning to Gary. 'I think I know where she is. It's no fancy cruise ship in the Caribbean, more's the pity; my guess is she's on a boat on the Norfolk Broads.'

Chapter 11

The dizzy fantasy that she might have been able to combine a
luxury cruise with finding Caroline fizzled out with the speed of
light. The Norfolk Broads had to be the place, and finding her
was the important thing.

'Are you crazy?' Gary said.

'Well, do you have any better ideas? We've eliminated every
other bit of the crossword, and these three clues are the only ones
that make any kind of sense. It has to be right. So what's the
problem?'

'When you've come down from your mountain-top,' Gary
said sarcastically, 'have you got any idea how many miles of
waterways there are on the Broads, and how many boats are
hired out at this time of year?'

'I should think there'd be hundreds—' Alex said, and then
stopped as she saw what he was getting at.

'Exactly. And you're looking for somebody you don't know,
who's kidnapped a woman who can't hear, and who's probably
got her tied up and gagged inside one particular boat that could
be anywhere in any one of dozens of inlets hidden by reeds.
Simple, isn't it?'

She stared at him, unwilling to let the old suspicions creep
into her mind. But all the same—

'You seem to know a lot about it!'

'I do, but I'm not about to confess that I kidnapped Caroline
Price, if that's what you're thinking. I had a week's holiday on
the Broads with my parents and sister a couple of times when I
was a kid. It was great.'

'Good Lord. It's not often you mention your parents.
Sometimes I wondered if you had any,' she added, since talking

175

about something else momentarily took away her acute sense of deflation at his description of the Broads. As far as she knew, it was just a section of England she knew nothing about, and her education was obviously lacking in that department.

'Thanks,' he retorted. 'I've been called a bastard in my time, but never quite so classily.'

'I didn't mean it like that, but we're getting away from the subject, and you've really given me a downer now.'

'Why? By saying the Broads is no picnic when it comes to searching for a single boat? You must know that.'

'I don't know anything about it. I was born on a farm. We didn't have boats in the Dales,' she said abruptly.

He eyed her thoughtfully now. 'It's hardly like braving the Amazon, but if you want company, I might be willing to come with you.'

'What about work?' She put her hand on his arm. 'I really would appreciate it, though. God knows what I'd find when I got there – if I ever got there.'

She was more jittery now than she had believed she would be. The end might be almost in sight, but there was still a long way to go before she could locate Caroline, and if Gary knew something about the Broads he could be very useful.

The knowledge that she could be in danger herself didn't escape her, either. She had no idea how many people might be holding Caroline captive, and she was pretty sure Gary could get tough when it was needed. It was always an advantage to have a strong arm around, and she revised every bad thing she had ever thought about him.

'I'll need to get a few days off work,' he told her. 'But I fancy seeing this through now. So how about it?'

'If you mean it, Gary, then I really would be grateful,' Alex said huskily.

He leaned closer, his intention clear in his eyes, his fingers making a sensuous trail around her cheek.

'*No,* darlin'. I mean *how about it?*'

'There's something I have to do before we leave,' Alex said over breakfast the following morning.

'Again?' he grinned.

'I must phone Mrs Selby-Jones and ask her to look at

Caroline's latest envelope. There would have been a postmark on it, and it may confirm that whoever posted it was somewhere in Norfolk.'

'Hey, I hadn't thought of that.'

'That's why I'm a private investigator and you're a delivery boy,' she said sweetly.

It came to nothing, though. The envelope had the familiar Bishop's Stortford postmark on it, so whoever had posted it had been canny enough to send it from the usual place.

'Oh well, it was worth a try,' Alex said, hiding her disappointment at not having Norfolk confirmed. 'So let's start planning. You'd better arrange for your time off, and we'll need a detailed map of the area. What then?'

She looked at him helplessly. They hadn't had much sleep last night, and she had wakened early, desperate not to disturb Gary – sprawled across her bed and taking up far too much room – since she knew what his morning reaction would be. And she hadn't needed that.

'I'm thinking,' he said. 'The bike will be an asset since it'll reach the parts that a car can't, but I doubt that you'd want to ride pillion all that way, and in any case we'll need a car to bring the girl back when we find her.'

'Good God, you're making it sound very complicated!'

'It *is* bloody complicated. The hardest part will be to find out where the mooring is, since we don't know the name of the boat or the guy who's hired it. You'll need to ask some very delicate questions at the boatyards. But I definitely think we should travel separately. We'll arrange where to meet up, park your car and use the bike for the last part. There are umpteen narrow lanes and flat-lands where we can cut across country to reach the mooring.'

She kept her eyes lowered, not wanting to betray the fact that for the life of her she couldn't rid herself of the suspicion that Gary knew exactly what to do, and how to go about it. Despite everything, there was still the chance that he could have been in on this all along.

There was the night he had virtually picked her up on her first meeting with Norman Price at the Rainbow Club; the fact that his courier job often took him to Price Chemicals; the way he had thwarted Jeremy from questioning her too much at the cottage; his helpfulness in decoding Caroline's diary.

177

Everything could make him a suspect, and yet she knew that everything could be just as feasibly innocent. She had already decided to trust him – and she must. She had to see it through now, whatever the outcome.

'Well? Have you come to the great decision?' he said, in a totally impassive tone.

She nodded quickly. 'We do as you say. Go separately, and meet up wherever we arrange that I should leave my car.'

It could be a case of the spider catching the fly, maybe. But she was in it now, for good or ill, and if the end result was finding Caroline Price alive and well, she knew she had no choice at all. And Gary had better remember that she was in charge of this case. He was just coming along for the ride, she hoped.

'I've got a lot of things to do, Gary, and so have you,' she said firmly now. 'Meet me at my office after lunch and we'll get started then. OK? And 1 don't suppose you've got any old maps of the Broads hanging about from your old holidays, have you?'

'Doubt it. That would have been up to my folks, and it was a long time ago, anyway. See you later then.'

If he *was* involved, Alex thought, he would surely have said he was sure he could find some maps at home. The fact that he didn't reassured her a little.

But she was glad when he left. She had a lot to think about, and not least was whether or not to inform Norman Price that she had a pretty good idea of where his daughter was. It would raise his hopes, of course, and she had learned from experience that it was often better to keep the client at bay until there was definite news.

The other thing was whether or not to bring in DI Frobisher. It would most likely turn out to be a police matter in the end. Norman would probably come clean by then and want to press charges, if only to prove that he was a Caring Father at heart who had instigated the search for his daughter.

Despite whatever dubious reasons Norman Price had for keeping the police out, Alex knew that if *she* had been the one who was missing. she would have wanted her father to move heaven and earth to find her. And that would have meant bringing in the full force of the law, not a female private investigator whose name she was sure Price must have picked at random out of Yellow Pages.

The police would have been combing the countryside long before this; there would have been Missing Persons bulletins on the television; Wilsingham would have been scoured, the villagers questioned and putting their solemn views across to the world at large; massive resources would have been put into operation.

In any police hunt on TV you only had to watch the dark-blue chain of officers threading their way through the undergrowth to know what they were looking for – and half-hoping not to find. They were human, after all – well, most of them – and some discoveries could be pretty gruesome.

But single-handed, it had taken Alex weeks to get this far, and the more she thought about that, the more her self-confidence was undermined.

Added to it was the disquieting fact that if Caroline had been in captivity all this time, then the time might well have been shortened had Alex gone over Price's head and confided in Nick. If there wasn't a legal reason for doing so, in her opinion there was certainly a moral one.

But Caroline must still be alive and sensible, since she had sent in the crosswords – or somebody else had. There was no doubt in Alex's mind now that she was being kept somewhere. The crossword clues had confirmed that. And she must have insisted to her captor that the grids had to be sent out. If he hadn't posted them, and Alex hadn't been cute enough to follow up the freebie lead, they might never have found her, she thought with a shudder.

But they hadn't found her yet. It must be considerably more than a month that she had been away from her cottage, but since she only had confirmation of Norman's infrequent visits down there to go on, she didn't even know the timing of that for certain. The Wilsingham folk obviously hadn't missed the occupant of Greenwell Cottage. If they had, they hadn't been curious enough to bother about a recluse who preferred her own company to anyone else's. The cloistered nosiness of village life obviously hadn't reached as far as Wilsingham.

Alex had assumed, like Price, that Caroline had been missing for all this time, whether by choice or by force. But now that Alex had a shrewd idea of her whereabouts, she began to abandon the timing thing altogether, and think more laterally. There was a more important thought that kept recurring now, and that was from something Gary said.

He had been on a week's holiday on the Broads several times when he was a kid. One week at a time. Presumably most people took a week's holiday in a hire boat – maybe two at most. She didn't know what you did on a small boat, though to Alex it sounded hideously boring. You could rule out any on-board entertainment like there was in the cruise brochures, or too much luxury. She tried to visualize it.

There would just be cabins and a kitchen – *galley*, she amended – and whatever else could be fitted into a confined space that must be pretty claustrophobic. It would be comparable to a caravan, Alex supposed, and she hadn't ever fancied that, either. She wondered if Caroline did.

But that wasn't the point. The point that was swirling around in her head now, was that surely nobody would hire a holiday boat for weeks on end? If they did, then it might make the job of finding out the name of the boat easier. And if they *didn't*, then the boat they were looking for might be a privately owned one, which presumably had to be registered for use on the Broads, and would at least identify it.

In any case, long-term hire boat, or private one, it narrowed the search – slightly. For the moment she ignored the memory of Gary telling there were miles of waterways on the Broads. The first thing was to identify the boat.

'Alex, you're a genius!' she told herself triumphantly.

Ever optimistic, she refused to let herself think of anything else but the fact that she had somewhere to start.

Until she remembered that she didn't have the faintest idea of the owner's name.

Not knowing how long she might be away, she repacked her overnight bag and left the flat. She called into a local travel agents and got all the Norfolk Broads brochures she could find, and began asking questions. It was amazing what people told you if you asked the right ones.

'Well, if you're looking for a quieter holiday away from it all, there are some nice secluded inlets starting off from Brundall,' she girl told Alex. 'Once you get down as far as Great Yarmouth the Broads can get as busy as the M1 right now. The northern parts are much prettier, and there are plenty of good pubs along the way, but it's very busy there too.'

'Do you have any detailed maps here?'

'No, but you can get one at any of the boatyards and booking offices in the area,' she was told.

Alex thanked her, bought a packet of sandwiches and a doughnut from a snack bar and took them to her office for lunch to give herself time to study everything she had found so far. The brochures included general maps of the Broads, and detailed interiors of the boats – and some of them were really swish, she admitted, if you liked that kind of thing.

They weren't cheap, either. Hiring one for a month or more just to keep somebody out of sight was going to cost a bomb. It revived her original idea that she could well be looking for a privately owned boat.

DI Nick Frobisher was up to his neck in paperwork when he heard the commotion in the outer office. Seconds later his WDC marched into his office, stiff-backed with annoyance.

'There's a guy outside who says he's got to see you and nobody else, sir. He's as drunk as a skunk and falling about all over the place. He's given me plenty of abuse, but I've told him you're busy and he'll have to wait.'

The man pushed past her and strode across to Nick's desk. planting both hands on it as if he intended to stand there for ever if need be. It was probably the only thing holding him up, Nick thought. He reeled back from the smell of whisky on the man's breath. He must have had a hell of a night of it and continued his drinking binge well into the morning. Maybe to give himself Dutch courage into coming here, Nick guessed, knowing the signs. The eyes were roaming with panic, the hair wild and unkempt. But he knew him at once.

'It's all right, Mary. Bring us some strong black coffee, will you? Calm down, Mr Laver. Take a seat and tell me what you want to see me about. And by the way, did you drive here?'

'Well, I sure as hell didn't fly,' he slurred, glaring at Nick through those bloodshot eyes. 'But never mind all that. I want to make a statement.'

Nick was too much of an old pro to show any surprise, while making a mental note to book him for drunk driving.

'Certainly. May I ask what it's all about?'

Laver banged his fist on the desk. With only one hand supporting him now, he was in grave danger of crashing to the floor, and he quickly recovered his balance. He spoke loudly and aggressively, but he was quite lucid, the words formed deliberately as if he had difficulty getting his tongue around them. which Nick could well believe.

'First of all, man, you've got to promise that what I'm going to tell you won't go against me. It's what they call a whatsit in America – a plea bargain – I b'lieve.'

He had Nick's full attention now. 'Well, we're not in America now, and I'm sure you know as well as I do, Mr Lavery that if any crime has been committed and someone comes forward to give information, it will always stand the informant in good stead.'

'That's not what I said,' Jeremy bawled. 'I want you to tell me I'll be kept out of the picture. It wasn't my idea, see? It was all his idea, and now it's gone too far.'

'I can't give you any more assurances until I know what this is all about,' Nick went on patiently, not wanting to push him into changing his mind. The man was in enough of a stew already. 'Now, just stay calm, and I'll arrange for someone to take down your statement and record it on tape.'

Jeremy's state of panic became more acute at the mention of a tape recording. 'Is that necessary? I didn't come here for that.'

'I assure you it is. It's for your own peace of mind, Mr Laver. You wouldn't want it said that the police tampered with the evidence now, would you? Once your statement has been recorded, you'll be given a copy of the tape so that you're quite sure you won't be misrepresented in any way.'

'Misrep—? Hey, no way, man – I'm not sure about any of this now.'

Mary arrived with two mugs of black coffee, and Nick told her coolly to take them instead to the interview-room.

'Ask DS Warner to bring the tape recorder, please, Mary. I'll also need somebody to take a written statement from Mr Laver, and you'd better send in a couple of the lads to escort him, since he looks rather unwell.'

He smiled encouragingly at the musician. He certainly wasn't letting this crap merchant off the hook now. He'd known all along there was something going on that involved either him, or his Uncle Norman, or both of them.

He'd also been gut-sure that somewhere along the line, Alexandra Best had a hand in it.

By the time DS Warner had got the tape machine set up in the interview-room and ready to run, and the DC was waiting to take down the written statement, Jeremy looked even more hunted. He had been told his rights and knew what to expect, but what had seemed like a good idea that morning and sent him off to find DI Frobisher in a blind panic, was suddenly becoming all too official for comfort.

'Look, man, like I said, I'm not so sure that this is such a good idea after all. I think I'll just leave it. . . .'

'You'll take a breathalyser test before you leave the building, so I would advise you to say what you've come to say,' Nick said more sharply, then added for the second time, 'Are you sure you don't want a solicitor present?'

'God, no! It's – well, all right. It's about my cousin. Caroline Price. It was just meant as a lark at first. Well, more than that, really. I mean, with all the money involved, nobody could say it was just a lark. But it wasn't my idea. I told you that, didn't I? I never knew he was a nutter though.'

He spoke jerkily. He wasn't making a lot of sense, and Nick knew he had to handle him gently if he was to get anything coherent out of him. But hearing the name of the cousin alerted him. Norman Price had implied that his daughter was missing, but he had never confirmed it, and no one of that name had been reported missing. It had seemed no more than a line that went nowhere. If you weren't informed officially that someone was missing, there wasn't much you could do about it.

'Why don't you start from the beginning, Mr Laver, and say what it is you've come to say? If it wasn't your idea, whose idea was it?' He still didn't have a clue what Laver was talking about, but that didn't matter. It always paid to sound as if you knew.

'Daneman's. He made it sound easy. Said he could make any woman fall for him, even dog-face.' Jeremy was bitter with angst now. 'I hated it when he spoke about Caroline like that. I mean, she's not that bad-looking. She just never attracted men. Never wanted 'em, as far as I knew. Not that I ever thought she was – well, you know. Daneman bet me he could have her any tir e he wanted, and he bought her all this flash underwear, the type that sluts wear.'

He paused, then said savagely, 'He even brought some of it to show me, used, of course, to prove that he'd been with her. It was disgusting, the way he kept wafting it under my nose. She fell for it all right. But everything began to go wrong, and it wasn't how it was planned.'

'How *was* it planned?' Nick said softly, and seeing far more into Jeremy Laver's character than he realized.

He revised his earlier opinion that the guy was probably homosexual. If his guess was right, he had no sexual inclinations at all. He was as tight-arsed as a eunuch. It was the other one – this Daneman – who was the perv.

Jeremy's words grew more rambling. His eyes were huge, his mouth trembling, and Nick knew he was looking on him as a pseudo-priest in the confessional now. His friend and mentor – God help him. He felt a swift resentment at having to soft-soap the whinger into telling him everything, but it had to be done. There were more ways of getting at the truth than by strong-arm methods.

'He was going to suggest that they went away for a few weeks on his boat, then he was going to keep her there until he got his freedom. That's what he called it.'

'His freedom?' Nick said.

'He had to say he'd marry her. Caroline wouldn't settle for anything less. She was living in fantasy land anyway, believing everything he said. But it all had to wait until his so-called divorce came through, on her birthday.'

'And he knew the date of her birthday?'

'Of course he bloody did. The birthday was important to the plan. He had to say it was the day he got his freedom and then they'd get married. Except that he was never married. He was a con-man, and it was just one of his tricks. Marcus had plenty of those. He kept making me listen to his tales of what they got up to; he was a real sicko – a psycho, I reckon. He enjoyed turning Caroline from a frump into a nympho, but then he started to get fed up with her.'

Nick could hear the alarm bells in his head.

'So what are you telling me? What was the result of him getting fed up with her?' Nick said.

He didn't want to lead him, but he was well aware of what a ruthless con-man – and psychopath – could do with a woman who wouldn't stop clinging when she'd got well past her sell-by date in his perverted mind.

Jeremy stared at him, the bloodshot eyes still wild and brimming with fatigue. 'Giving you all this information will go in my favour, won't it, man?'

'It won't do you any harm,' agreed Nick.

His brief moment of pity had gone. Privately he despised Laver just as much for betraying this Daneman as for conspiring with him over his cousin.

It was a strange old world he lived in, having to suck up to informants while hating their guts. But it had to be done. And he still hadn't got to the bottom of it yet. He knew there was a lot more to come.

'There was this bitch of a journalist, see? Well, that's what she said she was. Came to interview me, she said, for an American music magazine. Then Daneman saw her at Caroline's cottage, and described her to me. I knew it was the same woman, so what was she doing there? Tell me that if you can?'

'I can't, but go on, Mr Laver. What about this woman?'

He could hear the frustration and anger in the man's voice now. Laver was a small-time musician compared with the Lloyd-Webbers and Nigel Kennedys, but his manner was as egotistical as if he played his fiddle at the Albert Hall every night. And it was obvious that he felt stabbed in the guts that this journalist woman wasn't who she said she was.

'Toffee-nosed bitch,' Jeremy growled. 'Even took her fancy-man down to the cottage and was cavorting about with him on Caroline's bed. It was sick-making.'

'And how did she know about Caroline?' Nick asked carefully. 'Where does she come into all this?'

'That's just it. I don't know. I kept calling Marcus to make sure everything was OK, but he'd never give me a straight answer about anything. I'm still suspicious about that bitch of a journalist, though. Never trust a redhead, I say—'

'A redhead? What was her name? It may be important, Mr Laver.' Nick tried not to raise his voice, but his nerves were razor-sharp now.

If he went too fast Laver could so easily clam up and the inter-

THICKER THAN WATER ·

view would be finished. But there was only one redhead that he knew who had had connections with Norman Price and had telephoned the hospital to enquire after him, saying she was calling on his daughter's behalf.

'She said she was called Audrey Barnes,' Laver grunted. 'But about Caroline's birthday—'

'Yes, tell me about that,' Nick said.

Audrey Barnes. Alexandra Best. Same initials. Oh God, how corny can you get, Alex?

'On her birthday she's due to come into a packet from a crackpot great-aunt. If she doesn't claim it on the day it goes to somebody else. It was Daneman's idea to keep her out of the way so she wouldn't be able to get her hands on it.'

'Why would he want to do that? Who's next in line to get the money, Mr Laver?'

But he didn't need to be told. It was all there in the man's crazed eyes. He'd babbled out the rest of it, but he was still reluctant to give the final bit of information to damn himself, still putting all the blame on Daneman's shoulders.

'You've got to get to her, man,' Jeremy's voice rose in sudden hysteria. 'Marcus has got a bad reputation. He's fed up with my phone calls, and he came to my flat last night, threatening me with a knife and saying what he'll do to Caroline if things go wrong. If she drives him too far he'll sure as hell cut her. She's got a bloody awful temper. She's deaf, but she's certainly not dumb.'

'She's deaf?' Nick said.

He'd heard some bizarre tales in his time, but this one had all the trappings of a sick mind at work. He could see the other man start to shake. His putty-coloured skin had broken out into a sweat and his eyes were glazing. At any minute he was going to keel over, but Nick hadn't finished with him yet.

'What was the rest of the plan?' he asked urgently.

'When Caroline doesn't claim the inheritance, I get the money,' Jeremy mumbled. His lips shook uncontrollably now and he was starting to gag. 'Daneman's got several passports and he intends leaving the country as soon as he gets his cut. Hell, I don't even know if Daneman is his real name, man.'

'And Caroline?'

'I don't *know*. But I've got a real bad feeling about it. It's all gone wrong. I *know* it has.'

186

Nick didn't mince words. 'Well, I need to know two more things from you, Laver. Firstly, was Caroline's father involved in any of this? And I must have the name of this boat and where it's moored. We have to find it as quickly as possible. From what you've told me, there could be a murder charge here, and if so, you would certainly be an accessory.'

This time the shock tactic had no chance. Far from making Jeremy blurt out the final pieces of the puzzle, it served to have the opposite effect. It was a chance Nick knew he'd had to take. He just managed to scrape his chair back from the desk in time as Laver spewed all over it and then slumped to the floor, out cold.

Alex answered the knock on her office door, eager to tell Gary of her call at the travel agents and the girl's advice. She had barely finished her lunch, and was in the act of stuffing all the brochures into her overnight bag. Her heart jumped at the sight of the large figure pushing his way inside.

'Nick, do come in,' she said, hiding her nerves under the guise of sarcasm. 'What are you doing here? Don't you ever have any work to do?'

The moment he saw her, he cautioned his first reaction to wring her neck. He was used to summing up people at a glance, and she was definitely in a high old state and hyped up to the gills. If she was anyone else, he might think she was on something, but he was certain Alex wasn't stupid enough to get into that scene. He didn't miss the sight of the overnight bag and some glossies that she hastily hid from view.

'I'm working now. Going somewhere?' he said curtly.

'Oh, just out of town for a couple of days.'

She chewed her lip. Why was it, every time she was half-tempted to confide in him, he turned up, and she immediately reversed her thoughts? She wished she hadn't seemed so guarded – almost furtive – because she might have known it would arouse his interest.

'Business or pleasure?' he asked.

'A bit of both. I'm doing some research.'

And from her preliminary look through her road atlas, and the detailed brochures, she'd need to research the whole damn Norfolk Broads, which looked like an impossible task. Like looking for a needle in a haystack, no less, and there was simply no time for all that.

'Look, Nick, I'm in a hurry, so what do you want?' she said quickly, wanting to be rid of him before Gary arrived.

Nick smothered his fury. If she could be devious, then so could he, and a hundred times more effectively, he thought, anger making him more arrogant than usual. But he took the easy way out.

'I care about you. I haven't seen you for days, so I thought I'd check that you're all right – as a friend, since you don't seem inclined to see me as anything else.'

'Pull the other one, Nick,' she said, ignoring the innuendo. 'You're checking up on me, aren't you?'

'Now why would I do that? The only reason would be if I suspected you were involved in something heavy that you're not telling me about.' His eyes didn't waver.

'Well, I'm not,' Alex said abruptly.

And I know damn well that you are, he thought savagely.

Before she could think what he intended to do, he had pulled her into his arms and squeezed her tight.

'Just be careful. There are some pretty tough customers out there, so don't be too much of a fu— bloody feminist. Call me if you need me.'

Her voice was scratchy when she answered. He was just too hunky and macho to be called sweet, and he wouldn't thank her for saying so, but that was just what he was. And she had to keep the emotion under control right now.

'There's really nothing for you to worry about, Nick, but I'm touched by your concern.'

More than she could say, if he wanted to know. Their jobs could be highly competitive, but she was well aware that he thought deeply about her. Even if he still had his doubts about a woman doing what he considered a man's job, she knew he meant well.

There were some sleaze-bags in his unit who gave her occupation a far less complimentary name. At least she knew Nick was always on her side.

She was still held tight in his arms, and he suddenly kissed her hard on the mouth. She responded because he was her friend, and she loved him as a friend.

'Be careful, Alex,' he said again. 'And by the way,' he added casually, 'I don't suppose you've come across a character called Marcus Daneman, have you?'

'No, I haven't. What's he done?'

'Nothing – I hope.'

Moments later he was gone, and she stared thoughtfully at her door, wondering if there was any significance in the remark. He had a nose for a mystery, and he knew she was on to something. He wasn't averse to tantalizing her, or leading her up a false trail if he thought she was muscling in on his case. But this time he seemed intent on muscling in on hers, Alex thought indignantly.

But he couldn't possibly have any idea that she was on the trail of a woman called Caroline Price. He didn't know anything about her unless Norman had blabbed to him, and from his antipathy to the thought of any police involvement, she could count on that being a non-starter.

There was something about Nick's attitude that alerted her, though. Alex had known him a long time, and she knew when a throwaway remark was just a throwaway remark, and when it wasn't. She recalled it again, and was quite certain that she had never come across anyone called Daneman. She certainly didn't know anybody called Marcus.

Marcus. Hey, wasn't that the name of Dorien's husband in *Birds of a Feather*? Poor sap. . . .

God, she was doing it again, Alex thought, disgusted with herself for her TV addiction. She really should get out more. She finished putting the maps and brochures into her overnight bag, and then her hand froze.

Marcus. M. The possibility hit her so hard that she gasped. She should have seen it immediately. If this Marcus Daneman character was the mysterious M – Superstud himself, if Caroline's fruity comments in her diary were to be believed, who had apparently managed to turn her from a fairly plain woman into something of a sex bomb, then Nick definitely knew something she didn't.

She had no idea why he had mentioned the name, but his reason for calling on her was wearing a bit thin now, and she wished she'd had her wits about her enough to find out more.

He'd done her one small favour, though. He'd given her a

189

name to work on when she got to the Broads and made enquiries about any private boats registered in that name.

Chapter 12

Nick's earlier intention to storm in and demand that Alex told him everything she knew before the missing woman was mutilated or killed, seemed less favourable than his new policy. Her overnight bag and the hastily hidden magazines had decided him. She hadn't seemed to know Daneman's name, but he had a sixth sense about her next move, if not the exact location.

Laver's statement had made it a police matter now, and ironic as it seemed to him, Nick intended to virtually stalk Alex on the assumption that she had discovered where Daneman's boat was moored. He knew he was going against normal policy of calling in the whole team and setting the thing in motion to search for the missing woman. But this time he was doing it his way.

Laver was sleeping it off in custody, and hadn't looked like coming round for a long while, so he knew he couldn't get anything more out of him. God knew how much whisky the man had drunk before summoning up the courage to make his statement, but he was going to have a hell of a hangover later.

Once he had left Alex's office, Nick joined his three colleagues in his car, where they waited unobtrusively in a side street for her to come out and hopefully lead them to wherever Daneman was. After a while, when she still hadn't appeared, Nick called Price's factory number on his mobile.

On balance he decided that the father was unlikely to be involved in any kidnapping, especially since he'd guessed that Price was in dire financial straits, and that the girl was due for a packet, according to Laver. Price would need her.

But the fact that the guy knew his daughter was missing and that Alex had been hired to find her, was as obvious to Nick now as breathing. Price was a bloody unnatural father, but Nick had met plenty of those in his time. He'd also seen plenty of business dabblers who'd raise heaven and earth rather than involve the police in their affairs, and it took more than that to faze him about this one.

'Mr Price,' he said, when he heard the snappy response at the other end. 'This is DI Nick Frobisher. You may remember I spoke to you at the hospital after you were attacked.'

'I know who you are. What do you want?' Price said.

'Do you know a man called Marcus Daneman, sir? It's in connection with your missing daughter.'

There was silence at the other end except for the heavy sound of Price's breathing.

'Sir? We have reason to believe that your daughter may be in considerable danger, and if you know anything at all about this man she's been associating with—'

The next second he heard Price give an outraged laugh.

'Associating with a man? *Caroline*? You must be joking, Frobisher.'

'I don't think so. I've had it on good authority.'

'Oh yes? Who told you this nonsense?' Price snarled.

'Your nephew. Jeremy Laver. It seems that he and Daneman are well acquainted.'

There was a loud gasp at the other end. The penny was definitely dropping, thought Nick. He would obviously know all about the inheritance going to the cousin if Caroline didn't claim it. And if this slimy old geezer needed the daughter's money as he suspected, he'd be getting a shrewd idea now that his cringing nephew was involved in her disappearance, and that the money was in danger of going down the drain as far as he was concerned.

Price's voice became harsh and explosive. 'If that bloody female has been talking out of turn – she knew very well I didn't want the police involved – it's just a domestic matter. Nothing that I can't handle.'

'I'm afraid it could be far more than that now, Mr Price, but if you're referring to Miss Best, I would urge you not to contact her for the time being. Leave it to us now. She's no longer the only one concerned with finding your daughter.'

'Don't you worry. That's the last the bitch will hear from me; she can whistle for her fee.' He paused for a moment, and then his voice changed. 'But you don't really think Caroline's in any danger, do you? She never had much time for my nephew, but I never thought he'd hurt her.'

'You know as well as I do that greed can do strange things to people, Mr Price.'

'My God, you do think she's in danger! You think she's been kidnapped, don't you? I thought she'd just gone away for a while – you know what these bloody contrary women are like, and she's gone off before without bothering to tell me. Calls it interfering, when all I want to do—' Nick heard him swallow audibly. 'Christ, I even tried to learn – anyway, that's none of your damn business. But she's all I've got, Frobisher, and I don't want anything to happen to her.'

His panic seemed as great as Laver's now. Even his concern for his daughter's safety sounded genuine. Perhaps he did have a heart of sorts, Nick thought cynically. Price went on talking, although it was more like gabbling now.

'I thought she was just playing silly beggars, being too independent for her own good as usual. I'm going to her cottage to see if she's back, then I'm going home. From what you say it doesn't look good, does it?'

'I can't answer that yet, sir.'

'Christ man, you people are all the same,' Norman yelled. 'Can't you ever give a straight answer? You just call me the minute you get any news, do you hear?'

'Naturally,' Nick said coldly, thinking the whole of the factory must be able to hear him by now. So much for keeping his affairs private. 'Can you give me the address of the cottage and your home address, please, sir?'

Nick had already checked out the Chelmsford address, but he needed to hear Price say it, and the other man rattled off the details.

'There's no phone at the cottage. Since you already know so much, I suppose you know my daughter's deaf. So we'd better exchange mobile numbers Frobisher,' he said, taking charge.

Once everything had been accomplished, Nick ended the call, and turned to his colleagues.

'You know, just for a minute I thought the bugger sounded almost human. He seemed as frantic about his daughter as the thought of losing her money. I'm sure he had nothing to do with her disappearance, though. I don't think he'd even considered that foul play might be involved. Weird family. Still, providing he doesn't welsh on my instruction not to contact Alex Best, we're on.'

It had been a spur of the moment decision for him not to interrogate Alex in her office, and he certainly wouldn't want to scare the pants off her – Nick ignored the *frisson* of pleasure at the thought – but the information he had received that morning from Laver had been more than an eye-opener.

And now he knew that Alex was right in the thick of it, and he was prepared to sit it out in the car and play a waiting game until Alex led him to the missing woman and he could take over.

'Hello, what's this?' he said eventually, as a powerful Harley Davidson motor cycle roared along the street and came to a halt outside Alex's office building.

He couldn't tell who the rider was. He was dressed from head to foot in the obligatory biker's uniform of black leathers, an aggressive-looking crash helmet covering his head and face. But once off the bike, there was a familiarity about the swaggering walk that Nick couldn't place for a moment. And then he clicked his fingers as he remembered.

'Do you know him, sir?' DS Warner asked.

'No, but I'm pretty sure that the lovely Alexandra does,' he said, as the image of her way-out escort at Jeremy Laver's classical concert flashed into his mind.

Gary breezed into Alex's office, replete with a hefty meal of egg and chips from a greasy spoon café *en route*.

'Ready, doll?' he said.

'I've had a visitor,' she replied abruptly. 'And why do I have the feeling that it wasn't entirely coincidental? You didn't see a police car anywhere about, I suppose? But you wouldn't have done, of course. He doesn't use a marked one, our Mr high-and-mighty all-seeing, all-knowing superior—'

'What the hell are you talking about?' Gary said, as her voice began to rise.

'Nick. DI Nick Frobisher. A mate – I think.'

'A copper?' Gary's voice implied that nobody could consider a policeman for a mate. Alex glared at him.

194

'People aren't *born* coppers, Gary. They choose to do a bloody difficult job, and Nick's one of the best.'

'Fancy him, do you?'

'None of your business. Anyway, that's not why I mentioned him.' She dismissed her momentary irritation with Gary and the stink of tomato ketchup and vinegar emanating from him. 'He gave me a name that starts with M. I've got a strong hunch that it's Caroline's boy-friend, and that he's the one who's got her on his boat.'

She couldn't keep the note of triumph out of her voice now. She heard Gary whistle.

'So why did this copper give you his name? Is he in on the search? I thought this was just your case.'

'It is. I don't know if Nick's got wind of anything or not. All I know is that he mentioned a guy called Marcus Daneman, and once we get to the Broads I'm going to make enquiries about him. If he owns a boat and he's checked in, or whatever it is they do, we're definitely on to something.'

'Then let's get cracking,' Gary said. 'Oh, and I couldn't find any old maps.'

'I've got a few brochures with sketch maps in them, though they're not very detailed. We'll get better ones when we get there. We're heading for a place called Brundall to start with, by the way. A girl at the travel agents said it's less busy around there than the Great Yarmouth area, with lots of tiny creeks and inlets.'

'I don't think I remember it,' Gary said with a frown. 'But then, I was only a kid when I went there with my parents. But Daneman might prefer the busy areas so he can lose his boat among the hire boats – if it *is* a private one – and we don't know that for sure, do we?'

'Not yet. But my guess is that he'd choose a quiet spot in one of the inlets. Once Caroline realized what was going on she'd start yelling for help, and he wouldn't have wanted to risk her raising the alarm.'

She shivered, wondering what reaction Daneman would have had to that. 'Anyway, I've checked the map, and Brundall is also the nearest part of the Broads from Wilsingham and Bishop's Stortford for anyone who needed to go back and forth. So that's where we're heading,' she said again.

And it was her case, and she was in charge. She was driven by the need to find Caroline as soon as possible now. Nick's visit had filled her with new anxiety. and although she had been desperate to know the name of the mysterious M, he was no longer an anonymous and shadowy figure.

In Alex's mind he certainly wasn't the Adonis of Caroline's diary, either. He had assumed a much uglier life and form to her, and was a real threat to Caroline's safety.

From what she had learned of the woman so far – feisty, independent, bitterly resentful of her deafness and totally resistant to accepting help or sympathy or pity, even from her own father, Alex could imagine the devastating shock when her so-called lover proved to be a crook – even a killer.

She could no longer rule out that thought. Once they had started out and she was driving alone, with Gary's bike roaring along at some distance behind her, she had plenty of time to think about what Caroline's reaction would have been when she finally discovered the truth.

If everything Alex surmised was correct, then presumably she would have gone willingly and happily to this holiday on a boat with Marcus, never knowing until it was too late, that his intention was to keep her captive there until her birthday had come and gone, and her cousin could claim the inheritance.

Alex had no doubt now that he was up to his neck in the conspiracy. He was the one who stood to gain, no doubt promising to give this Daneman a hefty cut for his trouble.

But what happened then? What would Daneman do with Caroline once her usefulness had passed and she could identify him to the police? Alex didn't want to think about it, but she couldn't stop the horror of what Daneman might do intruding into her thoughts.

The chatty girl at the travel agents had told her that the waters of the Broads were deep in places and shallow in others. She knew from her own researches and from grisly observation that it didn't take much water to drown a body, or to weight down someone who was already dead. A body could remain undisturbed, entangled in the watery reeds for weeks or months, or for ever . . . bloated and distorted beyond recognition. . . .

A blast on a car horn behind her reminded Alex to concentrate on the road. She realized she was gripping the steering-wheel tightly and that her palms were damp.

But for those few traumatic moments, she had wished herself anywhere but driving towards a possible gruesome discovery and murder enquiry.

Whatever happened to the nice little domestics that Nick Frobisher teased her she was more suited for! And what kind of private eye was she now, letting her nerves get the better of her when she was hopefully about to leap the last hurdle?

At the thought, the tension began to unwind a little, knowing that she had to see this through. She had to find Caroline safe and well. That was all that mattered.

'Where the hell are they going?' Nick said, cursing as a lorry and then a boy-racer came between his car and the car and motor bike he was following at a discreet distance. Any other time, he'd have had him for speeding, he thought savagely, but he couldn't afford the time and energy on it now.

DS Warner studied the map spread out on his lap.

'They're heading for Norwich, sir. It looks as if it might be the Broads.'

'*Christ!*' Nick groaned.

It would have been difficult enough to trace a small boat anchored offshore – near impossible without the help of the coastguard – but on the Broads there were innumerable places where it might be hidden.

'We'll just have to hope the woman knows where she's going,' DS Warner went on.

'You don't have much time for her, do you, Sergeant?' Nick commented, his eyes still focused on the lorry that was still between him and the others.

'I think women should stick to the kitchen, and leave this kind of work to those more suited to it.'

'A chauvinist to the end, eh?' Nick said, breathing a sigh of relief when the lorry turned into a side road and Alex's car and the motor bike were in sight once more.

DS Warner grinned. 'I always thought that was why they called us pigs, sir.'

Nick ignored him. There were more important things on his mind than trying to put this charmer right. Some of them were just too blinkered to see beyond their noses. He frequently teased Alex himself, but it was never done with malice, and he had enormous respect for her – which this oaf didn't.

'Locate Wilsingham on the map, Warner, and see how far it is from Chelmsford,' he said instead.

'Within easy driving distance, I'd say – about forty miles.'

'Is that all? You'd think he'd have checked up on the daughter pretty often then, considering she's deaf,' Nick commented.

'It takes two to communicate, though. It could be that she's the stroppy one, not him.'

Nick recalled how Price's scratchy voice had almost hinted at something of the sort. And he'd overlooked it.

'Calls it interfering, when all I want to do—'

And what had he *even tried to learn*? Sign-language?

'You know, Warner, sometimes you come up with something really intelligent.'

The two DCs in the back seat sniggered. Warner gave them a few choice expletives in reply until Nick yelled at the three of them to stop acting like idiots and concentrate.

Alex was relieved to have a clear run up the A140 to Norwich, where a signposted offshoot off the A47 took her to the picturesque village of Brundall. She and Gary had arranged to check in at a pub for one night, and then see where they went from there. It wasn't difficult to find a pub. The difficulty was finding one that wasn't full.

They were finally offered what were virtually two attic rooms in a B&B well away from what the landlady called 'the activity'. There was every conceivable local map and mini-brochure available at the reception area. Alex was glad about the single accommodation, no matter what alternative thoughts Gary might have had. This wasn't meant to be a dirty weekend, and she needed to think sensibly without the sex thing getting in the way.

Once she had dumped her bag, she went into Gary's room and spread out the maps and leaflets on his bed.

'We're on the River Yare,' she said. Looking at its winding route, the river seemed to have as many hairpin bends as a mountain road, and her heart sank. 'There are several loops and dead ends and a nature reserve in this part alone. The boat could be anywhere.'

'Let's hope to God this is the right area, then.' He grabbed her hand. 'Give us a kiss before we do anything else.'

'Forget it, Gary.' Alex said crisply. 'I'm going down to ask the landlady where the nearest boatyard is. You can either come with me, or stay here.'

He couldn't miss the tension in her. This was no picnic as far as Alex was concerned, and somebody's life probably depended on it.

'All right, doll, don't get het up. Hey, did you see the way that prissy landlady looked so disapproving? You with your classy voice and me being me. Maybe she gave us the single rooms to stop any funny business. Fat chance!'

'Whatever. Come *on*, Gary, we don't have time for this.'

He was starting to get on her nerves now, and she knew it wasn't fair to feel that way. He didn't have to come with her, and she had to keep believing it was his good nature that had prompted his offer. But once all this was over. . . .

The boatyard was within easy walking distance of the B&B. In fact, everything was within walking distance of everything else. It was quaint, and the river was blue and sparkling in the sunlight, as idyllic and serene as anything you could wish to see. The pristine hire boats that were either moored along the banks or cruising elegantly up and down the Yare were enough to lure anyone on to the water. Except Alex.

In her opinion cruising meant a luxury boat with all mod cons, not one of these caravans without wheels. Not that she had ever set foot on either – yet. To each his own, she thought with a shrug, but this definitely wasn't for her.

She left Gary gazing nostalgically at the boats while she went into the boatyard office alone. This was her job and she didn't need telling that her plummy voice made it easier to get information than his East End one – depending on the circumstances, she acknowledged. It wasn't so much a snobbish observation as simply a fact of life.

The boatyard owner was large and bearded, and wreathed in smoke from an evil-smelling pipe, and Alex forced herself not to have a good cough in the dense atmosphere. She told him she didn't want to hire a boat, nor rent one of his houseboats. She was looking for someone who might own a boat and she needed to get in touch with him as soon as possible.

'It's an urgent family matter, Mr Stockwood,' she said, noting the man's name. 'I wondered if there was some kind of register for the private boats and if you knew of a Mr Marcus Daneman. I believe he'll be somewhere in this area, but I don't know the name of his boat.'

'The wife deals with that side of the business, my dear. She might be able to help you, and then again she might not.'

He was slow and methodical in his speech, but if his wife could come up with the right answers, Alex knew she'd be happy to deal with King Kong.

Mrs Stockwood spoke in the same comfortable Norfolk tones as her husband and didn't seem to notice the rank atmosphere. Passive smoking had a lot to answer for, Alex thought keenly, but she wasn't here to pass judgement. She smiled encouragingly at the woman and repeated her story.

The office was a jumble of papers and ledgers, and there was a huge wall map with flags stuck on it to indicate which boats were out and which were due to return. An enormous wall calendar detailed much the same thing. Alex was fascinated by the industry which appeared so haphazard to the outsider, but was presumably crystal clear to the Stockwoods.

'Daneman – Marcus Daneman,' the woman said, running her finger down a list of names in the book of private owners. 'No, he's not here, miss.'

Alex felt her bowels wrench with shock. She had been so sure . . . so certain.

'But he must be there. Please look again. Mrs Stockwood.'

'If you knew the name of the boat, it might be a help, but there's nobody registered by the name of Daneman. 'Course, he might have borrowed a friend's boat. They do, sometimes.'

Oh God, this was awful.

'Wait a mo',' the woman said. 'I wonder if 'tis the *Sandpiper* you're looking for. There's a weird chap who owns that one, big, rough sort o' chap, gypsyish I reckon, and the boat's only just about riverworthy. Not that he ever takes it anywhere, just leaves it moored in the reserve. It'll rot in the end, I dare say. But his name's not Daneman. Let me check – here 'tis now. He's called Peter Denny. Comes here now and then for the fishing and a bit o' bird-watching. So he don't sound much like your man to me. Sorry, my dear.'

She was sure it *was* the same man. Daneman – Denny. If people decided to change their name for any reason, an odd quirk often made them choose a new name with the same initial as the old. It was almost as if they couldn't bear to lose *everything* of themselves. She knew all about that.

'Thanks anyway. Oh – and do you have an Ordnance Survey map of this area, by any chance?' she asked casually.

' 'Course we do, girl. Every little crook and nanny, as they say,' Stockwood said, with a heavy attempt at humour.

Alex smiled dutifully. 'Could you photocopy the section where this Mr Denny usually does his fishing and bird-watching? He might be the man I'm looking for, and his family really do need to contact him urgently.'

She could have come clean and said who she was, but she preferred to use caution. As it was, the couple were looking at her with increased interest.

'Come into money or something, has he?' Mrs Stockwood said at last.

'I'm afraid I can't divulge personal information,' Alex said, but with enough intonation to make the woman nod sagely.

'Oh well, I dare say it's all right. I'll see to the photocopying for you, miss.'

'Any luck?' Gary asked her a little later when she tracked him down further along the riverbank.

'It's a long shot, but I think so,' she said jubilantly.

Then she stopped speaking, and her heart jumped. Not ten feet away from her was Nick Frobisher. He wasn't looking her way at that moment, and she grabbed Gary's arm and yanked him into the nearest souvenir shop.

'He's followed us,' she hissed furiously.

'Who?' Gary said in bewilderment.

'My copper,' she said, belittling Nick in language that Gary would understand. 'My bloody nosy copper!'

She heard several women tut-tut, and she lifted her hand apologetically. But how the hell did Nick know . . . and what was he doing here? For a raging moment she wondered if he'd put a tap on her phone or her answering machine, but she dismissed it at once. He wouldn't have. He wasn't that much of a rat. It decided her about one thing though.

'Gary, I'm going to call Norman Price and tell him where we are. For one thing he has a right to know, since he's paying me for this investigation.' The righteous tone slipped a little as she went on. 'And for another I'm not about to let DI effing Frobisher have all the glory of finding Caroline after I've done all the effing leg-work.'

The outraged gasps behind her became more pronounced, and she stalked out of the souvenir shop with her head held high, with Gary grinning along behind her.

'You really turn me on when you talk dirty, babe,' he taunted. 'Where now then? Back to the B&B?'

'Yes, and just to make that phone call and study this Ordnance Survey copy, so don't get any ideas. Then we're going walkabout – or rather rideabout.'

When she tried to contact Price she was told that he had left the factory and had gone home. She tried his mobile number, and was immediately met with a torrent of abuse. She held her phone away from her ear until he'd had his say.

'Just a minute. Mr Price. I assure you I have never given DI Frobisher any information at all. That's not the way I work; I respect client confidentiality at all times.'

'Then how the hell did he know so much?' Price said.

'You tell me,' she snapped.

'I know my bloody nephew's involved in all this somewhere, and he's told Frobisher a cock-and-bull story about Caroline and some man. But you must have blabbed even more—'

So now she knew why Nick was following her, Alex thought furiously. How he knew so much. *Damn* Laver's big mouth.

'I certainly did not. But if you want some relevant information about where I think Caroline is, then you had better listen to what I have to say.'

It was the accent that did it every time, Gary told her admiringly when she had finished the call. It stopped them in their tracks, and the more flustered she was inside, the more unintentionally clipped and cut-glass the accent became.

'I shouldn't have told him where we are, though,' she moaned. 'I certainly don't want him to come rushing down here until we've got results.'

'Wouldn't you, if there was a small fortune involved?'

She glared at him. 'Maybe. Or maybe he's got a smidgin of family feeling after all. Once he'd finished calling me a, well, never mind all that – he sounded genuine enough.'

'And I don't believe that any more than you do,' Gary snorted. 'So what's the plan?'

She took a deep breath. There were more urgent things to think about than Norman Price's tantrums. This Daneman sounded like a real nutter, which made things increasingly alarming.

'We use the bike. Frobisher knows my car but he won't know your bike. There are lots of inlets near this nature reserve. I reckon that'll be the place all right. The boat we're looking for is a bit of a wreck called the *Sandpiper*. That's if it's the right one, of course, and *if* Marcus Daneman is calling himself Peter Denny.'

'That's a lot of ifs, isn't it?'

'It's all I've got.'

And she hadn't yet worked out the plan of action once they reached the boat. She could hardly knock on the door and ask if a Miss Caroline Price was on board, either as a companion or a hostage. Especially if the guy was a nutter.

Maybe they could plead that the bike had broken down, and ask for help, or ask if the occupant had a mobile so they could call a garage – if such a slur on his mean machine didn't affront Gary's pride. It had definite possibilities. But what if the guy – Daneman/Denny – knew about bikes and came to look at it himself and found nothing wrong?

'If we needed to, is there any way to put your bike out of action temporarily?' she asked Gary carefully.

'Why?'

'Just a thought. You could ask Daneman or Denny if he knew anything about bikes—'

'Hey, I wouldn't need to ask anybody. I know this baby inside out.'

Alex sighed. 'Try to forget the macho image for one minute, will you, Gary? If the bike was out of action for a while, and you got Daneman off the boat to tinker with it, it might give me a chance to get on board and see if Caroline's there. But maybe there's no way you could fix it. . . .'

She gave him her best green-eyed stare, and he shrugged.

'Sure I could. I could always swap the plug-leads over to immobilize it. If the guy knew anything about bikes he might suss it out, or he might not. Like you're always telling me, you don't always notice the obvious.'

'But then you could reverse the plug-leads to get it going again?'

'Of course! Piece of cake.'

Nick smiled with satisfaction as he saw the Harley Davidson roar away down the main street and head for the minor roads. Alex was cute, but it took more than a female brain to fool him, even a mercurial one like hers. Anyway, he had been expecting something of this sort.

There were two figures on the bike now, both clad from head to toe in black leather, and with the concealing crash helmets hiding their identities.

A call to Mary back at headquarters to do a check on the bike's licence plate with Swansea DVLC had established the owner's name as Gary Hollis, and Nick didn't need a crystal ball to tell him who the pillion passenger was.

'Follow at a sensible distance, Warner. I don't want to alert them to our presence,' he said.

He preferred to be in the passenger seat now, with the map spread out in front of him. He didn't know the Broads, but he had checked out the major holiday areas, and discounted them as an unlikely place to keep anyone prisoner.

Laver had told him his cousin was deaf but she certainly wasn't dumb. If she could be as stroppy and contrary as the various descriptions of her suggested, then, once she discovered her lover-boy wasn't so loving any more, she'd have raised the roof at every opportunity.

He had also checked out the most likely places where a boat could be holed up without attracting too much interest. A nature reserve would seem to be the most likely.

Nick hoped to God Alex had done her homework and that this truly was the place. As far as the Broads went, it was the nearest point to what he called civilization, meaning Norwich. If not, he realized there were miles of navigable waterways spreading eastwards and then fanning out in all directions.

He had already toyed with the thought that a police launch

might be needed if they all had to be searched. But he had just as quickly dismissed the idea. Common sense told him that for safety reasons holiday craft would be prohibited from exceeding a low speed limit – around 7 mph according to one of the DCs. With all the family boats cruising at this time of year, Nick doubted that a speeding police launch would be exactly welcomed.

'We were right about them heading for the nature reserve then, sir,' Warner said a little later, having already done his share of checking and not prepared to let DI Frobisher have all the kudos.

'I can see that,' Nick said shortly.

And he could also see that the road they were travelling on was petering out into little more than a dirt track, and he could tell from the map that it looked like ending altogether pretty soon.

'We're heading towards the kind of country that a bike can cross and a car can't, sir,' one of the DCs said. 'It's likely to be marshy, and we wouldn't want to get stuck—'

'Thanks for your advice, Vernon,' snapped Nick. 'When that happens, we'll have to leave the car, spread out and do the last part on foot. That means we could easily lose the pair of them as well as losing sight of each other once we start combing the reeds and inlets of the nature reserve, so keep your wits about you.'

'We don't how many boats are likely to be moored around here either, do we, sir?' Warner said, his tone implying that all this was a good waste of time. 'It could be one or it could be dozens.'

'Right again. And without having Alex Best to lead us, we don't have a clue which one we're looking for, or even if it's here at all. But unless anyone's got any better ideas, we continue as we are, right?'

It didn't help his equilibrium to know that the rest of his team thought this was all a wild goose chase, and to suspect that part of it was a personal mission to score over Alexandra Best. It was far from being simply that, he thought, although there was always a certain amount of competitiveness in their dealings. But there was something far more serious at stake. A woman was missing, and it had become as much his business as Alex's to find her.

But then he added reason to his downbeat thoughts. If Alex knew exactly where she was heading, he doubted that she would want to alert Daneman to any chance of discovery by the sound of a powerful Harley-Davidson engine. In that case, they would need to dump the bike somewhere and continue on foot as well. At least it made them equal in that respect.

Chapter 13

The traumatized woman lay hunched up on her bunk in the tiny cabin. She was as terrified of the confined space as she had once been by the thought of going outside from her hermit-like cottage existence. Now she could easily believe that even hell could be no worse than this.

Caroline vowed that once she got out of this hateful little cell, she was never going to be afraid of open spaces again. She was never again going to give in to the self-induced agoraphobia and paranoia that had almost destroyed her self-confidence since her deafness had isolated her, making her lash out at everyone she had come into contact with.

Even her father. Especially her father.

She swallowed painfully. The two biggest mistakes in her life had been shutting her father out, and letting Marcus Daneman in. She was awash with fear every time Marcus came near her now, especially when he taunted her about what he was going to do when he came into money. *Her* money.

It was far more than mere hate that she felt for him now. She despised him totally, and she despised herself even more for ever having believed his lies. Being convinced that he was mentally deranged did nothing to appease her loathing for him.

Her self-esteem was at its lowest. She cringed at the memory of him touching her and of the things they had done together – sexually explicit, disgusting things – that had seemed natural and erotic at the time, because they had been done with love. On her part, at least.

Now that she knew it had all been nothing more than a cruel, sadistic game to Marcus, she loathed herself as well as him. She was totally degraded because of him. And discovering that her cousin Jeremy was involved in her kidnapping, and the reason for it, had compounded the nightmare.

Unless Marcus appeared with food, or drink, or to let her visit the toilet on the boat, she hardly knew if it was day or night. She had been shocked when she had first seen the poor state of the boat, thinking she was going on a luxury holiday.

She should have been suspicious right then, but she had been too seduced by love, and by the way he called it their little love-nest, all warm and cosy inside . . . and then he had boarded up the cracked window in her cabin, just allowing small slivers of light to come through.

She had tried prising the board away, tearing her nails and ripping her fingers to shreds, until he had effectively stopped all that by tying her to her bunk.

But the worst times, when she simply couldn't stop herself from screaming abuse at him for what he was doing to her, were when he not only gagged her to shut her up, but tied the vicious blindfold around her eyes as well. That was when she really knew the meaning of isolation and terror, when she could nei-ther hear nor see.

The cabin door opened, and her nerves jumped with fear as she adjusted her eyes against the brightness outside. She could see Marcus's dark unkempt shape moving towards her, and she opened her mouth to scream, in the hope, as always, that someone was near enough to hear.

'You bastard! *Bastard*! Why won't you let me go?' she screamed at him. 'I swear you'll never touch a penny of my money – and nor will Jeremy—'

'Shut up, you snivelling bitch,' he snarled. 'You make me sick, and who said you were ever going to get out of here?'

She went on screeching at him, not aware that he had spoken. 'You have to let me go, you maniac. People will be looking for me. They'll have called at the cottage, and wondered where I am. My father will send for the police.'

'Nobody's going to miss you, you stupid bitch. Nobody cares that much about you, especially your father. Haven't you got that bloody message yet?'

He was against the light, and despite his ranting, she still couldn't see his lips moving. She didn't even know if he was talking to her, although she knew that he would be. Yelling at her would be more like it. He'd be taunting her, shaming and degrading her, as usual. Abusing her with words now, since he'd got tired of abusing her body.

Because she knew it was so futile, Caroline stopped shouting at him and simply screamed. She kept on screaming at the top of her voice. She knew she was doing it. . . .

It was unnatural and heartbreaking that she couldn't even hear herself scream, except inside. Inside her, she was sure she was filling the cabin with the noise of her own voice.

The hurting in her chest and throat told her so, and she knew she must be making herself heard because Marcus suddenly struck her a savage blow across the side of her head with the back of his hand.

She whimpered with shock and pain as her head rocked, feeling the hot trickle of blood run down her cheek.

The next second she saw the glint of the knife he frequently threatened her with. The point of it was pressed against her throat, sharp enough to remind her that if she made a single move it would enter her flesh.

She daren't even swallow, she thought wildly. She couldn't do anything at all against this lunatic. For one agonizing moment, she was tempted to lunge forward against the knife and be done with it. Except that then he would have won. He and Jeremy.

But just as suddenly he drew the knife away from her.

'That's better, you whore,' he snapped, still uncaring that she couldn't hear him. 'Come on. Out for your usual, and then I'm getting out for some fresh air. I can't stand the sight and smell of you any longer.'

He untied her, yanked her to her feet and pushed her out of the cabin towards the tiny toilet compartment.

'I don't need—'

'Get in there, bitch,' he mouthed at her. 'Unless you want me to help you do it.'

He grabbed at her skirt, and she fled inside the box-like toilet compartment. She couldn't have borne it if he'd tried to remove her knickers and fondled her in the process. She started to wet herself at the thought, degraded even more.

She fumbled through her basic needs with shaking hands, knowing he would be listening. Aware of her own rank smell that so offended her. She had always been fastidious, and he had reduced her to this, she thought, weeping uncontrollably. He didn't need to stand guard outside the door, anyway. Her limbs were so cramped and unsteady she was sure she couldn't have run anywhere if she'd tried. She was dazed from the blow to her head, and her senses were still reeling.

When she had finished, she banged on the door and he let her out and pushed her back in the cabin and on to the bunk. He tied her up again and produced the gag and blindfold. Her eyes hurt so much from the unaccustomed light outside the cabin she was hardly aware of what he was about to do until it was too late to scream or beg him not to do this. Not to leave her with nothing. . . .

'*Bitch*,' he shouted close to her ear, aware that she couldn't hear him and couldn't see him. But from the way she flinched, he knew she could feel his hot breath close to her skin, and he took a sadistic delight in torturing her so.

Alex lowered her field-glasses from her vantage point, almost choked with unexpected emotion to realize they were in sight of the boat at last.

'That's it, Gary. Bit of a wreck, isn't it? I wonder why they allow it to stay on the Broads at all.'

'It probably only needs a cosmetic job. It wouldn't be so bad with a lick of paint and some TLC.'

'I doubt that it can move, anyway. What on earth must Caroline have thought when he brought her here?'

'She'd have been too blinded by love to notice,' Gary said sarcastically, demeaning her.

'Not for long, I'll bet,' Alex said, refusing to be riled by his insensitivity.

They gazed silently across the marsh and scrubland at the shabby-looking motor cruiser that had seen better days. It was moored at the head of a secluded, narrow and sluggish inlet that was probably rarely frequented. The reeds surrounding it were lush and tall and the boat could remain half-hidden for ever, unless anyone was especially looking for it.

'What does it remind you of?' Gary went on.

'I don't know. What?' She probably shouldn't ask. . . .

'*The African Queen*. Any minute now, Humphrey Bogart will pop up from the water, scraping leeches off himself—'

'Shut *up*, Gary. I don't need this now,' Alex hissed. 'Let me think. If Daneman's on board. we have to make a distraction so that you can get him away to take a look at the bike. You switched the thingys like you said, didn't you?'

'They're called plug-leads, and yes, I did. What am I supposed to do with him, anyway?'

'Use your brains – and your fists if necessary.'

Seconds later she caught her breath as she saw movements on the deck of the boat, and a large, shambling figure came out, looking all around him before making a move. She and Gary crouched down among the reeds.

'He's coming out. God, how could she ever have fancied him? He looks a real thug. Wait until he's well away from the boat, Gary, and then you have to get him as far away as possible. Once it's clear. I'll go in.'

'Listen, Alex, are you sure this is a good idea?'

'Unless you've got a better one, it's the only one we've got,' she said. 'Don't let me down now.'

She waited until she saw Daneman striding well across the marshy ground before giving Gary the OK to head him off and lure him away as far as possible. But she couldn't wait too long. She didn't know how much time she would need, or what state Caroline might be in, she thought with a shudder . . . and the further away they were when she found her, the better.

But when she saw that the two men were within sight of one another, she sped off towards the boat. Once on deck, she called Caroline's name quietly, and immediately realized how stupid that was. Even if she'd shrieked it out, Caroline wouldn't hear her.

Ignoring caution then, Alex kicked in the outer cabin door and peered inside. The smell that hit her was vile, and she wondered briefly how anyone could exist in it. Trying not to breathe too deeply, and with one hand covering her nose and mouth, she pushed open an inner cabin door and gasped as she saw the figure hunched up in the foetal position on the bunk.

Alex would hardly have known that it was a woman except for the long skirt that barely reached her cracked and blood-encrusted feet. There was blood from her forehead seeping into the blindfold. The sight of her smothered any sense of revulsion Alex felt at the stench. Caroline Price was in dire need of help.

And the fact that she hadn't even moved . . . didn't even know anyone was there . . . was just too terrible.

Alex rushed across to the bunk and pulled the gag from her mouth. The woman immediately opened her mouth to scream, and Alex clamped her hand across Caroline's mouth before wrenching the blindfold from her eyes. She crouched down so that Caroline could see she wasn't Daneman, and stroked her face with her free hand, trying to calm her.

Alex could see that her eyes were wild to the point of dementia, and she wouldn't like to guess how much longer she could have remained sane in this captivity.

'It's all right, Caroline, it's all right. I'm here to help,' she said, choked at the sight of the pathetic figure.

She knew Caroline couldn't hear her. It hardly seemed to matter, providing she realized she was here to help. But they daren't waste time. God knew how effective Gary's motor-bike ruse would be. Gently, Alex removed her hand from Caroline's mouth and quickly began untying the ropes that bound her.

'I thought he'd come back,' Caroline babbled at once. 'He means to kill me. He has a knife – he's a maniac—'

Alex helped her to sit up and then faced her sideways to the daylight so that the deaf woman could read her lips.

'Nobody's going to kill you. I'm getting you out of here. But we have to be quick. Your father contacted me—'

Caroline suddenly gripped her hand. Her eyes were huge. She had lost weight and her face was gaunt and angular.

'My father won't want to see me,' she wept. 'I wouldn't let him help. I hated him. I shut him out.' Her voice grew husky. 'How long have I been here? Does he know?'

'He knows. And you'll see him soon,' Alex said.

She was stunned as well as shocked. This was certainly a turn up, but she had no reason to doubt Caroline's own words.

All this time she had believed Price was the villain of the piece, having little time for his daughter, when it seemed now as if it had been Caroline holding him off, feeling victimized and defensive because of her deafness. He still needed her money, of course, but still . . . it could be that blood was thicker than water – or bank-notes – after all.

'We've got to get out of here, Caroline. Can you walk?'

'I'm not sure,' she mumbled. 'I'll try.'

She stood up, swaying and still dazed. She gripped Alex's arm tightly, and then sank down on the bunk again.

'It's no good. He hit me, and my head is swimming.'

'Sit still a minute,' Alex said. She punched out the numbers on her mobile phone and called for an ambulance. But she knew she had to get Caroline off this boat herself. She couldn't afford to wait for outside help. If Daneman came back they would both be prisoners. She was strong, but she would be no match for him. A maniac assumed unnatural strength, and she had no doubt now that Daneman was deranged.

'Lean completely on me,' she ordered.

Caroline tapped her shoulder, and Alex realized she hadn't heard her. She faced her again, pity overcoming even her revulsion at what Daneman had done. But there was no time for any sort of emotion now. That could come later. The need for urgency was uppermost now.

As usual, Daneman needed to get away from the boat for some peace. Every time the bitch had exhausted her bloody awful caterwauling, she'd started kicking the bunk to try and attract attention, until he'd taken her shoes away. Then she'd carried on kicking and head-butting, until she was in danger of doing herself in.

She'd never been much of a looker, but she hadn't been a bad screw, he thought, remembering. Still, he'd be bloody glad when the thing was over and Laver had collected his money and they had completed the deal.

He'd have to go to ground until then. But then he'd be off, with a new passport in a brand new name. The anticipation of it took his thoughts away from the irritating bitch. Once he was enjoying the good life, she could rot in hell as far as he was concerned.

He was well away from the boat and thankfully breathing clean air, then scowled as he saw the young man in black leathers walking towards him. The guy had appeared from nowhere. Daneman noted his biking gear, and assumed he was a bird-watcher, though he didn't look much like one. Not that they came ready labelled, he reminded himself, and it took all sorts. He nodded and made to move on, but he didn't get the chance as Gary stepped squarely in front of him.

'Hi there, am I glad to see somebody. Do you know anything about motor bikes? I've broken down, and I've got to get to Great Yarmouth by tonight,' he invented.

He knew he was a hell of a lousy actor, but he was doing his best, in view of this lout's glare.

'I might, but it's not my line of country—'

'Do you have a mobile phone then? I could call a garage and ask them to come and help me out.'

'I don't have my mobile with me,' Daneman snapped. 'Look, I can't help you – you'll have to find somebody else—'

'There's nobody else around, man. Is that your boat back there? Can I come back with you to use the phone there? I'll pay for the call,' Gary said, feeling desperate now.

But he knew there would be no invitation on to the boat. He saw Daneman's eyes narrow, and if he read his expression correctly he knew the guy would be deciding that taking a look at the stranger's bike and sending him on his way was the safer proposition.

'Where's this bike then?' Daneman said at last. 'I don't have much time for all this—'

'It's not far.' But Gary knew the guy was going to get suspicious any minute now. He hoped to God Alex had got to the boat and was getting the woman out. He didn't object to tackling this thug, but he didn't fancy having to get into a fist fight and risk ruining his leathers.

Daneman walked silently beside him for some way, and then stopped, his voice full of aggression.

'I still don't see it. What's going on?'

He turned his head quickly, and in the distance he could see four men advancing cautiously in a wide circle towards the inlet where the boat was moored. His face was puce with rage as he turned on Gary.

'You bastard, this is a trap, isn't it? I can smell a copper a mile off—'

Gary gave a forced laugh. 'You must be crazy, man. I'm no copper—'

He didn't get the chance to say anything else before Daneman's fist caught him right between the eyes and he sank like a stone. He didn't even hear Frobisher's shout, or see Daneman race back towards the boat with every intention of holding the woman hostage now. She was his insurance.

His sides were hurting like hell by the time he reached the boat, but desperation was urging him on. He flung himself on board and wrenched open the cabin door. He'd pull the bitch outside and hold her to him with the knife against her throat.

It took him no more than seconds before he registered that the cabin was empty, and knew what he had to do. There was no time to think. There was no way he was going to be caught either. No way he was going into captivity himself like a rat in a trap.

He'd been there and done that, and he always told himself that when it came to the final choice, he'd rather take the other way out. The one way where nobody could touch him.

Somehow he had always known it would be this way. He felt the excitement of an inevitability that was stronger than fear, more climactic than sex. He was going to cheat them all. And crazed by the knowledge that capture was imminent if he didn't move fast, he turned on the gas bottle and all the taps on the cabin stove and the tiny oven.

And once the smell of the gas became almost sweetly tangible, he threw a match into it.

Alex saw Daneman turn around, and she had also seen DI Frobisher and his men forming a trap from which he would never escape. All her resentment at Nick's presence vanished in an instant. Thank God, she thought. *Thank God.*

She didn't see what happened to Gary, and she couldn't wait to find out; they weren't safe yet. She and Caroline crawled as quickly as possible through the tall reeds to comparative safety, well away from the boat.

A few minutes later, Alex's senses were blasted as she heard the explosion. For an instant she felt as if all her nerves had splintered along with the shock-waves. She clutched the other woman to her, and then realized that Caroline had never even flinched. In the midst of everything else, Alex registered it as the most poignant fact of her life.

'What's wrong?' Caroline mumbled.

Alex lifted her head cautiously. She looked back over Caroline's shoulder to see the flames leaping up from where the boat was moored. She saw Nick and his men racing towards it, shouting to each other. Shouting her name.

She tried to shout back. To tell Nick she was all right. She was safe. But her voice stuck in her throat and she couldn't utter a sound. She could just watch the horror of that boat going up in flames, and wonder who, if anyone, had been on it. If Daneman had seen through Gary, and dragged him back there . . . oh God, what had she done. . . ?

'Alex, are you OK?'

At what seemed like an age later, she seemed to turn her head in slow motion at the sound of the voice. Through a blur of tears she saw a ghostly figure staggering towards her and she blinked the tears away to see Gary's bloody face.

'Thank God you're safe,' she croaked. 'I thought you might have been on the boat. You look a hell of a sight.'

'Never mind that. What about her? Is she dead?'

Alex swallowed hard, then realized she was still holding Caroline tight to her chest and that the woman seemed content to stay there, still clinging to her as if she was a lifeline.

'No, she's not dead.'

Intuition told her that Daneman had been killed. But no matter what he had done to her, it would still be a shock to Caroline. They had meant something to one another once. Alex looked directly into her face so that she could understand the words. She tried to speak as carefully and calmly as she could, considering that her own nerves were still juddering all over the place.

'Caroline, the boat has blown up. I'm afraid it was very likely that Daneman – Marcus – was on it—'

Alex turned her around so that she could see the billowing smoke and flames across the flat expanse of land.

The reaction was not what she expected. Caroline's hysterical laughter was blood-curdling, and her eyes lit up with almost demoniacal pleasure. Her nipples peaked against her torn dress as if she was experiencing a sexual orgasm.

'My God, she's flipped,' Gary muttered.

'Wouldn't you, after what she's been through?' Alex retorted, folding Caroline in her arms again.

She was aware of other voices then, and she saw Nick Frobisher running towards her. Thank God he was safe too, she thought . . . she registered the fact while feeling oddly detached from it all. She had to hold on to her senses as tightly as she was holding on to Caroline, because if she didn't, she knew she was in danger of flaking out.

And she needed to see this through to the end. It was still her case . . . and she had won.

'Christ, Alex, you gave me one hell of a fright,' she heard Nick say roughly, and then somebody else's hands were prising Caroline away from her, and she could hear the sound of an ambulance siren somewhere in the distance, or maybe it was in her head . . . it was all going away from her anyway . . . receding into the distance. . . .

Alex came round to find herself lying on a hard flat surface and with the sickly sensation of moving over bumpy ground. Or as if she was on a small boat. For one horrible moment she knew she should be remembering something very significant about that thought, but she couldn't.

She felt very strange. And a guy she didn't know was smiling down at her, his dark glasses and green shroud making her wonder for a moment if she was dead.

'Feeling better, miss?'

'I'm not ill,' she said. 'Where the hell am I?'

But she recovered fast. She registered that the green shroud wasn't a shroud at all but some kind of official garment. So she wasn't ill and she certainly wasn't dead. She turned her head sideways and saw that there was someone else lying in a similar position. There was an older man leaning over the other person and holding its hand.

At the sound of her voice the man turned around, and she could see tears in his eyes.

'Good God. Mr Price,' she stammered.

She vaguely remembered phoning him, and presumably Nick had done the rest to get him here. She looked beyond him, to where Caroline lay on the second ambulance cot, still ashen-faced, but practically radiant – well, sort of – compared with her defeated appearance on the boat.

Alex struggled to sit up.

'Are you all right?' she asked.

But it was a superfluous question. She saw the way Caroline held on tightly to her father's hand, the way she had held on to Alex's. It was startling, to say the least.

The memory of why she had been searching for her rushed into Alex's mind, and she only hoped this family feeling wasn't going to be crushed when Norman revealed why he had needed to find her safe and well before her birthday.

'I'm much better now, and I know I have a lot to thank you for, Miss Best,' Caroline said huskily.

'For goodness sake, call me Alex. You hardly know me, but I feel as if I've known you a long time.'

'So I understand, and I won't forget what you've done.'

Alex felt her face go hot with embarrassment. If she was intending to reward her, she felt doubly uncomfortable, knowing Norman's prime reason for wanting his daughter found. Or maybe it hadn't been his prime reason. Some people found it hard to communicate with one another, and these two seemed to be pretty good examples of that. Maybe.

'Where's Gary?' she asked Norman. 'And what about the other person?' she added delicately.

'Daneman's dead,' he said briefly. 'Your young man refused any medical help and has gone back to where you were staying to wait for you there. DI Frobisher's dealing with all the other details and said he'd be in touch with you shortly.'

'Right.' And that seemed to sum everything up neatly. Thank you and good-night.

She felt an odd sense of deflation again. It was ridiculous. As far as Alex was concerned, it was a job well done, and yet it wasn't finished yet. If she was a man, maybe she could have left it at that.

But she needed to know that these two would be all right, and that Caroline wasn't going to be exploited by one con-man, having just been saved from another. Even if this one was her own father.

Caroline's voice was still shaky. 'It's all right, Alex. I know Marcus is dead. And I can't pretend to be sorry. He was an evil man, I know that now. All he wanted was my money.'

'So did young Laver,' Norman said grimly, avoiding Alex's eyes. 'But at least he made a statement to the police, which I suppose we must be thankful for.'

218

'So that's how Nick knew! You see, I didn't betray your confidence, Mr Price—'

'I know that, lass, and I'm sorry for doubting you.'

'It doesn't matter,' Alex murmured. But she was fully alert now and wanting to be out of here. 'Where are we going, anyway? I have to get back to London.'

The ambulance man spoke again. 'We need to check you both over at the hospital in Norwich, miss.'

'I don't need any checking over. I only passed out. Miss Price is the one who needs medical attention.'

'Mr Frobisher insisted that we should take you as well, and I'm sure he was right,' the man said. 'You both had a nasty shock back there.'

Well, God bless Nick, Alex thought in some annoyance. She was fine, and she wanted to be home. The fact that she knew she was ungrateful towards him didn't help her feelings. She thought Gary might have come in the ambulance too, but if he had any sense he'd clear off and be thankful he needn't have anything more to do with Alexandra Best, Private Eye not-so-extraordinary. . . .

Conversation dried up after that. They must be nearly there, Alex thought thankfully, as the outskirts of Norwich came into view. All she wanted was to get this over and take a taxi back to collect her car. She glanced towards Caroline to tell her it wouldn't be long now, and then her intention was stopped in mid-thought.

Norman was making signs to his daughter now, and she was looking at him intently. It took a few seconds for Alex to realize that it was the sign language Caroline pretended not to understand, and she groaned inwardly.

From what she had learned of Norman's daughter, she had wanted none of that. Caroline hadn't even wanted to acknowledge to the outside world that she was deaf or had a problem. Caroline was the feisty one, the fiercely independent one. . . .

And Norman could be blowing it all now with this clumsy attempt at being the Caring Father.

She saw Caroline's face flush with colour. She wasn't so bad-looking when she wasn't scowling or glaring at people, Alex thought. As Gary would say, she'd probably scrub up quite nicely . . . she saw Alex watching her and smiled faintly.

219

'What's he saying?' Alex said, knowing she had to ask.

'I love you,' Caroline said softly. 'And I love him too.'

'It was bloody creepy, I can tell you,' Alex told Gary, when she had got the all-clear from the hospital and they were both at the B&B preparing to leave. 'I mean, all this time I've thought Norman didn't have a compassionate or fatherly bone in his body, and there they were, hugging one another like two lost souls.'

'It'll never last,' Gary said cynically.

'Maybe not, but that's up to them. I've done my job.'

'Except for getting paid.'

She smiled. 'Oh yes, there's that. And I do want to thank you, Gary, for everything you did, especially facing Daneman. He was completely mad, you know, and you were marvellous.'

'And that's it?'

Alex turned slightly away. 'For now. Let's see how it goes, shall we? Unless you were expecting a cut?'

He laughed. 'I wasn't. We had plenty of laughs along the way, didn't we? I dare say you're glad to get the Prices out of your hair, and you deserve to take some time off now. We'll be in touch again sometime soon.'

About a month later, Nick Frobisher came breezing into Alex's office. Life had been fairly mundane since then. She hadn't seen Nick for some time, and she greeted him cheerfully.

'Got over your little jaunt yet?' he asked.

'I'm fine, thanks, Nick. So what's the latest? I'm sure you're not just here for your health.'

'One of these days, Alex, I'll tell you just why I'm always hanging around, but I've a pretty shrewd feeling that you're not ready to hear it yet.'

'So why are you here now?' she said, not denying it, and knowing only too well that he was right.

She loved him as a friend. Someday it might be something deeper, but not yet. Any more than she loved Gary, whom she hadn't seen since the day of Caroline's rescue. A fine fair-weather friend he had turned out to be, but she had to admit she was secretly relieved about it. In her business, it was better if you walked alone . . . most of the time.

'I thought you might like to know that we've been keeping tabs on Norman Price's business affairs. It seems he was in debt up to his eyeballs, but now his daughter's got him off the hook by way of her inheritance.'

'Really?' Alex said incredulously. 'Then I'm disappointed in her. I didn't think Caroline would turn out to be spineless after all she'd gone through—'

'She's not. Far from it,' Nick said. 'Your Caroline has got a business head on her shoulders, and it seems she put certain conditions on paying off Daddy's debts. She's become a partner in Price Chemicals, and has come out of her shell enough to work part-time in his office. I reckon it's mostly to see he doesn't cheat on her, though.'

'Well, good for her,' Alex said. 'And what about the slimy cousin? I hope he'll get a good long sentence for his part in all of it.'

'Don't worry, it's all under control. Unfortunately, Caroline has refused to nail him, and she and her father want nothing more to do with him. And since Daneman fried on his boat, there's no one else to come forward.'

'But you had Jeremy Laver's statement. He admitted it! Damn it, Nick, you can't leave it like that. He's got to go down for it!' She felt close to tears, remembering how terrorized Caroline had been, and that her cousin was just as responsible for it as Daneman.

Nick shrugged. 'If the Prices won't testify there's not much we can do to force them. And you have to remember that Caroline never actually saw Jeremy at any time. She didn't know he had anything to do with it until she saw Daneman's reflection in the mirror and read the name Jeremy on his lips. But if you think about it, he ends up with nothing. No inheritance. No family. No funds for his theatre. He's a loser all the way.'

'Well, that doesn't satisfy me,' she said angrily.

He came around her desk and pulled her into his arms. She stood there rigidly, not prepared to be mollified.

'Let it go, Alex,' he said coolly. 'As far as you're concerned, the case is finished. But don't worry. We haven't done with Jeremy Laver yet. As you say, we've got his statement, and he'll get what he deserves. So why don't you shut up shop for the day? Go home and take a break – and have dinner with me tonight.'

She hesitated for a few minutes, and then she nodded. Why not? She knew he was right about one thing, anyway. As far as she was concerned, the case was well and truly over. Norman Price had lived up to his word and paid her fee, and he had added a nice fat bonus into the bargain.

Presumably he'd allocated all her expenses before Caroline's inheritance had come through. Now that it had, she guessed he was laughing. And so was she.

But since the two of them had formed a new and apparently amicable alliance – she mentally crossed her fingers at the thought – she might as well forget them. It was nothing to do with her now. She let out her breath without realizing she had been holding it in, and smiled at Nick.

'Dinner sounds great. I might have something interesting to tell you by then.'

'Oh? What's this? Another baffling case you want me to help you with?' he said arrogantly, his eyes becoming keener at once.

Alex laughed. He wasn't the only one who could keep someone guessing.

'You'll have to wait until tonight to find that out, won't you? In any case, I haven't sorted out the details yet.'

When he left her office, after she had succumbed to a very satisfactory kiss, Alex decided to do exactly as he had suggested. Shut up shop and go home. Then she was going to take a long leisurely bath, relax with a large glass of vodka and lime, and drink a silent toast to Caroline Price for her strength of character and her determination to survive.

But first of all there was somewhere else she had to go, and something else she had to do.

'Hello again,' said the chatty girl at the travel agents where she had been before. 'Have you decided to take a holiday on the Broads after all, then? You've left it a bit late for this year. The season's more or less over, and the weather's on the change now, so next year would be your best bet. Not that you can ever guarantee the weather in this country—'

Alex stopped her in mid-flow, with the feeling that if she hadn't, the girl would have gone on with her sales pitch for ever.

'Thanks for the advice, but I'm not worried about the British weather right now. What I've got in mind is as far away as possible, and something rather more exotic than a boat on the Norfolk Broads. So tell me what you've got in the way of winter cruises. Luxury, of course.'